Hotel Mirabelle and the Wonderful Wheelchair Company

Valerie Sinason

(Advance Reader Copy)

Advance Praise

I strongly suspect that had Jane Austen met Sigmund Freud, the two of them might well have given birth to Valerie Sinason, the author of this extraordinarily moving book. Both a writer and a psychoanalyst, Dr. Sinason has drawn upon her multiple talents and her extensive experience, and she has crafted a stunningly heartwarming text about the complexities of being an ageing human being. Every single mortal person will be deeply absorbed by this amazing novel and will have much to learn from Sinason's lifetime wisdom."

—Professor Brett Kahr, Senior Fellow at the Tavistock Institute of Medical Psychology in London, Visiting Professor of Psychoanalysis and Mental Health at Regent's University London, Honorary Director of Research at the Freud Museum London.

This is a deeply moving and humane book. Only someone with Valerie's lived and professional experience could have written so truthfully and tenderly about disability, ageing, and what it means to care for and about another person.

Valerie captures the heart of love and dependency, commitment, trust, and truth—the realities that come into sharp focus when we live alongside those we love, including in their final years and days. Her writing honours human frailty and courage and our shared need to survive, to belong, and to be held in relationship. These are precious moments, described with great care and compassion

—Baroness Sheila Hollins, former President of the Royal College of Occupational Therapists, Former President of the Royal College of Psychiatrists, Former President of the British Medical Association, and current Emeritus Professor of Psychiatry of Learning Disability at St George's, University of London

Hotel Mirabelle and the Wonderful Wheelchair Company

Valerie Sinason

ISBN (hardcover) : 978-1-917898-03-4
ISBN (paperback): 978-1-917898-04-1
ISBN (EPUB): 978-1-917898-05-8

First printed March, 2026
by Sul Books (an imprint of Sul Books, LTD)
Lewes, UK / Rodenbourg, LUX
Cover Image and Design: Ivana Mjunda
Interior Design: Sul Books
Editorial: Rhyd Wildermuth and Mirna Oliviera

Find our books at SULBOOKS.COM

Dedication

With thanks to the International Psychoanalytic Association Culture Committee for permission to reprint "Eskimo" (2023) from *The Analyst as Storyteller*, IPA Culture Committee, New York, which became the basis of the first chapter

To Helen Lewis for helping me realise the book I needed to write and Martin Pettit who first sharpened it.

To Ivana Mjunda for the beautiful front cover and Rachel Gillies for the photograph that felt true.

To Marsha, Barry, Sally, Greg, Hilary, and Pete for precious family support, to the memory of my parents who showed me the power of love in sickness or health and to all those engaged in making new memories with those who are losing them.

To friends and helpers Adah, Aideen, Alina Care, Angela, Angelina, Anka. Arnon, Brett, Btn Wellbn staff and home visiting team, Cecilia, Cynthia, David, Dehra, Don, Duke St. dentists, Embassy Court book club, Elizabeth, George, Guinevere, Hayley, Hugh, IPD, Isabella, Jeni, Joan, John, Judy, Kim, Leo, Lynn, Maddie, Marianne, Paul, Penny, Pier Luigi, South East Coast Ambulance Services, Stella, Stephanie, Steve, Sue, Susie, Sussex Royal Hospital Respiratory unit, Speech and Language, Community and district nurses, Cardiac diagnostics and cardiac rehabilitation,Tony and Vicki, for the right support at the right time

To my publishers Rhyd Wildermuth and Oliver Rathbone of Sul Books for believing in Hotel Mirabelle and Rhyd for his fine sensitive editing, as well.

To Marsha, Barry, Sally, Greg, Hilary and Pete for precious family support, to the memory of my parents who showed me the power of love in sickness or health and to all those engaged in making new memories with those who are losing them.

But above all this book is dedicated to my husband, David Leevers, creative inventor and engineer who has managed his severe mixed dementia and COPD so pragmatically and stoically. From inventing a smart phone to finding any phone too hard to use he has retained his kind, loving and curious self. He has been the inspiration for this book and gave me the blessing of his openness and approval.

Act 1
The Group Gathers

Chapter One

A cold morning after days of sun, she sat quietly by the side of the bed, head in her hands; fifteen minutes, that was all she wanted. He was asleep. A calm on his face, peaceful on his side of the bed with soft pillows cushioning his neck and shoulders. It was the serenity she cherished before he woke. She loved looking at him when he was asleep, having a quiet and comfort he did not have in the day.

He was breathing. Alive. His face, his eyes, the little dimple at the side of his mouth, the graceful frown lines on his forehead that she liked to stroke, the silver richness of his hair. Her Tom. And each morning she experienced that moment of joy.

It did not last long, especially with moments of bitterness that had entered his moods recently. The community nurse had whispered to her that his behaviour changes were due to the illness, not his character, which stayed calm and loving, and that she should try to stay as calm as she could.

Should she make a phone call? No. And look, he was already waking up.

His eyes settled on the TV news, which was always on at 7.30 am, and then fixed on her face. A slow smile lit up his face.

"You're awake, darling," she said. "Tea?"

He smiled warmly.

Standing up, Geraldine wrapped a shawl around her shoulders, covering her favourite kaftan and hiding the burn mark on her left arm. She carried the tea to him in his favourite mug. Their grandson had designed it for their diamond anniversary — a cat and mouse.

"You are Tom and Jerry," little Sam had chortled. "Do you get it, gran? But your Gerry has a G instead of a J!"

"Mug of tea coming, Tom darling," she trilled. She was becoming an expert in this. She smiled wryly at the family photographs along the way — son, daughter-in-law, and grandson — nodding to each in turn. The "Gallery of FaceTime Phantoms," as they lovingly called them.

Half-light was coldly entering through the bedroom window slats as she placed the mug on Tom's side of the bed. She noted, as if in slow motion, the swirls of heat rising from the mug fighting the cold air and the spillage from his evening drink all over yesterday's newspapers that he had not read — or could not read. *The Times* and *The Guardian* appeared to be melting over the duvet.

Over forty years of sleeping together and now: this. He in his adjustable bed with metal bars on each side to stop him from falling. But he was alive. Even when he didn't want to be sometimes. He was alive. Alive.

Slipped down the side of his indoor wheelchair, which doubled as a coffee table when he was in bed, was a full-page colour advert — Wonderful Wheelchairs — covered with his spidery notes. These days his handwriting was shaky and unreadable. Another sign of ageing. All the television programmes they seemed to like now had adverts for wheelchairs or recliners. Oh, and adjustable beds, commodes, wet wipes, Zimmer frames: not the brand names she took any pleasure in or wanted to be connected to.

"You are an algorithm gran," Sam had explained.

How could he even pronounce such a word at his age? But as the bright only-child of a bright only-child, his verbal skills were astonishing. And as the only child of older parents and even older grandparents, no wonder his vocabulary was so rich, even though theirs — or Tom's — was diminishing. Would they meet in the middle?

She picked the leaflet up and was tempted to throw it away, but she changed her mind. She would leave it there. It had his writing on it. She would preserve anything, everything as long as she could.

With the kitchen roll and anti-bacterial sanitisers from the bottom of the bedside cabinet, she gently wiped what she could. Such an immaculate man he had been, never went anywhere without a shirt and trousers pristine and ironed.

First, it was a collect-from-your-home laundry and ironing service. Then it was Rosa. If ever there was time for a housekeeper-cleaner, it was now, but their trusted Rosa was not allowed in. She had a cold and might bring in an infection. Thirty years of once-a-week. And now they were a plague house. Every time they arranged for their family to come, one of them had a cold. What had happened to natural immunity? No arrangement could be guaranteed, including the loan of mortality.

"You having one with me, Gerry love?" he asked. "You haven't had your second one yet." He struggled into a sitting position, his red velvet dressing gown pulled tightly around him. "Better than a water bottle," he always said, "a smoking jacket without the smoke."

Better a dressing gown and an old mohair shawl than calling in an engineer for the broken central heating. Any visitor could cause their death. They were better like this, together in God's waiting room. And it was such a comfortable waiting room — and with the best company! They were at the stage when friends were getting too old to drive and too vulnerable to travel. The mobile phone was the new magic wand allowing access to anyone, anywhere.

She propped the cushions behind his head, stroking his still-luxuriant, curly hair. Her Tom Cat. He had never been willing to go to the local barber, even before coronavirus, and her hair-cutting skills were poor. They had left the state of his hair somewhere in-between them, her jagged pruning and his thick sprigs of life.

"Silver fox," their son Brian said, admiringly, on yesterday's video call, pointing to his own balding head. "My hair hasn't lasted that long," Brian had laughed.

"Even though you are my son and hair," Tom had joked, an old joke he never forgot.

"Son and hair," little Sam had laughed. "Did you know granddad that h–a–i–r also means h–e–i–r, and it sounds the same but is spelt differently?"

"Gerry? Angel?" Tom repeated, "Your second drink?"

Her attention slowly returned.

"Of course," she replied.

All her responses had slowed. Maybe it was since Covid, or because she was tired. Or was it age or worse? a hidden, internal voice whispered. She closed her ears to it, and instead spoke. "I was thinking about Brian calling you a silver fox."

He smiled and kissed her hand. Such courtly gestures he still had. He has, she corrected herself. They were living on so many time levels. Each day they shed petals from their old selves. Sometimes, she felt too close to see it. At 5 pm today, they would have their weekly video call with little Sam. Would it be like time-lapse photography? Each week they would see his petals open while he would see theirs fall. Dorian Gray — she must read it again. How quickly did his face change? How was her face transforming? She hardly dared to see the age changes on it. She only looked in the mirror before a family video call.

She stood up uncertainly, her back to him as she went out of the room. "I'm having chamomile," she added. "I should have put them both on a tray."

"We can't have your brain going along with mine," he laughed.

Such kindness in his voice. Such understanding. That was the voice she had known for over sixty years. She must store these moments for both of them, these diamond moments. How was her brain, really?

Back in the kitchen, she wiped away a tear. A small pool of hot water, still steaming, surrounded the kettle. It trickled down onto the dustbin lid — the damp remains of the morning post — atop a torn envelope sticking out at the side with a familiar hospital insignia. A sharp intake of breath. The cold entered her. There was a limit to how much reality she could bear at once.

"... and can you bring me that suitcase, angel?"

"Suitcase?"

"Bag. In the kitchen."

"Big bag? Little bag?"

"Bag!" he shouted.

"What's in it?" she asked, trying to find another way in.

"Things. Bag things! You know!" he shouted, irritably.

Where had his kind voice gone? This was the new one when he was in a panic. An SOS from his struggling brain. Such a brilliant brain it had been.

"Things. In a bag? To eat?" she asked slowly and calmly.

"Of course to eat! To have with my tea."

There was a tense pause.

"Biscuits?"

"No!"

"Nuts?"

"No. No. You know. Bag. Shiny top. Eskimos, Sweet Eskimos."

"Shiny top?"

"Of course"

There was a deep moment of tension. Him in the bedroom and her in the kitchen. Two tired old brains.

"Icing!"

She shouted delightedly

"Icing!"

She felt like dancing. Her voice burst through the hall into the bedroom.

"Of course!," he called back, rocking with laughter.

And how they laughed! Two joyous spirits. Years of skiing, surfing, dancing, cheering their children, children's concerts, graduations, weddings, grandchild, diamond anniversary, death of a brain. Death of brains?

"Clever angel! That is why I thought of Eskimos," he called. And they carried on laughing together in the different rooms, in their different bodies. When the laughter stopped, she found a bigger wave of movement running through her. She found herself uttering a huge sigh and then holding tissues tightly against her eyes, where they slowly started to contract as the water seeped through them.

She found herself running back to the bedroom to give him a hug, his right hand clutching the burn mark on her left arm.

"Now isn't that fascinating, angel," he smiled, not noticing her silent flinch. "My mind found a meaningful link and jumped, and you found where I had jumped to. My language detective! What a diamond you are!"

He burst into song with a shadow of his fine tenor voice, "I sing, icing; I scream ice cream." Choirs and concerts, pantomimes and parties. And then he was singing "What a Wonderful World." Somehow, when he sang it, the world did become wonderful for a moment. "Oh, wonderful wheelchair — oh, wheelchair, my love, what a wonderful wheelchair you are."

And then the moment passed. How she wished she could polish it and keep it. She watched it fade in her heart and disappear before her eyes. She went to the kitchen, put two cupcakes on a plate, and walked back to his side of the bed. The hurrahs were over. All was quiet again.

Some of the new tea had already stained his dressing gown, a darker red showed through. Some had transformed the white sheets, a faecal stain. A stain that matched the sheets that had just been put in the washing machine. His eyes were closed, and a familiar furrowed collection of lines ran down his face. Her old Tom Cat, Silver Fox, Eskimo. The new word was now held on her necklace of names. She took a deep breath.

His eyes opened and crinkled. He looked at her in pleasure, instinctively pulling the clean sheet from her half of the bed over him.

"Where is your tea, angel?" he asked in his most able loving voice.

"Oh, goodness!" she cried, taken totally by surprise.

"And why have I got two Eskimos?" he smiled.

She adjusted the shawl more carefully around her shoulders and left without a word. Touching the family photos like a last Braille of hope, she made her way back to the kitchen. Angel. He had never called her that before this year. Gerry, Geraldine, Deeny, darling. He only started to call her angel when their mortality had hit them in the face with his stroke and dementia. Angel. Was she alive? The torn envelope, its hospital insignia still visible, albeit soggy, reached out its clammy palm towards her from the dustbin. It had her name on it.

Chapter Two

Summer 2023. The previous year, a national review by Bad-Holidays.com had singled out Sunville as the "worst-kept secret" of surf and turf in the UK, with each part of that combination failing equally. If Brighton, nearly thirty miles away, was a place helping police with their enquiries, Sunville was on the run from the law, hiding down grubby back alleys and living off bin detritus, which was also often found strewn around the sea front.

Sometimes it felt even the tide had gone on the run, and the pier, famous for being vestigial, like the Burnham one, rarely bothered to appear. The pier housed an old arcade of fruit machines, a doughnut kiosk, and a fish-and-chip shop. And it closed at 8 pm, one hour later than the chippie on the Parade.

Brightening the gloom was the lit-up seafront terrace of Charlene's twenty-bed partially-restored Hotel Mirabelle. Ahead, the small Sunville Grand Parade could just be seen snaking its way to the left of where the pier stood. *How on earth could it ever have been given such a name?*

Poor Sunville. She loved it. It was her hometown, her childhood home. It was where she went to junior and secondary school, and even that building, that place of learning where she had spent many happy years, had now been turned into council flats. Bob's flit to Marbella, before they even knew of her pregnancy, before Della's birth, was a brief interlude drowned in gin. Everything else in her life, before and after, felt rosy.

The Mirabelle did its best to light up the gloom, and all the roads of terraced B&Bs watched with fascination. Since the bar had opened a week ago (albeit with limited hours, until the whole hotel had its grand opening in a week), it glittered at night like a down-market Versailles or a miniature Blackpool Illuminations. She couldn't reduce the electricity bill. The lights had to stay on, whatever the cost. Mirabelle Hotel, no; Hotel Mirabelle (much classier), had a fifty-year history of slowly sliding more and more downhill, becoming ever more darker and drabber, losing one star after another. *Lose any more*, she thought, and *we'd be in perpetual night.* But she liked a challenge.

She had taken it on just as Covid struck, and at an almost give-away price; it had slumped so badly, and the owners had decided to swiftly retire. It housed twenty-five bedrooms, now turned into twenty to make them all *en suite*, perched, like the afterthought they were, on top of the original and much larger ground-floor base. The ground floor, with its intercommunicating meeting rooms, lounges, dining halls, and toilets, also boasted a large separate owner's flat.

It had been a popular wartime restaurant and dancehall; first, with comedy acts and dancing girls at the weekend, with additional private function rooms available for weddings and parties. Then, it was slowly adapted into becoming a hotel, too. "To save guests having to dangerously stagger back from the Hen and Horse after closing hours," Charlene's dad always used to say, adding, "why couldn't the Hen and Horse add some rooms to help us?" And now she was providing all he wanted in one place, even though he was no longer there to enjoy it.

Sunville was on the top of the list of "The 20 worst holiday resorts in the UK" on Bad-Holidays.com, under the huge headline WHERE NOT BE BESIDE THE SEASIDE. Some teenagers revelled in the name, and one enterprising girl had started selling "The Last Resort" T-shirts on the parade. Other resorts went from poor to posh with gentrification, or grand to dated, but Sunville had stayed consistently at the bottom for the last half-century.

Charlene wanted to change all that, for Sunville, Hotel Mirabelle, and all the people stuck in wheelchairs who have never had any chance of a proper holiday. *This will make Sunville history,* she thought.

"Wheelchair users," not "people stuck in wheelchairs," her daughter Della always curtly reminded her.

Wheelchair users! Charlene thought that made them sound like drug addicts. As if these new-fangled words made any difference to the condition.

Their new holidaymakers were due in just a week (if all went well with Wonderful Wheelchairs' first bookings in Sunville). All those people, and their loved ones, just stuck in chairs, or wheelchairs, plonked in front of the telly with no hope of a normal holiday. Unable to travel. Like her mum and dad, who had passed away three years ago. Even in their 80s, dealing with Alzheimer's and spending all day in twin recliners, they still wanted to travel, to go out to eat. And ramp-less Mirabelle, like so many others, had been inaccessible for them. That situation was even worse now, especially after Covid. It had never occurred to them, or her, to complain before or, alternatively, to set up fundraising to secure ramps. How could that be?

She had managed to sell her two hairdressing salons, one in Sunville and one in Brighton, to help accommodate the new venture, but it was her parents' money that made it possible. Who would have thought they would have left so much money? Money in their savings accounts, ISAs, pensions, a separate fund for Della (their only grandchild), let alone their bungalow (fully paid off). Maybe it was only because they lived in Sunville and there wasn't anywhere to spend it.

It was all left to her.

"Don't you worry about that bastard, B," her father had said, unusually swearing, "We will see you right."

And they had, and it was now invested in the Mirabelle, thanks to that chance meeting.

The 2020 Ageing Excellence Exhibition was held in a former car showroom with dirtied bright blue carpet tiles everywhere and a lone kiosk for entrance tickets; it was an unlikely setting for the gleaming new wheelchairs, commodes, hoists, gadgets, and throne toilets, along with the never-ending piles of leaflets. There were also small clusters of people around the different exhibition spaces, some in bright colours and some in hospital-style overalls to lend more authority to their wares.

Charlene had gone alone. And like an ageing mermaid sitting on a rock in the ocean, there was Irene Hanson, perched on the highest wheelchair with her big hoop gold earrings, tight blue-and-yellow "Wonderful Wheelchairs" T-shirt, holding a mirror and covering her mouth with yet another layer of red lipstick.

Irene! She would have recognised her anywhere. Sunville infants and juniors, best friends from 6 to 10, nearly five decades ago, inseparable. She never had a friend like that again.

Irene. That spark, that cheekiness, and that cleverness could never fade. She had neatly bobbed dyed white hair (one way of dealing with grey) that looked almost identical to the blonde bob she had as a child.

A few cups of tea and many gin-and-tonics later, the old photographs, the memories, and the tears followed. What a fast-forwarding of years and lives: Irene suddenly disappearing from school with no notice or forwarding address, teens, Bob, pregnancy, Della, Bert's and Betty's deaths, Southern Highlights. And from Irene's side, pulled from school to school according to where her mother's boyfriends lived, terrible teens, her mother's death, a string of unsuitable men, and no family of her own.

"Taken after my mum, haven't I?" Irene had said, raising her last gin-and-tonic. "She only took me away from Sunville to follow a useless guy around, and I did the same for years. But not anymore. But you are lucky. You have a kid. Too late for me."

Irene worked for Wonderful Wheelchairs, a brand-new business run by a brother and sister, Naresh and Maanika. Naresh had been badly injured in Afghanistan and lost both his legs. Making it possible for other people with disabilities to have a holiday was his personal Invictus Games. His sister, Maanika, did most of the administration and probably provided lots of the funding too, thought Irene.

She explained it all to Charlene, and then the obvious appeared before them both. The hotel and the travel company should work together.

Chapter Three

I want a holiday," said Maureen, smiling at her key worker, Alice, who had just arrived.

"Okay," said Alice, smiling back. "Can I take my coat off first?"

Maureen nodded. "Yes! But what does 'okay' mean? Why did you say 'okay' when I said I want a holiday?"

"It means I hear you. You want a holiday."

"Yes. But you know, I don't get a holiday without help."

"That's right, even though we already know you can manage to go on a holiday without any of us."

"I do, don't I, friend Alice? I have been to the swimming pool by myself and for a weekend in Eastbourne. And then there was the big holiday. A whole week."

"Yes," agreed Alice. "Can you remember where that holiday was, Maureen?"

"Holiday in Cornwall."

"Yes. You had a holiday in Cornwall two years ago. And you surprised us all by going away with a travel company without any of us there."

Maureen lived in a sheltered-accommodation studio flat in Cherry Tree, a new development for people with disabilities. There were ten studio flats and a resident manager as well as a community lounge. But-there was no cherry tree on the small grounds of Cherry Tree, which had felt a wasted opportunity to Alice and the other staff and volunteers. At least it was better than those facilities with sunshine-cheery names to wipe out any sense that disability carried a shadow with it. Just a shaved piece of grass with a gravel path around it and three wooden seats.

"Cornwall!" laughed Maureen. "But there was no corn in the wall."

"No. There wasn't," laughed Alice.

"But there was sand in the sandwich," chortled Maureen.

"Oh, you are so punny," smiled Alice, putting her arm around Maureen. "I've got bad manners, Alice. Would you like a drink? I got tea, and I saved a little milk for you, and then I have to go to the shop to get more milk."

"Thank you, Maureen. I would love a cup of tea this morning. And I have found something you might be interested in: a hotel in Sunville. It's a holiday company called Wonderful Wheelchairs."

"Oh," Maureen paused while pouring out the boiling water. "That is true. Wonderful Wheelchairs. Because wheelchairs are wonderful, aren't they? Cos I couldn't walk without one." She finished making the tea. "I didn't spill anything and took care with the boiling water, Alice," she said, proudly.

"You did, and you remembered I have this bad habit."

"Very bad habit, Alice. One teaspoon of sugar. Not good for your teeth."

"I know," said Alice, folding her hands over her plump stomach. "That's why you have stayed so healthy, Maureen, and can even walk a bit without the wheelchair," she added.

"Do you know, Alice, on the last holiday there were all these people there who didn't have a learning disability, and they couldn't walk like I can. I was the best walker. Me!"

"That must have been very strange," Alice said.

"It was. Because my neighbour, Christine, who had Down's like me, in her family she had a clever dad in a wheelchair and a mum who couldn't see properly, and her sister had a big fight with her boyfriend and had to go back home to live with mum and dad."

"Whereas, you are living very successfully here and are good friends with your neighbours, and you can help people who have got good brains because you have a good heart. Even though your parents didn't."

There was a long pause as she sipped her tea. "Alice," said Maureen tentatively.

"Something else. I didn't say it."

There was a pause. "Yes?"

"Yes. There was a man on the holiday who was a teacher. At my college. For my class."

"Your special enrichment course at college?"

"Yes. Mr. Grass. Spelt the same as grass in the garden, but there wasn't any grass on him."

"No," agreed Alice.

"Like Cherry Tree doesn't have a cherry tree."

"He was a nice man in college, and he said I had — potential. He was proud of me."

"Yes. I remember now. You got a certificate."

"Yes," said Maureen, pointing to the framed certificate on the wall. "This is to certify that Maureen Anderson was awarded the student of the year certificate for her all-around progress in all subjects."

Alice looked at the small handwriting at the bottom right, his signature: Edward Anders Grass.

"I didn't realise his middle name was Anders," said Alice.

"Yes. Maureen Anderson got a certificate from Edward Anders Grass."

Maureen paused, and then added, "He was on holiday in Cornwall."

"You never said," exclaimed Alice. "That is amazing."

"He didn't recognise me," said Maureen.

"Oh, that must have been hard," said Alice, struggling to find the right words. "But it was years ago, isn't it? He must have seen so many people in that time. Brains get older, too."

"No, Alice. You are not being amazing now. You are not getting it. He got that thing — Alzheimer's. He doesn't remember people and he couldn't walk."

"Oh, so your brain is working better than his, and your legs."

"Now you're thinking, Alice," said Maureen and she burst into tears.

Alice coughed. Maureen never failed to amaze her. She reached out to offer her hand. Maureen held it for a moment, squeezed it, and then let go.

"Oh, Maureen. How strange for you. Do you know what it makes me think about?"

"No. You have not told me," said Maureen

"My dad was so very strong. He could lift me. And you know how heavy I am."

Maureen laughed.

"And then he got a problem with his legs, and he could not lift me anymore or any of the heavy bags of rubbish he used to carry out to the bins. And it is so strange when someone you have always looked up to, who can do all the things you can't do, suddenly can't do those things anymore. He used to feel like a giant to me when I was small and now he felt so small."

Maureen looked at her very seriously. "You loved your dad, Alice, and I loved Mr. Edward Grass, so it feels very sad. But if it had been Miss Jenkins — who was horrid to me in infant school and called me a 'mad mongol' — I would have been glad I could do more than her, and I would not have wanted to help her. Is Jesus cross with me for saying that? Am I bad?"

"Oh, dear Maureen. You are a person. A proper person with feelings. And those feelings can be happy or angry or nasty or anything. And Miss Jenkins was terrible and should not have been allowed to teach. Jesus would know you are an honest person who tells the truth."

Maureen banged her fist on the table so hard that everything on it bounced. "So, friend Alice, now I can go on a holiday because Jesus forgives me, and if Mr Edward Anders Grass comes again I will be very nice to him even though he forgot me."

Alice hugged her, and then Maureen added, "Jesus wants me to do this trip, Amazing Alice. You see it will be my birthday. I will be 64 in a few weeks."

Alice was drinking a glass of white wine, which was highly unusual on a workday. She had texted her supervisor, Tony, and he was about to call her back. What luck that he had had a cancellation! Her counselling course for social workers had accepted her volunteer hours at Cherry Tree and included her work with Maureen. And there was the phone ringing. She answered and, hearing Tony's voice, immediately let loose a torrent of words with hardly a pause.

"Tony. Thank you for ringing back. I know we haven't got supervision for another few days but I had to ring. It is Maureen. She gets me each time. She makes me weep. She has such a heart and a brain and is trying always to make sense of such difficult things. Today she told me she wanted to go on a disability holiday — it is called Wonderful Wheelchairs. She loved that and said she could travel because of wheelchairs, and they are so wonderful. She never denies her disability and she expresses appreciation for anything that helps her.

"Well, it turns out that two years ago when she went on a one-week holiday, there was a man on the trip who had been a former tutor of hers at college. He had been her favourite tutor and really recognised her achievements. She received a certificate that was signed by him that still has a pride of place. His middle name 'Anders' resonated for her with her surname 'Anderson' and was a way she hoped to make them more connected, related.

"He did not recognise her. She realised their positions had reversed and that she was now both physically and mentally more able than him. She did not triumph over this, as she cared about him but then thought about an abusive teacher where she would have enjoyed that reversal. And then she worried Jesus wouldn't like her. I was just gob-smacked. Her emotional understanding is outstanding."

There was a pause.

"Tony?"

"I'm here. Just thinking. That was a really powerful concentrated burst that came out of you."

"Sorry. I was gabbing away."

"No, you weren't gabbing way. You were faithfully transferring a mass of deepest feelings about identity and disability to me that Maureen had transferred to you."

Alice sighed. "Oh boy. I feel better already."

"She is a remarkable woman. In her 60s, isn't she?"

" Sixty-three — and she will have her birthday while she is away."

Tony sighed. "Birthday — a painful day for many people with a disability who have been told or think they should not have been born. And look at her willingness to engage with you on a deep level. She really knows you are listening to her. You can encourage her to think more about the people she might meet on this trip — there might be real-life

Mr. Grass or Miss Jenkins kinds of people. She might be tempted to look after everyone because of her guilt. She was brought up in a convent, wasn't she?"

Alice nodded, though she knew Tony could not see it. "Yes. After her mother rejected her at birth and left her as a baby on a convent step."

"So there might be more religious issues, too. What a trip for her. A kind of pilgrimage, in fact. I'm glad you'll be there for her."

Chapter Four

Mary Mullins had been head of maths at a prestigious South West London academy for 30 years until her retirement arrived at the age of 60, which neatly appeared just as dementia took hold. That saved a lot of embarrassment for the school and her.

Mary loved the school, the children, and the work. And children loved the witty illustrations and words as much as the clever and sharp way she taught problem-solving in the maths textbooks and books she had written and edited for them. The school library had a whole section of them, including *Everything Adds Up*, *Don't Let Problems Multiply*, and her text on subtraction, *Don't Let Everything Get Taken Away.*

Deborah Stott, her live-in companion, an involuntarily-retired widow, was also a writer and had previously worked as an editor in a children's publishing company. Her husband's untimely death from cancer and her consequent breakdown led to the loss of her job. They kept her on as long as they could, but redundancy couldn't pay her mortgage and she lost her home.

Finding an advert in *The Lady* for a live-in companion seemed a shining possibility for a new direction. The woman advertising was an academic, a single woman and a wheelchair-user. She already had a daily carer for personal needs, as well as a weekly cleaner, a community nurse, and an occupational therapist. She just wanted a companion and had large high-ceilinged room with an en-suite, along with a reasonable salary, to offer in return.

That's how she came to live and work with Dr. Mullins, an author she'd already adored. Deborah gained a new home, and a place where her skills were valued: she had had proofread Mary's last two books. Despite the sharpness of Mary Mullins' tongue, there was a deep closeness between the two women after four years of working and living together.

"You always were my favourite author, Mary Mullins," was Deborah's regular refrain — a duet they both enjoyed.

"That is correct and it is *Dr.* Mullins, and don't you forget it," Mary would reply in a mock reprimand.

But the last time she said, "And don't you — don't." There was a pause, and then, "I forgot 'forget.'"

That was when Deborah first realised Mary Mullins had Alzheimer's as well as cerebral vascular dementia. They both wept and hugged each other, because neither of them did crying.

The doorbell rang, and then came the creak of the door opening.

"Just me," called the morning carer, Lizzie.

"Just a housewife, just a cripple, just me — there's no 'just' about it," mimicked Mary, waving Deborah out imperiously.

"Okay," said Deborah, an edge entering her usually calm voice as she stood up to leave. "I get it. It's zero day, and everything ends up to nothing. So, I better get out of your way."

Because Mary had not replied, Deborah said, "Don't worry" to the uncertain Lizzi hovering by the door and putting on her plastic gloves. Deborah thought of this as her condomised spaceman attire. "It's alright. She's all yours. All yours."

Lizzie reached for the remote to start their morning ritual. "Good morning, Dr. Mullins. Would you like the TV on?"

Mary's bitter laughter darkened the morning air, a response increasingly common and harder for Lizzie to manage. Ignoring climate change, train disruptions, and wars, Mary handed over a weekend supplement from under one of her pillows, folded down to display a full-page colour advert.

"I went to sleep laughing at this. Look at this rubbish. It must have cost a fortune. Look. Wonderful Wheelchairs! What a — What's the word? What a ...? " she finally shouted. "Call Deborah back in to see."

Lizzie rang the bell at the side of her bed, and Deborah came rushing in.

Mary waved the advertisement to her. "Look! Read that!"

"What a description!" said Deborah in a falsely jovial tone. She had been determined neither to always fill in the words for Mary nor to leave her stranded too long on the shores of memory.

Dr. Mullins laughed, spittle curling out of her mouth. "Exactly. Description. What madness. What fakery. It is just so — so — *wonderful* being in a wheelchair."

On the page were pictures of smiling men and women in wheelchairs against different scenery: sea, beaches, forests, and mountains. There weren't photos of the rooms. Hoists and commodes and standing aides would rather spoil the aesthetic. Most of the holidaymakers were in their 60s, white, clearly affluent, and couples. Deborah could see what she was looking at. All the holidaymakers looked so happy — no signs of upheaval nor the effort to even get there.

Wonderful Wheelchairs. What a wonder it was, Deborah thought. Pavements with curbs to attack the disabled, restaurants with small doors, and disabled toilets needing a key or being "out of order." Friends' homes being fortresses against her and her kind. Oh, brave new world! She focused on the page again. Most of the people were couples, with only a few singles thrown in.

"Noah wins again," Deborah sighed, turning back to a previous joke between them. "Everyone comes in twos. Well, us going together, even though we are both singles, makes us a two, makes us normal again!"

"Not twos. One-and-a-halves," said Mary sharply.

For a moment Deborah was stunned by her clarity and could not bear it. She didn't reply.

"Don't give me your joke about my brain compared to yours," Mary shouted. "Be real, for God's sake. It's all we have got."

Deborah sighed. The jokes had stretched so thinly in the last few months. Why couldn't she just shut up? Why did she have to try and lighten the mood? Mary had reason to be depressed. And so did she.

"You know what I mean," said Mary solemnly, seeing she was properly listening. "And I am, or was, the mathematician."

Deborah picked up a tissue and dusted the nearest bookshelf. She knew better than to interrupt at such a point. She recalled Mary's response to a similar moment shortly after her arrival.

"We are typical Brits," Mary had said. "We know problems multiply and things get taken away and we don't get surprised when they do."

"And things always end up with zero," Deborah filled in.

"Or even minus," Mary had added.

It certainly seemed a minus moment. Lizzie timidly helped Mary wash and dress. Getting her out of the wheelchair seemed to take longer than usual.

Clearing her throat, Lizzie looked worriedly at her employer. "Are you okay, Dr. Mullins? Something seems wrong today."

Mary found herself unable to speak. Her hands hung heavily; her head bowed down. Leaning on Lizzie, she reached for the bathroom stool to sit down. The truth was that she had woken up shocked from her dream. What a dream! Thank goodness that stupid advert had distracted her.

In her dream, she had been swimming in the sea. It was serene and warm. And she was swimming exactly sixty-four strokes in each direction: sixty-four strokes to the left to go past the groyne and the deck chairs and then back again. She could recognise the seafront blocks, the shapes that came and went with her even breaststroke. All was peaceful except for her breath, so she floated for a moment, doing her yoga breaths to calm herself. Even in her dream, she lucidly understood that 64 stood for the years of her life.

And suddenly, she was changing direction, turning around to go: but was it forwards or backwards? She did not know. She could not find the numbers. Where were they? How could she swim without them?

Her arms and legs were stupid, irrelevant accessories. It was the numbers that held her. And they were going.

She woke up silently weeping for her numbers, her beautiful numbers that used to dance around her brain all the time.

Why couldn't she tell Deborah? She would have understood. She understood her deeper link to numbers. And she had let it out on her —

poor, long-suffering Deborah, who tried to keep their spirits up with stupid jokes and a cheerful voice and getting the television on the right channel in the morning.

She looked again at the photo of Brighton Beach in the Wonderful Wheelchairs brochure. She had always swum with her mother — up to even a year before her mother's death. She had not felt ready to enter the sea since.

Renunciation? Sacrifice? She deserved such a crazy place. *Let's minus it together. Once more into the minus.*

"Lizzie," she said in a softer tone. "Could you ask Deborah to come back? I lost my tongue this morning. Big decisions. There's a holiday I want us to go on."

Chapter Five

It was a sunny Sunday morning in summer, but Joan Moreau had already been working for hours. Since 5 AM, she had been in her small immaculate kitchen watching with pleasure the wrinkles disappear from blouses, skirts, bedding, dresses, and shirts as she ironed them. She still felt like a magician each time.

She had been only 6 years old when her mother, Bess, carefully introduced her to the magic. Her pink pillowcase lay on the pristine ironing board like a crumpled petal, and then her mother had said, "Watch." Her right hand gracefully moved the iron up and down. It glided like an ice skater over the pink cotton, and all the crumples and wrinkles disappear.

Once ironed, they were folded with grace to join a fragrant pile building up on her Formica chair. Bess's folding was as magical as her ironing. When Joan opened her wardrobe and chest of drawers in the morning, everything was folded there like new. It felt like Christmas, but one that came every day.

It was the home that she had been born in, that her parents had managed to get a mortgage for soon after they married. She kept it the same way her mother and father had left it. No need to change what worked well.

She softly hummed to the music accompanying her from her faithful old wireless. She still couldn't get used to the word "radio." With the early morning shift, she was used to turning the volume down. In a few more hours she could enjoy it blaring out.

Maurice, her father, had been a car salesman who loved to understand everything about what he was selling. Before his untimely death from lung cancer, he had brought in a new wireless telephone with a party line, and a black-and-white television, then a colour television, and a SodaStream. Home carpet shampooing, a vacuum cleaner; the biggest surprise was the Kenwood chef. Bess said she was the first woman on the street to have one.

Joan, the only girl on both sides of the family, as well as the only grandchild, had all these new inventions in miniature size, toys to ingratiate her into her mother's role. She understood immediately how serious they were. Her toy ironing board was her apprenticeship into her mother's magic skills. Only girls who understood the beauty of it were then allowed by Joan to play in her bedroom. Otherwise, she would show them into the small, neat garden. They then knew they were consigned to the swing or slide but not allowed to put dirty dolls' clothes in the tiny washing machine, or lay the tiny table with cutlery and miniature food. Later, when she had grown up, Joan had these toys — now collectors' items — carefully and available for her daughter, Susan, long before she'd known she'd arrived.

Winston had left her — them — twenty-two years ago without notice. No. He hadn't left them. It wasn't Susan's birth. He didn't even know she was pregnant. One dance was all it took to change her life, and then only one month of her mahogany man. His gleaming gorgeous man-skin was like polished wood.

But that was twenty-two years ago. Bess and Maurice did not speak about him. They had only met him once. A whiff of his strong after-shave and a deep voice, his car engine left on outside the house when he whisked Joan off to a dance. After he disappeared, Joan did not speak about him, and nor did her parents. They put her and her baby at the centre of their protection like pearls with their attention a shell closed around them.

It was such a surprise when little Susan showed herself to be so clever in her learning. From her first days, learning to read and write, all those ticks and gold stars, and all those beautiful toys were ready for her attention. But Susan lost interest in them very early. Books took over all the Barbies and toy kitchens, then it was GCSEs and awards and university.

Joan and her own mother had been known and admired for their domestic skills by neighbours, who would knock on the door for advice on removing stains or cleaning doorsteps. But this did not transfer to Susan, nor did Susan's love for learning transfer back to her mother or her grandmother.

Where had her brains come from? Her father was never mentioned. School didn't seem to notice or mind she came from a single-parent home, although friends of hers in similar situations had experienced all kinds of welfare intrusion. Bess and Maurice were so omnipresent, and they had space in their family home for their daughter and her daughter.

And then they died. Those two solid parents and grandparents. Maurice with lung cancer and Betty with Alzheimers, and then there were only Joan and her clever child. Not that her cleverness was everything she hoped it would be. She still had no job, but Joan had her regular low paying jobs. It was alright.

At 7.55 AM, Joan would have a cup of tea and a cheap biscuit from Poundland and would read the free local paper that had come through her door. Maybe even a crossword. Then she would fold the paper neatly, ready for other purposes. Susan was still fast asleep. She would let her have until 8.30 AM.

Who would believe it? The last member of the Moreau family, Susan had gained a first-class degree in French. The first in their family to go to university, let alone learn another language, and Susan had seen it all through. Ignored all those dangerous dances, drinks, and outings. But the university term was over, and there was still no job to show for it. Joan had willingly supported her for twenty-two years, bit now it was really time for her precious girl to find her own paid work.

To be fair, Brexit had messed up some of the previous chances. Some of Susan's group were now working as baristas or volunteering in climate change work. It was like the gap year idea — but after the degree. Some people had more money than sense. Who needed a gap year? Who could afford one? What was the gap for?

French. The Moreau name. No-one knew where it came from. But it meant dark-skinned. Or even – Morin-dark, or "the sea." Joan loved that exotic-sounding name amid their ordinary life. Perhaps it had been that name that had made Winston so beautiful to her. Dark-skinned. And she was so pallid, with her mousey blonde hair and dull blue eyes.

Susan had taken up the French that showed so mysteriously in their history, wherever it came from. Susan Camille Moreau. Joan hadn't dared to give her a French first name. It might have led to a dance club and another baby. She'd be a grandmother by now, and still only middle-aged. She never used Winston's surname. They were only together one month.

She finished ironing the last blouse before making her cup of tea. It had been Bess's, one that fitted Joan perfectly. Beautiful green leaves and dark purple flowers that showed up even more after the ironing.

How she loved ironing. Watching all the wrinkles and creases of time disappear before her eyes, thanks to the efficiency of her hands. Some people liked mowing the lawn to watch evenness and symmetry. Give her the iron or the hoover, any day. All was peaceful in her domain. She did not envy Susan her pages, written in a foreign language. And Susan, bless her, had never looked down on her.

Joan sat down with the newspaper, carefully turning over the pages. She turned the pages slowly, but her eyes were working fast like her hands when sewing. She could spot, even in the small print, something that might benefit her family. Vouchers, free tickets, quizzes, she was queen of all of them.

And there it was, hidden under a full-page colour advert.

"Susan!" she called abruptly, narrowly avoiding bumping into her ironing board and the organised piles of washing she had taken in.

"Susan!" she called. She knocked loudly on the bedroom door, ignoring the "NE PAS DERANGER" sign on the door. "Susan, wake up!"

"Do I have to?" came her sweet, tired voice.

Poor girl, thought Joan, oblivious to all the extra hours of sleep her daughter enjoyed. "I waited as long as I could."

Susan stumbled out of the room in her "Bon Soir" pyjamas with the Eiffel Tower all over them. Giving her mum a quick hug, she walked into the kitchen with bleary eyes.

"Can I have a coffee first, maman?" she asked.

Joan handed over the advert to her daughter.

"It's a holiday advert, mum. I can't afford that. It's a job I want. And that's not the right age-group for me anyway. Are you telling me I'm old? Do you want me to come on holiday with you? Is there something I can do?"

"Look again — read the last line," said Joan, quickly filling the kettle and putting coffee in Susan's Baudelaire mug.

Susan collapsed onto a kitchen chair holding out her hands for the drink. Joan brought over the mug of coffee.

"Wheelchair Wonderland!" read Susan in a throaty French accent. "Join our Wonderful Wheelchair Team, as a visitor, driver, or skilled helper. French and Spanish language skills are particularly welcome. Specialist training is provided too."

"You see," said her mother. "It might even get you a paid holiday now as part of it. You were really good with grandad before he passed. And grandma."

"It's in the UK, so not really likely to use my French unless they have French clients on the tour, and if they are advertising this late they probably don't— it will pay peanuts."

"But nothing is using your French right now, and you need money while you look for a proper job. The point is," and Joan beamed here, "this is a late holiday and, as you say, they are only advertising now — *today.* So they have seats left on the coach, and they are going to be short of money if they don't fill them. And to manage the replies that come in, the bookings and the trip, they need staff."

"You're right," agreed Susan with a spark of interest. And they have only just advertised and most people will still be asleep!"

"The early bird catches the worm," smiled Joan.

"Okay. I will ring tomorrow."

"Susan Camille Moreau," emphasised Joan, "There isn't always a TM. To Moreau."

Chapter Six

It can't be the bank or the accountant," called Maanika, as the sound of the company phone filled the room. "Not on a Sunday and not this early. And Irene and Charlene would have used the personal number."

"It could be another cancellation," said Naresh.

"Staff sickness. Resignation. The coach needing a service."

"What about acts of war? Storm damage? Climate change?" added Maanika, "I can think of plenty more for you."

"I can't face it, can you?" replied Naresh, his face torn between humour and depression.

"In return for? "

"Anything," he replied.

"Anything?"

They laughed.

She picked up the phone. "Wonderful Wheelchair Company," she answered, "Maanika speaking."

"Oh. Wow. I mean, you are the Maanika that started Wheelchair Wonderland."

"Yes," smiled Maanika, putting it on loudspeaker so Naresh could hear. "Together with my brother—"

"Naresh," finished Susan. "I mean, sorry. I am just excited. I didn't think I would get you. I thought it would be a secretary."

"That's me," said Maanika. "Secretary, reception, bookings, holiday research, disability research—whatever is needed."

"Oh, wow. That is just like my mum."

There was a pause, and then Susan continued. "I am sorry. I am not being myself. I am applying for a job. I saw it advertised in the paper. I have just passed my French degree, and I am looking for a holiday job while I start looking for—"

"A job that isn't a holiday!" finished Maanika.

They both laughed, and Maanika then said, "Let's start from the beginning. Tell your name, address, date of birth, and send me an email with your CV. You should have the email on the advert. So we can spend this call on more important things. Apart from needing a job right now, what is it about working with the elderly? And we usually have at least one French tourist on her trips."

As comfortably as that, Susan told her all about her grandparents, and how she had looked after him with his lung cancer, and how Bess had struggled with Alzheimer's and how Joan could do everything to help her daughter. And just half an hour later Susan had been offered a training contract with a two-day induction that would explain how the company worked and would teach her how to use wheelchairs and standing aids correctly.

Maanika then rushed back into the lounge to alert her brother.

"Dr. Tom and Mrs. Gerry Finch, Ms. Maureen Anderson, Dr. Mary Mullins, and Mrs. Deborah Stott. We have started. It is going to be all right. And our first new local care assistant: Susan." Maanika sat down gracefully on the gold brocade sofa. "Just in time for the Mirabelle opening next week, and I have all the paperwork to show you here." She unzipped her case to produce a pile of papers and unopened letters. "Hard copy and not just email!" she added.

"Well done to you, little sister — and you have done all the paperwork brilliantly. Dadaji would be so proud. But I don't need to see it. I trust you completely."

"And she is a real gem," Maanika tried to inconspicuously wipe away something from just under her eye. Dadaji had died a year ago, the last member of their original nuclear family. Now there were only Naresh, Sunil — her husband — and her.

"I have a really good feeling about her. I told you. The other staff are going to be so pleased to have her join. Susan Moreau."

Naresh limped uncomfortably to the sofa, running his right hand through his silver-flecked black hair.

"I don't want Sunil to be angry with how much time you spend here. I am sorry. I know I am leaving some things for you to complete, but I cannot keep up with everything. That is why I asked you to join me at the start. I apologise, I have not met Charlene yet in person. She is key to our immediate plans. I will see her tomorrow with Irene. Wonderful Wheelchairs needed a home fast after our Hastings disappointment, and Sunville is close enough to the other visits we had planned and much cheaper."

"But?" she asked playfully

"But our employees have only been with us for two years!" he smiled, equilibrium temporarily restored. "And they thought they were joining a thriving concern. Irene is great, I'll give you that. And how amazing that she was acquainted with Charlene. Sometimes the universe is behind us. But the others have hardly had a moment, and Muhammid has only just joined."

Maanika sighed. Her husband had warned her she would be taking on too much in going into business with her wounded hero brother. They both knew his "delegation of tasks" was a sign it was too much for him, and he had been passing more and more to her. And not surprising with all he had gone through in Kabul. Sunil, a newly qualified accountant, could offer help with the business plan, but had no time to offer anything else. And his task was to build up their finances so they could start a family. At 35 years old, it was the right time.

"Yes. But that is true for the whole world, brother. Everyone thought they were in a thriving concern before Covid struck. Just be grateful you are not in Wuhan, Ukraine, Palestine, or Israel. Or, worst of all, back in Afghanistan. This is not a thunderbolt from the universe aimed just at us. Everyone has suffered and it is our duty to welcome and know all the people who come to us."

There was a pause. Maanika only said such things when she felt her older brother was giving in to despair and depression. It didn't work for him, letting it all out. He needed a military structure around him with carefully planned aims and times.

"Well, we have sent it all out now for good and bad and that's all my rainy-day money," he added, "and some of yours. Just the press details and adverts." He looked at her guiltily. He knew she still hadn't told Sunil about the savings from a private account that had been given to the venture. And she had sworn him to secrecy.

"Yes, we have," she agreed, "And it is a rainy day now, and what better way to use it but to turn other peoples' rainy days into sunshine? Do you know, I am so excited just about the toilets? Do you realise how revolutionary Charlene is — and she doesn't even know it? More cubicles in the men's toilets, a door for the urinal area, and a special toilet for men bringing small children in. It is the way for the future. It is good for LGBT people, too."

Maanika smiled, her usual sweet tone returning. "Our precious message in a bottle," emphasised Maanika. "Wonderful Wheelchair Company. I hope the waters of the world will be kind to us." She smiled at him, toasting him with a glass of water.

"How can you smile? How can you be so calm? Thousands of pounds," he emphasised, gesticulating wildly with his hands. "We never used such money before. All our future security."

Maanika sat on the sofa next to him. "And you never had to manage without legs before, Naresh," she said gently. "They are priceless. You are priceless. You were injured. You could have died. Have you any idea what that was for me? For my husband? Our tiny little unit, with Dadaji and Babaji dead? Your life was all that mattered. And you came back, my dearest brother. You came back, and you had this dream to fulfil. Others didn't come back. Nadia waited and waited for a body bag. After that, nothing can be so bad again unless we enter another war."

He sighed and reached out his right hand to hold hers. At least his hands worked now. Naresh had been wounded in Afghanistan. A roadside explosion. He had intended to leave the army after the last tour of duty. Just a broken right arm then. That was when they had the idea for Wonderful Wheelchair Company. Well, he had the idea, and she had the name and the advertising experience.

He had always been an active man, a walker, a mountaineer, a boxer, a shelf-stacker, an army man. Not having use of his right arm had frustrated him intensely. Every sport, DIY, television advert, and film seemed to involve two-handed people.

"You could always be a one-armed bandit," Maanika had laughed.

He was lucky. He hadn't had a girlfriend since they came to the UK, and she did not know if he had ever had one before. He had not wanted to marry while he was in the army. He did not want there to be someone who would have to mourn if he died in battle. He did not think anyone would ever want him now. Maanika and Sunil both told him they would put details about him on an internet dating site, but he could not go through with it. Fate had given him these injuries to protect his country. But he was lucky with Maanika, sometimes, he feared, at the expense of her kind husband. Somehow, in her sweet gentle way, she was the person who could break through his despair. "You had to hand it to her," he used to joke. Disarmed. In need of a hand, a hand-out. He couldn't handle it.

"Think of Invictus," she had urged him, "think of your friends who did not make it. Think of all the people with no holidays. We can do something powerful together. I am fed up with all my personal assistance work. I can be a PA for you instead. And I have some savings."

Sunil, her husband, knew there was no point in trying to stop Maanika. She was unstoppable. Wonderful Wheelchair Company was born. She found the first hotel and Irene, an experienced retired care worker ready to come back and do more. Then a coach driver and a disability personal assistant. She waded through the army pensions, created a charity and access to all kinds of grants and awards appeared. Wheelchair Wonderland. Wonderful Wheelchairs. Television interviews, newspapers, seeing sparks of life in the eyes of wounded men and women. And then an explosion. And then Covid.

Naresh was smashed up — a roadside bomb in Kabul. Both legs were amputated above the knee. And then Covid destroyed their first-year plans. Christmas 2020 was to have been their start, their first plan for the year. Everything was cancelled. Staff disappeared except Irene and Les, their coach driver. Suppliers became ill. The hotel in Hastings had let them down.

Sitting next to Naresh, Maanika opened an envelope from her small pile.

"Lady Hermione Lambton — goodness! An aristocrat." She then opened the second envelope. "Maureen Anderson." And then she passed an envelope to Naresh.

"Jane Edwards," he looked confused and bewildered, and then looked again. "It is a booking. A woman with an intellectual disability," he said, tears in his eyes.

And just then, the phone rang. Naresh and Maanika looked at each other, and Maanika smiled wryly at her brother. "Hello Universe," she said to him, then picked up the phone.

"Wonderful Wheelchair Company."

"Is there still time to book?" asked the voice on the other end. Breathless, excited. Maanika now knew the tone well.

"Yes," she said warmly and calmly. "Yes. There is."

Chapter Seven

Hermione slipped her long, elegant legs out of the satin covers. It was her 70th birthday. Would anything be any different? The king-size bed looked hardly ruffled in the morning.

That's because it is just me, she acknowledged to herself, her gaunt sculptured face and body and untidy rivulets of silver hair facing her in the ornate mirror.

She did remember a time when she felt beautiful. But not now. Not after the two years he had turned against her and the two years of loss. She reached for a brush on her bedside table to tidy her hair. Almost waist-length, within moments it flowed like a silver stream. She had refused to cut it on ageing, and James had applauded that — until it all happened. Now she quickly twisted it into a bun and clipped it to her head. All virginal, spinster, and safe.

His side of the bed was empty and had remained empty. James had died two years ago. The bedroom, with its rich olive-green carpet and its old gold brocade-draped curtains, was silent and immaculate. Not a speck of dust. Not a sign of life.

"Like a museum," she thought bitterly. "Like me. A museum of old age. Widow section. Dangerous Artist Widow." There. She had said it. The curse needed to be named on this day.

Slipping on her silk kimono, she reached resolutely for her golden walking stick. Before it all happened, she slept naked, rose naked. All that had changed. Even with nobody there. Time to get out of bed to get the papers. She had brushed her hair. Papers. Coffee. Wash. What a sterile routine.

The walking stick had sparkled at her in a dull beige disability shop. James had refused to come in. He stayed outside in the car, strapped into his wheelchair. He said he had had enough of death by beige, recliners, and incliners. He was a "decliner," thank you very much. Despite her nervousness, she walked in, saw it with relief, bought it, and left. Any future shopping would be done alone or with Juanita, her help.

James had mocked her savagely in the car, oblivious to the presence of John, his former groom, who was driving. John's face stayed frozen and neutral while his employer's raging voice sliced into her. One after another, the hurtful sentences came like gunshots. *She was minimising his real injuries. She had given herself an infantile magic wand. She had a mental illness, Munchhausen's. He had no choice but to be in his wheelchair after his terrible accident. She was making it about her, making a mockery of the real damage he faced.*

A riding injury, a leap into the air, had destroyed him. In one moment, he lost mobility, sexuality, identity, love, and hope. He also lost his kindness and their history. At 68, after a lifetime of riding, Fortune, his favourite horse, had failed him. After two decades of their marriage, a first for her and a second for him, he had suddenly closed the doors of his heart to her and opened them to Covid as violently as he had leapt into the air. At only 68, Covid had taken him.

He had the king of wheelchairs, the best that money could buy. He could turn, reverse, speed up, slow down. She had been so thrilled to discover it. He had just mocked her.

"A moving coffin, and it can go fast — nowhere and for nothing. But you knew all about it, witch. Your damned art. I should have known."

He had turned against her, closed his heart to her until he had drifted away completely. His strong muscular protection and attention had left her, and she was deserted.

After hospital, he stayed in his study with a hospital bed placed there for him — his beautiful study, with its brown leather chesterfield and the distant smell of cigars. Portraits — recent family members, ancestors looking down on horseback, paintings of his horses: even Fortune, who had failed at the last fence and nearly killed him. Even Fortune had a place on the wall, even though he was shot after the accident. It was only her paintings he had removed; or, rather, had gotten John to remove. Her self-portraits, portraits of him, and the cursed painting. *No. Don't go there. Not today. Not yet.* He allowed his former groom, John, to wheel him out to the south terrace when it was warm and dry to bring him meals she had cooked, and that was it. The other horses were all sold and passed on as quickly as possible.

She was careful. Always had been. The neurologist had warned her. A couple of minor falls for her were enough of a warning to reach out for a walking stick. Or two: alpine walking, which used two sticks, was apparently all the rage.

She needed her hands for her painting. Juanita was right. She didn't have anyone else.

Tying the belt of her silk kimono, she slowly walked out of the bedroom to the front door. All the papers were there. She had not cancelled any of them. Just reading through them all on a Sunday morning gave her a sense of James still being there and how he used to be. She must not let two years of altered behaviour destroy the memory of two decades. "It was not him," the doctor had said. "It is his condition." But it was, a small voice in her head replied.

Reading the papers would take her almost up to lunch. And he would normally, even on the good days, have been reading in his study. So, until lunch, she was used to being solitary. And, of course, in his last two years, after his fall, he did not like her being near him for long. And he did not go into her studio to see her painting. Not after that. And then it lodged in her like a curse, a taboo, and she did not go into her studio, either.

Putting down one of her sticks to pick up the papers, an advert fell out. "Wonderful Wheelchairs," it said. She burst into tears. Her studio was her wonderland. Something extraordinary and amazing. But instead of a rabbit hole, it was a place of connection. "Wonderful Wheelchairs—Wheelchair Wonderland."

He could never connect to a disability. He was not made for stillness and contemplation. Everything about him was action and vigour. How she wished he could have accepted disability. They could have curated an exhibition and used art as a key to understanding it. The man he used to be would have loved that. His old bank would have hosted it. Or, they could have travelled and cruised anywhere in the world, maybe even visited his daughters in Australia. But Virginia and Emma would never have seen him, let alone her. Even though James and his first wife, Lucinda, had been divorced for years before Hermione met him, the daughters still accepted their mother's twisted narrative. Through this murky lens, Hermione was the marriage-wrecker, seductively stealing him from them all, and then making him leave them. Lucinda had managed to create a completely new narrative, eradicating her regular infidelity and loudly denouncing his "affairs," the brief relationships that followed their divorce.

"It was my 'tryathon' time," James had joked. "I was trying to see who could live with me and who I could live with. And you ended it." She had laughed. She loved his sense of humour. He did still have a sense of humour, didn't he, even after the loss of his girls? She wasn't imagining it?

They fell in love with violent suddenness in the presence of her painting. It was transformative. Within a month of meeting her, he had sold his Knightsbridge bachelor pad and bought their St. Johns Wood Georgian house with its famous ballroom. They celebrated their 45th birthdays within two weeks of each other and were married six months later. It was obvious to them both that no children would come from this marriage. Neither of them wanted adoption, and Hermione had long since abandoned the idea of being an elderly mother, but James wanted a family home because he felt part of a family for the first time in his life. And Hermione felt his certainty, his strength, like a healing ripple that went through her and took her over, making her arms and fingers reach for brushes and paint again.

Her heart was so ready to welcome his daughters, anyone he loved, but the girls, Virginia and Emma, 10 and 8 years old then, never came to visit. And he had hardly seen them for five years. Lucinda had found an elderly millionaire from Sydney and was happy to take them as far away as possible. She didn't want money or shared custody. She just wanted to get away.

And now he was dead, and they had missed the chance. Despite all the emails and letters, there was never any response. They would be 33 and 31 now. Not girls anymore. She had given up sending birthday cards and presents in the last decade. Disappearing daughters, vanished just like her dream babies. She was ready to take legal action, and hire a private detective, but he would have none of it. He had a box in his study where he noted the dates of cards and letters sent. There was also a fund set up for each, but only if they make contact and understand what had happened. If they were true daughters of his, they would grow to understand their mother's perfidy and trace him. He had the same email address and was easy to find online. So, she had let go of them, too.

Hermione still had a website. Her name—it was a joke that had worn thin. Hermione at winterstale.com. Her mother, the late Lady Cressida Lambton loved Shakespeare and especially his play *The Winter's Tale.* She somehow identified with Hermione. What a name to inflict on her daughter. Poor Hermione is wrongly seen as unfaithful by her husband King Leontes, just as she had been turned into an immoral woman by his family.

Slowly and nervously, after placing the papers on her bed for reading later, she found herself walking to her studio door, holding onto the gold walking stick like a diviner. Perhaps it was magic! It seemed to have a life of its own, guiding her to her studio. Yes. 70 years old. It was time to open it. She was not Dorian Gray. She was not Bluebeard's victim. There had to be some beauty in this, some new light. She was old and had some wisdom.

It was dark in the studio with the heavy blinds lowered and the curtains secured over them, but there was still a familiar, encompassing smell. Her loyal cleaner, Juanita, still cleaned and polished the studio, and put new water out into shiny jars as if feeding a plant.

"You will paint again, Lady Hermione. You are alive. Your room is alive. He is dead. You are not," Juanita had said.

Turning the light on, her remaining paintings twinkled at her from around the room. These were the paintings she had not included in her last exhibition, either because she only wanted her best paintings to be passed on, or because there was something about them that she could not bear to let go of yet. She was entranced. She always was. It was a ballroom, a beautiful ballroom with ornate cornices and acres of wall for her paintings from which to shine intermittently. They came out of her, but they were their own creatures, objective, separate. She felt she was sitting in a rowing boat in a vast sea, and the paintings were small lighthouses pointing the way. There, on the easel, carefully varnished to stay protected, waiting for her, was the unfinished canvas that had been calling out to her ever since James died. There was her palette and all the colours of the world calling to her, bushes of brushes. Her wonderland. And there, a huge painting, her largest, wrapped neatly in bubble wrap (thank you John) was her curse painting, waiting on the wooden stand.

She could not face it quite yet.

Let's take this one first, she thought. Taking off the dust cloth, there on the easel in the centre of the room was her last painting still unfinished. There was the backdrop of battle and war, harsh hills and valleys, all brown and dry and scorched grass. The foreground was a large black wheelchair. A man sat on it as if it were a magnificent stallion. His hands held onto the controls. He looked as if he was flying. But his face was unfinished.

"Because you were unfinished, my poor darling," she said to herself. "You could not stay on, you could not face it."

And then she craved the real light, the light outside. She opened the floor-to-ceiling curtains and then the blackout blinds.

How she loved this room and James for finding it for her. "I have found your art studio," James had said. "It will be your wonderland." She could not believe it when she first saw the room. Every part of her being yearned to paint there. And she did. Frozen by her previous lover's disappearance, this room thawed her and she continued to paint until the accident broke James. The curse. What did it mean? And she could not bear the freedom of her beautiful room and craft when all his joy had left him.

How could she notify Lucinda, Virginia, and Emma? There had never been any response to the emails and letters. Who even knew if they still lived together? The girls were not girls any more, they were women now. They might even have children. A pang hit her. She might even be a step-grandmother and would never know. A further pang. The ballroom was hurting her. Could she manage to go on?

At 21, she had fallen in love with a fellow art student, Vadim. His face was fading all the time, fading under layers of oils, of landscapes, and seascapes. Were his eyes so dark? Did he have real human skin? It was thanks to James she was freed from him. Before James, she painted him all the time. She imagined the babies they would have had. She painted them everywhere. Victorian cherubs on ceilings, on vases. They all had the same dark eyes. He laughed at her, stroking the oil paint hair of his latest paint-child.

"How many have I got now?" he would ask each time they met.

"You have tribes, you have peopled the world." And she would laugh before they rolled back into bed.

One more year of college left and she wanted them to holiday together in the summer recess. But he had to work in London to add to his student grant for the last year. Suddenly, he stopped phoning her, and then he did not return. After two years of being soulmates, bodymates: just silence. And then a curious formal letter sent to her, stating that he had to urgently return to his own country in mysterious circumstances. And that was it for another two decades.

She had to paint him out of her system, paint the babies out into their world of sunlight and air, and properly have the goodbye he had not granted her. And that was it, until she met James two decades later. She was too loyal to her spirit babies and her paintings to try for real babies again. It was almost a relief that they both felt too old to start again.

But while they felt too old to start a family, they were enthused by each other's vitality. Indeed, it was the restless power in James that drew her when she saw him lost in thought in front of one of her paintings. It was "wonderland."

Yes. Let's go there. Do it. Now.

Slowly, slowly, sitting on the wooden chair and putting down the gold stick, she began to unwrap the canvas. The sound of the bubble wrap crackling as she pulled at it felt like tiny gunshots into her heart. Could she bear to see it? The painting he fell in love with, that made him fall in love with her, and then turn against her.

There. *Wonderland,* her largest canvas, depicting a stone wall of an art exhibition graced by three paintings, each the same size and in a golden frame. Each of the three paintings invited you to wonder about its meaning and placing. One of the paintings included her missing babies. Babies on shells floating in the sea, babies in the petals of flowers, babies playing on puffball clouds in the sky. They all had the same shining dark eyes and blushing skin. Was it the place where she would lose them or claim them? Were they frozen there, or were they free? In the second, a beautiful lake with calm trees around it, transformed, halfway along into a dangerous waterfall with jagged rocks. It showed the way her first love had turned to horror. But James claimed he fell in love with her looking at her Icarus, the third painting.

In the painting, Icarus was high in the sky but on a black stallion. On the ground was a small wheelchair. Somehow, James recognised himself, the dangerous shadow-side of his yearnings. The painting struck him at the deepest level. He bought the painting and that was it for the future. She had been seen and recognised at the deepest level, and so had he. He had lost his children through a scheming ex-wife and she had lost her spirit babies and her eternity lover. Were they the same? Had he let go his of real children too easily? Four years had gone by since her Icarus had fallen — and from a black horse. No wonder he had turned against her. No wonder he said she had cursed him.

Two years had gone by. Wonderful Wheelchairs. Wonderland. Her studio. Having a ball. "My kingdom for a horse." And this holiday leaflet. There was synchronicity here. Would it help her to finish the painting? If he could not bear to think of himself disabled, could she help him even now?

Chapter Eight

It was a muggy morning and Marion was not feeling happy about the 6AM start. Sun hats, lotion, sting relief cream, comb, *The New Yorker*, *Granta*, and *The Times Literary Supplement* were strewn on her side of the bed. Steve lay on his side, dodging the printouts of directions and tourist schedules. All this just for a long weekend in England.

The bars on his right protected him from falling out of bed, but those on the left kept her away from him. Or rather kept his incontinence pads away from her. Kept him in his bed-castle high and dry.

Wonderful Wheelchairs! Steve had enjoyed the alliteration. It had set him off on a humorous journey: charismatic commode, handsome hoist, nefarious nappy. To say nothing of Alicia in *Terra Mirabile*. She ought to be grateful. Wonderful Wheelchairs had provided Steve with more light relief than the last hospital visit and the black humour of the Do Not Resuscitate.

The consultant had come to offer a "dignified respectful talk" about it. With a practised compassionate gaze and sweet voice she said, "I just want you to think about the benefits of dying naturally, rather than having heavy dangerous procedures for resuscitation that could leave you in a worse state."

Marion raged silently. How seductive this could sound to a poor elderly person in a confused state, or those with a learning disability, or those unwanted.

They had only come for a review after his last fall — one of the joys of cerebral vascular dementia. Steve was elegant and slim as always in his corduroy trousers (he had worn them since the 1960s) and polo neck jumper. Even though he was in a wheelchair, he still looked like the Anglo-Saxon scholar he had been. They both stared in amazement at each other and then at the doctor.

"Are you aware," began Marion, "that if I wanted to die naturally we wouldn't take any pill or have any operation or go to hospital."

"Exactly," echoed Steve. "And no removal of gallstones or taking of antibiotics or having a trespass — no, bypass."

They high-fived each other as the consultant nervously left the room.

"It's worse than *One Flew Over the Cuckoo's Nest*," said Steve.

"The cheek of it," said Marion.

They went home with vigour and clarity and drank a glass of champagne that night.

That was a month before Steve saw the leaflet for the Wonderful Wheelchair Company.

"We can't resist anything as wordy as this," he laughed. His good mood at the booking had lasted. He felt as if his memory hadn't been slipping away as much as it had been before.

Marion had gone ahead and booked. She knew she needed more help. Her own leg problem had gotten worse, along with the stress incontinence.

"It will take me a day to get over this, getting up this early," muttered Marion. "And then it is almost time to return. I never tutored anyone before 9am, except for a brief period nearly half a century ago, and now, outside of hospital or war, I never will again! To start this early for a holiday weekend is mad."

"*Calme-toi!*" he called merrily.

"Not long now and we can have a good sleep on the coach. But, yes, we don't need such an early start again."

Marion saw only four students a day now and never started before 10 AM. "Students" might not be the right word. They were not children studying for exams or undergraduates. They were largely well-paid, highly educated midlife or post-midlife adults needing to learn French, or to brush up their French for major life events like moves or promotions. She tried not to notice the lengthening queue on her waiting list. Brexit had ruined work for many language teachers, but with her textbooks and podcasts, she remained in demand. What she had reluctantly stopped was her previous high-level diplomatic translating. She did not have the stomach for that now — not in this age of disinformation. Poor

Macron. Who would be a French leader to a country still re-enacting the revolution?

She slammed the large suitcase shut. All the extra pills that had to be taken with them now were like a travelling pharmacy, to say nothing about their incontinence pads or the spares, creams, and Velcro tops. Very romantic. Perhaps they should have two suitcases, she thought: one for them and one for their disabilities. But then she noticed she was having a lesser moment and would be all right in a minute. She was never good this early in the morning.

"Marion! We are supposed to be making marvellous new memories for me, remember!" remonstrated Steve, laughing. "Recollection, recall, retention, reminiscence, remembrance, mind, retrospection — antonyms for the word memory: amnesia, amnesic ..."

"Stop," she called to his English lecturer self, all her irritation gone. "That was brilliant! You are frightening me. My memory is going faster than yours!"

"Competitive to the last!" said Steve. "Wondering who will get to the Grim Reaper first? In the words of the immortal Emily Dickinson:

> Because I could not stop for Death –
> He kindly stopped for me –
> The Carriage held but just Ourselves –
> And Immortality."

Marion wiped a tear. His precious memory. Just listen to the wonderful man. *Vouloir c'est pouvoir* — to want is to be able — and when you couldn't be able? What happens next?

Qui craint de souffrir, il souffre déjà de ce qu'il craint. "He who fears suffering is already suffering that which he fears." How she was helped by Jean de la Fontaine, the famous poet and fabulist in seventeenth-century France. Marion regularly quoted him.

When she briefly went back to therapy, after Steve was first diagnosed, she remembered something similar from the great British psychoanalyst, Winnicott: "The catastrophe you fear will happen has, in fact, already happened. When we worry, we're naturally fixated on what will occur next. It's the future with its boundless possibilities for horror."

Horror and comedy. The GP had also come around for a little talk. She didn't know about the consultant. "It's about your DNR," she said in a practised chatty tone.

"We are R," enunciated Steve.

"We are!" agreed Marion, giggling.

"Resuscitate," they both sang, the two former senior lecturers made to feel delinquent for wanting to stay alive.

She relaxed, picked up the papers from the bed, lotion and sun hats, and went into the kitchen to check the travelling bag. Before, he would have helped her with it. Before — stop, no need to go there. She stuffed the papers into the transit bag. At least there were no passports to find or Covid certificates.

"I mustn't forget my Beowulf," he called.

"Your Beowulf?"

"Yes. I still haven't finished my paper on Grendel."

There was a pause. Marion returned to the bedroom and sat gently on her side of the bed.

"Darling — you finished your paper on Grendel and his link to Cain."

"Well, I have some further thoughts on the impact of Christianity on Anglo-Saxon myth," said Steve, rising up into a sitting position and with renewed vigour in his voice.

Not Grendel again. He had wrestled with that paper for years before it was published. No other piece of work had affected him like that before. It was the last paper he had published. Five years ago. When he was first diagnosed. Grendel, the monster, the lonely one, the outcast. Poor Steve. Marion shuffled in her seat. The GP had said it was important not to disagree.

"Good idea!" she said and kissed his cheek.

He smiled. "Have you called the aubergine?" he asked.

She burst out laughing. This is how they were now. The English lecturer and the French lecturer suddenly segueing into two old cripples. The precious jewel of memory is either sharp and diamond-like or dissolving into the air.

"Do you mean Uber?"

And there he was restored. They both roared with laughter.
"I did."
And this was how it was.

Chapter Nine

Lavender in the air. A fragrance of memories. How could he do it? Was this holiday a dare gone too far, even for Desperate Dan (as his family called him)? Booking a holiday at a time like this, an anniversary. Nobody did things like this.

Doris and Daniel were, as usual, in their neat-and-tidy front room. She had polished the silver Sabbath candlesticks — one of the few family heirlooms her grandmother had managed to bring out of Russia. Now she was polishing the marble mantelpiece and would next be returning the family photographs to their allotted places. Already polished, they were queuing neatly in their silver frames on the dining table, waiting to be put back in order. On the table in a lead crystal vase, bought on an Austrian holiday, were the crimson blooms of dahlia and white astrantia flowers edged with deep pink from their small south-facing garden. Even the flowers came to full bloom at the right time, their water already changed.

"You are so careful, it is like watching a goldfish bowl being cleaned, taking care not to frighten the fish," laughed Daniel, but he watched with pleasure. He did not know how, but it calmed him. Doris could get so anxious about everything, especially after the death of their son, Daniel Junior. But this task showed her at her most competent and calm.

He was on his recliner, intermittently reading the papers and watching her fondly despite his growing panic at the secret he was about to tell. His grandmother and grandfather, their photos, came first. All stiff in a ghetto photographer's studio. Times were different then. That was the only photo of his grandparents' life post-pogroms and pre-Holocaust. Their time.

Then came his mother and father. Bless. Look at their smiles. Just after the war. The Battle of Cable Street — they were there. So were Doris's parents. The East End managed to revolt against the Blackshirts and mounted police. Smiles were different then. It was the dawn of a new age, they had thought. How he missed them. They were all grouped on the left-hand side.

Then came her wonderful parents. Unlike him, she didn't have wedding photos of either set of grandparents. Lost in the war, and lost to life. But there was a profusion of carefully archived photograph albums. What a photographed child Doris was. To prove she was alive. To make up for all the empty spaces, the pogroms and gas ovens.

"Well, we had the real thing," his father-in-law had said, lighting his pipe. "Chin up. No need for copies."

Their wedding day was forty years ago. His mother-in-law had learned to play "My Old Dutch" on the piano especially for the occasion and then "My Yiddisher Mama." Everyone cried. How Doris had loved that out-of-tune old piano. Her mother had passed it to her when rheumatism put an end to her own tinkling. But the music gene had passed by Doris completely. She loved listening, but it was Dorothy, their daughter, who loved playing it. Even though the piano tuner had now given up on it, she could not bear to remove it, despite their promises of buying her a new one.

"She's a chip off the old block," Daniel had laughed.

"It's got Buba and Zaider in it," Dorothy would protest, polishing the beautiful mahogany wood. And, of course, her own family photographs sat on top of it now, continuing the tradition, albeit with wooden rather than silver frames.

Daniel could not help laughing, and on one occasion had said, "Well you better open the lid and let them out," and Dorothy had run out of the room crying. She was a sensitive one, Dorothy, always had been and not surprising given the circumstances, losing her twin.

He moved quickly on. Him and Doris. His family loved Doris and her family just like he did. Daniel and Doris. "Dan Dare," Doris called him. And he did dare. Until the stroke obliterated his ability to walk more than a few steps. He didn't want to think too much about that. It upset him to think about his disability. And now this new decision to dare to bring up the holiday.

And then their twins, Dorothy and Danny Junior. You could feel the gaps, the deaths, the grandparents, one after the other, falling like ninepins. All their lovely relatives who made the world secure and who you could not imagine leaving the world. Such a close lovely family. How perfect it had all been.

Doris paused her polishing as she always did. Daniel felt it in his heart.

A photo of Daniel and Dorothy. Daniel Junior, proud in his football kit. Daniel Junior at his bar mitzvah. How beautifully he read and sang. Dorothy at her hockey match, Dorothy in her school play. And then Dan Junior's funeral. Just like that. Just as it had felt. A bright life suddenly extinguished: 18 years old, struck by a drunk driver, killed within minutes on a sunny August, just before his first term at university.

Pause. Fast forward. Dorothy's wedding to Jeffrey. No brother to rejoice. Dorothy's children DJ (named Daniel Junior, in honour of her dead twin and her dad) and May (in honour of Doris's birthday) — and no uncle to look on proudly. Could you have two juniors? Daniel struggled with it. It was alright that his son was Dan Junior. But his grandson? Or did you need a Dan Junior Junior? They called him DJ instead.

Dan returned to focus on Doris. How would she take his news? She had taken his stroke with her usual grit, and everything that happened because of that. But this?

Doris had not brought the next photo up.

"It's August again, Dan " she said.

"Yes. I wondered when you would notice."

"Did you know for a while?"

"Well, there was more lavender than usual." He looked at her fondly. "You know love, your polishing is a better calendar than our grand-babies." He pointed to the wall calendar Dorothy had made with photos of their children on each page. August and May, their "namesake" months, were always a special photograph. For August, Dan Junior was in fancy dress singing "My Old Dutch." Dorothy had been excited that it was Chevalier's brother Auguste who had written the lyrics.

Doris's eyes returned to the mantelpiece. "When DJ and May get married, we won't have room up there," she said worriedly.

He grinned. "They might not get married. People aren't, nowadays."

"Well, our people are," she insisted.

"Well, mine will have come down before then," he laughed.

"Don't you say things like that, Dan Rickstein," she remonstrated,

"Well, we can put them up on the wall," he suggested.

She looked at the wall worriedly.

"We could always move and get a larger front room," he said.

Doris looked shocked, and then roared with laughter, and Dan joined in. Duster in her right hand and smoothing her apron with her left, she sat on the armchair next to him.

"You know, your mum and dad were right, Doris love. We have the real people. We don't need the copies."

She put the duster down. "I wish Dorothy hadn't called the nipper, Dan," sighed Doris.

"That's why we call him DJ," said Dan.

"One Dan Junior was okay. But we lost him and had another one."

"You can never have too many Dans," said her husband, squeezing her hand.

"But it could be a burden for the poor kid," she worried.

"And what about May for your birthday?" he asked.

There was a pause. "Do you think it could be their — well, that they are like — well, it is like our mantelpiece for them?" asked Doris. A sharp intake of breath at this thought. "Like her and the piano too," she finished.

"Oh, my goodness. You have got it in one there!" said Dan. Come on Dan. I dare you, he thought. Dan Dare, Desperate Dan. "There must have been something like this on my mind," he said. "Damn it woman, you have always been my mind-reader."

"Well, what is?" she asked, quickly putting the remaining photos in place. "Don't leave it hanging in the air."

"Well," he said, shifting uncomfortably on his chair. "I've got something for you this August," he smiled hesitantly.

"Now Daniel Rickstein, you're always getting me things, you generous man," smiled Doris.

"Be my legs and bring me the envelope from my top drawer," he said.

Doris hurried to their bedroom. He was the one losing his legs. How had he managed to surprise her yet again? He was amazing. In the top drawer was a large envelope addressed to both of them. The envelope had ornamental writing across the top "Make Marvellous Memories: From the Wonderful Wheelchair Company."

What was this?

"I dare us," he said simply. "It's time."

Chapter Ten

Another coach load of cripples for the weekend. I have had enough of it," shouted Les Dawkins. "Just to make an honest woman of you. I'll be dead by the time the day comes."

Tracey Miller was sitting by the kitchen table surrounded by several editions of *Bride* magazine, notes, and felt-tips, her double D size breasts spilling over the pink "Bride's Notebook." She held a pen with a pink fluffy heart on it in her right hand.

"What's that, love?" she called, yet again not focusing on him.

He walked behind her and squeezed both breasts. "Beep, beep," he called.

She turned around to hug him. "It's going to be the best day of my life," she said. "I'm fifty-six, Les, and you are the first guy to properly get me to the altar, to really stay with me for that. I have waited so long for this, and I know everything I want to make it perfect."

He belched. An anger built inside him despite the foolish smile on his face. "I've got another fucking Wanking Wheelchairs because of you next week. Picking them all up, taking them on all the outings, and then taking them all back again. And they kill me. Fitting all the chairs properly in the coach, dealing with the hydraulic lifts, the stupid questions all through the driving. And I don't get paid any extra for being a bloody comedy act. As if wheelchairs are wonderful, and as if there are wonderful memories. It's queuing at the disabled loo, queuing at the Costas, queuing to go down the coach lift, queuing to come back up it. It is a bloody British obstacle course."

"You know you love them, poor bastards," said Tracey, offering him a crumb of meaning before putting on some more red lipstick. "And you are part of their holiday. You are marvellous and you do it to give me marvellous memories, too."

A rare and honest smile covered his face. She stood up and turned round to face him, planting a perfect pair of red lips on his cheek. "That will make them turn round at the Hen and Horse," she laughed.

"Now how did you know I was going there?" he asked.

"We should go on Mr. and Mrs.," she said excitedly, "Bet I could answer anything about you."

"You think you know your Master's Mind, do you?" he grinned, feeling her silicone implants. He had paid for them as a Christmas present for himself and her, and they had both enjoyed them.

"I don't have to go to the Hen and Horse for company now, do I? I don't have to put all my eggs in one basket."

"Or you could go with me to celebrate your extra job and then we come back here early. You've got a relatively easy job tomorrow, haven't you?"

Les turned his head away for a moment, experiencing a pang of something unfamiliar that made his eyes water. All those years of no-one. Driving up and down different motorways with different coaches. Schools, stag nights, hen nights, and now a cripple carrier. No-one knew he had no-one. He could chat with the other drivers at all the motorway cafes in the UK. Name any cafe, and he would be sure to find someone he knew to chat with. And then home. And strangely he did have a home. Somehow he did save all his money for something undefinable. A small two-bed bungalow with a nice lounge, kitchen, and bathroom. His. How had he done that? But no-one to share it with. And no-one who knew. Mother dead, dad drunk and disappeared. No-one until Gwyne, who appeared on one of those awful hen night drives, chatted to him at each stop, and then decided she didn't want to go to the hen-do, as her mate was marrying her old boyfriend. She asked Les if she could travel back with him. He had felt sorry for her little drunken self, with the mascara running down her small, pinched face. He took her back to Hen and Horse and, of course, it turned out she had been sofa-surfing and had nowhere to sleep.

The men at the Hen and Horse were all oohing and aahing. They had never seen him with a girl before, and it seemed amazing to him that he had a real home, his own flat, his own mortgage, and could invite her to stay — just for the weekend, mind. Just to help her over the wedding blues. "Mouse," he called her, little Gwyne. She was tiny and damaged, with straggly, black-dyed hair. He could ignore it at first, the shifty guys lurking outside his door. He knew what they kept in their pockets and the way his savings disintegrated to a powder. He knew the holes in her body. The little portholes the powder could disappear into. And at the Hen and Horse, they just pitied him now. All the whisky. But she kept his kitchen tidy. She polished the dining room table. And she made him feel proud he had a home.

Just a day, and another day, and then a last weekend and then a last week. It was her old frenemy getting pregnant that did it. Screaming and crying. And in the Hen and Horse. That was it for him. He told her to fuck off, just fuck off. That was it. The end. He had had enough. And she shouted at him that she was pregnant, too, and it was his, if it was, and ran out. Ran out and swallowed up by the dark sky. He was 30. It was a year before he went back into the Hen and Horse. The well-insulated nest of men greeted him without comment. The circle closed around him. They had all been there or somewhere worse. Then it was back to more and more motorways, saving every penny he could and another couple of decade before Trace.

Now he was 55. Where did that time go? And how did he get Trace?

Everything happened in his coach. He could write a book about it. He was hiring a stretch limo at that time, so he could do weddings too, a little sideline. It was Trace who booked it. He was impressed with that. Most of the wedding cars were booked by the groom or in-laws or bridesmaids. She did it herself. She knew what she wanted, too. Sparkly water and juices for the journey to the church — she didn't want anyone to be drunk before the wedding. And it could be champagne on the way to the hotel after. They settled the price very straightforwardly, and she paid her deposit. He picked her and her two best friends up at Coach Lane in Hayward's Heath. He liked the name of the road. Regardless of all the other vehicles he could manage, coaches were his life. "Even though it can feel like a pumpkin," he joked.

Exactly on time, she came out, all in white, flanked by her friends. A vision of bouncing blond and warmth and acceptance. Her beaming smile and thanks for his punctuality warmed him in a way he rarely felt.

Her friends were not memorable to him, but kindly, and not drunk, and they laughed together in a genuine way.

When they got to the church, there was a handful of anxious people standing outside.

"It's his brother and family. They must have worried I wouldn't come," laughed Trace.

"Well, there is still time to change your mind," laughed her friend Mo.

The car slowly pulled up and Mo and another friend helped Trace out, shaking the long white train and setting the tiara and veil on her head. The brother and family came nearer. They were all frowning.

"Dave — anything wrong?" asked Trace. "He hasn't crashed his car has he?"

Dave stood silently and took out his iPhone. He scrolled down and handed it to Trace. Les could feel it as if it was his own heart breaking again. The bastard had jilted her. Right at the altar. He was sure of it.

Tracey read it out. "Tell her I can't go through with it. I'm sorry. I don't love her. Better admit now than later."

He jumped out of his seat, moved through the small, dumbfounded group and put an arm around Trace. She sobbed and sobbed.

She got back in the limousine. Asked her friends to go and deal with any problems in the church and to cancel the catering and, if it was too late, get the local homeless charities to come.

"Just drive," she asked Les. And he drove. From Hayward's Heath to Brighton, along the coast and back to London. He parked outside a clothes shop and she told him what to get. He bought her clothes to wear, a nightie, and overnight things, and then it was back to his place. And she never left.

And this wedding really, really mattered.

Chapter Eleven

Fuck you!" shouted Roland. He kicked his case open and flung his glass tumbler, filled with orange juice, with all his force, onto the hard floor. Splinters of glass flecked with orange liquid exploded everywhere. A volcano of hurt.

Andrzej and Olena raised their eyebrows at each other despairingly and sighed. They had never wanted the glass to be anywhere near him, and warned him this would happen, especially with a change to his routine.

"I know a holiday is good for him," emphasised Olena, "but it is a change, and even a 2-to-1 staffing will find it hard if he breaks crockery and glass. Especially glass."

Nonetheless, the behavioural psychologist, Dr. Brown, had said Roland would not know the consequences of his actions if he did not see something break. Removing all glasses could make him more violent.

"Perhaps he needs to see me dead on the floor to know how much he hates women," said Olena, angrily.

Andrzej glanced at her sharply. She looked exhausted. Pushing his suitcase to one side, she was busy sweeping up with the brush and dustpan. First the main glass shards, then the mop. Then she would vacuum. Even the tiniest splinter of glass could damage bare feet. She had a duty of care. Her face was determined. She would not let Roland's disturbance get inside her and destroy their work.

Andrzej thought she should not be allocated such a violent young man, especially with her family still living in Kyiv. He still had family in Poland — he was the only one here — and already the tensions were building with Russia. And what an irony: as well as improving their English, he and Olena spoke to each other in Russian. He had learned Russian and English at school, and Olena and her family had never learned Ukrainian, and now in Ukraine the Ukrainian Russian speakers were seen as unpatriotic.

Andrzej listened. There was no more noise coming from Roland. The packing for his holiday had clearly disturbed the poor man. He would be rocking quietly in his room by now, his expression would be a clown face of anguish.

"I'll go and check on him in a minute. We have half-an-hour before the coach," he said.

"And then it is the two of us all the time with him, and a plus-one carer from them. This will be our easiest week. Maybe it will be a holiday for us."

"Yes," she replied, tossing her long blonde plait and wiping a tear from her eyes. "And when they see how bad he is — expel him from the hotel perhaps — our agency will realise he needs a closed ward, and cannot be kept in the community. That he is a danger." Emptying the glass debris into protective cardboard, she put it in the bin and then went out for the mop.

Andrzej, meanwhile, zipped the case up quickly after folding the clothes that had been disturbed from the top. Poor Roland. An elderly mother — Farida — had him at 45. Now he was 25 years old and vastly obese, and his mother was 70. Her husband had run off, upset they had given birth to "an ugly cretin." And she was left to bring him up as best she could, alone and unsupported. Poor Roland — he had T-shirts with Star Wars pictures on them. A little teddy bear was fitted onto an outside zip pocket. The bear wore a little T-shirt with a well-known logo — Rolo — the name of a chocolate sweet as well as Roland's nickname.

How hard to be a young man with such severe disabilities. "Roland," Andrzej called gently, walking towards the bedroom further along the corridor. "Everything is ready. Can you help me with the cases? I don't think I am strong enough."

Understanding what was likely to happen, Olena quickly withdrew into the kitchen taking the mop with her. The hoovering could wait. Roland charged out from his bedroom into the dining room, arms outstretched to hug Andrzej. Andrzej tensed his whole body ready for the onslaught. Roland being affectionate was as frightening as Roland being angry. Only 25 years old and twenty stone.

"Sorry! Sorry," shouted Roland, weeping copiously, clinging onto Andrzej.

"Okay! Don't get me all soaked, Rolo. You are like a fountain when you cry."

"Sorry Andrzej, sorry Olena — bad manners to women."

Olena moved further back into the open-plan kitchen. "It's good to say sorry and even better not to do bad things so you don't them have to say sorry." She looked at him seriously.

"I know you are worried. It is a holiday. Different people. We don't know them. It is different to what you usually do. Andrzej and I don't know them, either. We don't know what it will be like. So it is the three of us together. We want a quiet holiday and not violence."

Roland sat down breathlessly, leaving Andrzej to wipe his T-shirt.

"Love you, Olena," he said. "Still coming on holiday with me?"

Olena paused, hiding her hand behind her back as she realised a small shard of glass had pricked her finger and she did not want his guilt to be increased.

"Of course, she is coming with me and you," said Andrzej. "She wouldn't let you down, even though you couldn't manage your feelings."

Roland moved a step nearer her.

"Don't come any closer," said Olena. "I must hoover now."

"So, are you ready for a holiday, Roland?" asked Andrzej. "The cab will be coming to take us to the coach stop. I will be sitting next to you."

Olena flashed a smile of relief at him.

"High five, Big A," said Roland. He moved closer to do a high five.

"One minute for the hoover and then we say goodbye to your room," said Olena.

"Can I hoover?" asked Roland.

Olena paused with uncertainty.

"Promise. Pretty please. Little finger promise. Piggy promise," he pleaded.

Andrzej sighed at the incongruence of child-like promises and the violent behaviour. He stood up and brought the hoover in from the hall cupboard. "I will put the plug in first, Roland, and then you are going to be helpful and hoover the floor. I swept up the glass, but we have to make sure there is no danger to your bare feet. Little bits of glass can almost be invisible."

Roland held the hoover like a precious object, and slowly made his way around the dining room. Every moment or so, a little tinkle signified another tiny piece of glass caught. "I am catching them, Olena and Big A. I broke the glass but now I am catching the pieces. Sorry."

"Thank you, Roland. That helped," said Olena, feeling confident to move forward and take the hoover from him.

"Chocolate biscuit for good boy Roland, Olena?," asked Roland.

"On the coach, there will be good things we have brought for the journey, we have your pens and paper, carrots, and a cheese and egg sandwich," said Olena, trying to sound cheerful. Please do not have another tantrum, she thought.

"And we must say goodbye to your room now," said Andrzej, getting up and walking out of the dining room.

Roland followed him. "Say goodbye to my room, and make sure it is all nice and ready for me to come back to," agreed Roland.

Olena sat down on the kitchen high stool and looked again at the information page. The cab would arrive in five minutes. Morris, their local one, to keep continuity. And then a twenty-minute drive to the coach stop. And the driver's name would be Les. It was not clear how many others would be on it.

They would be alright for the journey, Olena concluded. Roland liked sitting down and watching the view from the window. It would not be too long until the stop at the services.

Roland had a new wheelchair to cope with his extra weight. It was all folded up in the entrance hall. Olena's case was right next to it, on top of Andrzej's larger one. It seemed strange, the first holiday since she had come to England. It was work, but that felt much better than a real holiday. Her family had no more holidays; Kyiv had no more holidays.

Chapter Twelve

Muhammid jumped excitedly on his bed at the Hotel Mirabelle, bursting into song. "And I think to myself, what a wonderful world."

Ibrahim winced. *Oh no. Where did he get this taste for old songs from the West?*

"Did you see, brother? They brought a piano into Betty's Restaurant today. And they have one in Bert's Bar. Perhaps they will let me sing and play, and just look, brother!" laughed Muhammid, "a bed each, free food and lodging, and money to save."

Ibrahim frowned at him, but the excitement was in him, too. "Calm yourself, little brother. If we break the bed, it will come from our salary." They burst out laughing together, Muhammid sitting cross-legged on the bed and Ibrahim on the armchair.

"You are so clever, Ibrahim," sighed Muhammid. "A job that is also a holiday! And my English will improve."

"Yes. This is what we have to do! Learn whatever we can," emphasised Ibrahim.

"Then we can have a car and a house," added Muhammid.

"Gently, gently. It takes time. A few years at least to get a mortgage. And remember, we do not know if next week will be fully paid for."

Ibrahim stood up and pointed to the shiny hoist in the corner of the large double room. "Let's go over your handling skills here. We could have a lot of people who will need hoists."

Muhammid got off the bed reluctantly.

"Then, if there are enough bookings, when we have the lists, we will go through the of people on it and I have to think about allocation and meet with the other helpers and the—"

There was a knock on the door. Muhammid crossed himself, while Ibrahim walked to the door and opened it.

Irene Hanson — neatly bobbed white hair, large dangly gold hoop earrings, safari tight top, and leggings — bounced into the room with the confidence of a spritely grandma. Muhammid beamed back while Ibrahim watched with concern.

"You must be the Hussain brothers," she smiled. "Hope you had a good journey here and have had some time to relax before the excitement starts! I am Irene Hanson; and you," turning to Ibrahim, "are the older one and my deputy for WW for this trip, if we get the green light."

Ibrahim bowed his head with pleasure at this recognition. "Please sit down," he said, pointing to one of two smart wipe-clean chairs on each side of the little table, which was also a wipe-clean. Unlike the ground floor area, the bedrooms were all new and modern.

Irene picked up his expression as she sat down with a large sigh. "Yes. Really spic and span here. Makes keeping everything urine-safe much easier."

Ibrahim suppressed his shock at hearing a woman speak so naturally about human waste. But this job demanded such openness so long as there was dignity for the person.

"And it makes our guests, if we get them, feel less nervous and shamed. If we do not get them for next week, we will have more practice for the one after!" she added.

"Coffee, tea, or water?" asked Muhammid proudly, pointing to the little fridge and the crockery above it.

"Well, I was going to invite you to the staff lounge. It used to be the biggest bedroom on this floor, the last one down the corridor to the left. First time we have ever had one in a WW hotel. But since I am already here, thank you. Black coffee, please."

"Staff lounge," mused Ibrahim. "I did not know that."

"It won't be in our handouts yet. Too quick for all the changes. Poor Maanika and Naresh will have been rushed off their feet; well, pardon the expression — because of, you know. Covid flatlined our bookings, and now we hope people will be suddenly desperate for a holiday. I know this hotel really well. It's in my blood from living here. What a history it has had. From wartime dancehall, it has lost more stars than you've had hot dinners! Got really run down. My bestie, of all people, my infant and junior-school bestie, a marvellous woman, Charlene, the owner, bought it and has done it up real nice, and now Wonderful Wheelchairs has selected it for its Sussex holidays. Take a look at Bert's Bar. Check out the toilets, men's and women's, so you can tell our guests and the staff where they are. Get a look at Mirrorland today before any visitors get there. It is already becoming a thing! That is unique. Meals will be served at the tables now instead of self-service, so we don't have to bob up and down doubling as singing waiters."

"Singing waiters? I sing and play piano," said Muhammid excitedly.

"We might need that," said Irene with a friendly smile. "But the point is we can stay talking to our lovely lambs while the food is served, and to us as well. And it will be really good grub. Local produce."

"Very good for me," smiled Muhammid, stirring the coffee.

"Yes. Still growing," agreed Irene. "Whereas I need to stop growing." She patted her ample stomach, noticeable under the tight top and leggings. Ibrahim looked embarrassed, but Muhammid smiled back.

"You are a beautiful older lady," he said.

Irene tossed her white bob and giggled loudly. "Not so much of the old lady, young Muhammid."

They both laughed as he handed her the coffee. Ibrahim then pointed to the hoist at the opposite corner. "I was about to give Muhammid a further handling lesson," he said gently.

Muhammid's face instantly became serious. "Sorry brother. Thank you."

Irene sipped her coffee and then gently placed it down. "Sorry, Ibrahim. I can get carried away. I was so excited to see you, see you both, in fact. I am one of the oldest care team members since Wonderful Wheelchairs started. Of course, we will get down to the training needs of everyone. One delicate question I had for you, Ibrahim, and I will ask it in front of Muhammid.

"We take the confidentiality of our clients very seriously. They come from all walks of life, aristocrats and council estates, universities and learning disability homes, all parts of the country. But what they have in common is a mobility problem. Normally we take the privacy of our bodies for granted. But when you have a disability, other people are involved.

There are gender issues. Women who feel nervous about a man helping them with their personal care, men who feel nervous about a woman helping them — or the other way round."

"Yes," said Ibrahim sadly, "I have worked with a woman who had a very cruel mother, so she needed a man to help with personal care."

"Exactly," said Irene candidly. "And we have to talk to each other about first needing a pad, and second needing new sheets. And we need to share details as we go on the trips all together. But there is also confidentiality between staff, in that senior staff — Ibrahim and I — also need to talk about how new care assistants are managing. And because you are brothers and sharing a room, it may be, Muhammid, that you sometimes, however hard we work on it, might hear things that are not meant for you as a first-timer. But right now —"

Her mobile phone ringtone interrupted the conversation. A huge smile crossed her face "Yes. Yes. Yes! Right away," she shouted.

"Boys! We are on! The names have all been emailed. I need to go over the lists of participants with Ibrahim and allocate carers. It is all right for you to stay in that meeting, Muhammid. We will have that in the staffroom in fifteen minutes because no-one else will be arriving tonight. End of the corridor on the left. The door that says private."

She stood and faced Ibrahim. "If you think it is okay for you, I think it could be helpful for him to be familiar with the names before we hand them out, so he has a more comfortable start. But only if you think that is okay."

Ibrahim nodded. "And then he will finish his last training on the equipment today and be on time to join the coach at its last pick-up point tomorrow to help with the wheelchairs."

Irene nodded and walked out briskly, leaving two shell-shocked men in her wake.

Act 2
The Journey

Chapter Thirteen

Two women burst into the cloakroom in fits of laughter and made their way to the make-up counter and mirrors. There, they perched on the spare chrome and red velvet high stools as if they were settling down at home. Large bags were dumped at their sides on the floor, and small make-up bags miraculously appeared on the counter.

"Free nibbles and booze when it formally opens, and we know how it all works here now. We can get here first. Go on! I dare you!" laughed Di.

Zen applied the last flicks of mascara and studied her face critically in the huge, brightly-lit gilt mirror. Her brand-new bright blue push-up bra (or "push-off," as she called it) was her new armour. Hair done with cornrows for another seven weeks without having to do anything to it, bright red lipstick on, tight low-cut blue summer dress, and trusted blue high heels.

"Not bad for nearly 50, even if I say so myself," she laughed at the mirror, feeling the rows and then stroking her small gold crucifix lovingly.

"Why are you doing that?" asked Di.

"What?"

"You touch those gaps of bare skin on your head and then your cross," said Di.

Zen turned away. "Leave my cross out of it. That's for another day. When you get more of a brain. These are cornrows, not gaps of skin."

"Cornrows? It is hair. Why don't you do those nice long braids you did when we did the Pagoda."

Zen remained silent.

"You could catch a rich one on these holidays here," argued Di, changing the subject, running her hand through her newly blonde curls.

"Better than trying to be cruise-bait," she added. "Their wives have either just died or are about to, and they are too lazy to go looking so you just have to be there. Plop. Splat. They will drop onto your lap like soft fruit."

"Dried-out prunes more like," laughed Zen, coming away from that painful subject of hair.

"It's worth the money," continued Di. "Only one-night full board. Cheaper than a cruise too. You can afford a pampering day in the spa and get yourself ready for a really rich one this time."

Zen looked at her friend sceptically. "It's what you want to do, innit! You are shoving me to do the moves because you are one scared cow."

"No, I'm not," said Di. "I'm on to Ted, but he takes his time."

"Which he hasn't got much of," emphasised Zen. "And I think you are too late. That Meals on Wheels bitch has already got her teeth into him. The way he is, a soggy cucumber sandwich and he's yours. None of this matters anymore anyway," she added, pointing to her ample cleavage.

"It always matters," said Di, shoving her breasts up higher in her sports top. "It was worth doing it — even if it reminds them of milk instead of sex."

They both laughed loudly.

"Let's both do it then," offered Di.

"Take your pick gents! Chocolate or milk. We could do with a girls' night out. A 60s night," she giggled. "Can you imagine, Zen?" continued Di. "A 70s music night with 70-year-olds, and 80s with 80-year-olds."

"I'm not thick. You don't half go on," complained Zen.

"Then come with and we do it together. We can do it tomorrow."

"Me?" said Zen aghast.

"I can't manage all that mess," said Di tentatively, "You already have."

Di's husband had left her in her early 50s. Whereas Zen had managed her husband's cancer for years until his death.

"Oh, so I can go down shit alley again and you stay clean and dry?"

The two women sat silently for a moment, primping their hair. "Look, if you net an oldie and go on a cruise, you can bring me along to share wipe-up duties," said Di, as if offering a gift.

"If I net one, it will be one who brings a nurse with him. Otherwise, it is drinks at the bar only and not here," said Zen emphatically, pointing to her large cleavage.

"Okay. That makes sense. Let's do it then," agreed Di.

"You're like a dog in heat," complained Zen. "I don't know I want to go anywhere with you until you have cooled down.

"Bitch," muttered Di.

"Right, that's it," shouted Zen. "You can go back in the bar on your bloody own, because I don't want to be seen with you — you twisted gas-lighter. You clearly got me here tonight because you fancy your chances, don't want to admit it, and want to lumber me with the work. If you want me with you as Black age-bait tomorrow, you are going to have to do better than this."

And breasts aloft, she picked up her capacious handbag, thrust the make-up bag into it, and walked out, leaving a shocked Di lost for words. Cornrows! Bitch. Thick blonde bitch.

Without a pause, Zen walked angrily into Bert's Bar. There was a low but happy hum of conversation. A smell of leather. Still new. She paused to take it in. Instead of relishing the tap-tap of her sharp stiletto heels drumming on the wooden floor, she walked more gently. A small group had already congregated by the bar. There were men and women of all ages. Her eyes scanned the Chesterfield sofas and wing chairs. Lots of empty places, but once the grand opening happened, this would be packed.

Ah. Bingo. A silver fox on his own in the corner. He had dark skin; not as dark as her. She liked his look. Lots of empty beer bottles on the table in front of him and gin glasses as well. Could be in luck. She made her way to the corner, head held high, ignoring the looks that came towards her. She didn't care what they thought. The art deco lamps were on and the waiters wore bow ties. This place was classy, and so was she.

Just as she moved to the empty wing chair next to him and started to mouth, "This one free?" she suddenly saw he had no legs. None at all. She had never seen anything like it. Half of him was cool, brown, sleek — and then he just ended. Cut in half. Did he have a willy? Did it matter?

"Afghanistan," he said, with a tired smile.

"What's that when it's at home," Zen asked. Some bloody African country he thought she came from?

"Where an explosion got me," he said, amused by her response. "War," he added.

She took a deep breath. Slowly her eyes took him in.

"Yes. They are still missing," he said.

She burst out laughing. "It's easier looking the second time," she said.

"Try a third," he offered. He watched her eyes move up and then linger. "Yes. I have got one."

"Well, thank heavens for that," she said. "How would anyone know?"

He raised an eyebrow. "Well, they'd have no business knowing, would they, however curious they were, and if they did have a business to know they would find out or could ask me."

Zen put her hand to her mouth. "Oh, my God — it's the pot calling the kettle black. Except I am the Black one and she is the blondie."

Naresh frowned in bewilderment. "Pots, black, blondie?"

She burst out laughing. "It's my hair."

"The cornrows?," he asked.

She sat upright, absolutely shocked. "You know about cornrows?"

"I should hope so. My sister, among many other things, used to be a hairdresser."

"God help me. A light brown man with an English voice who knows cornrows."

Naresh could feel an extremely rare smile beginning to spread. Looking up, he saw a white woman of a certain age in skin-tight, low-cut clothes walking towards them with a frightened look on her face. This must be the friend.

"Zen," asked the woman. She looked at Naresh without flinching. "Can I join you both?" Zen shifted uneasily on her chair and then wordlessly signalled to the empty adjacent one.

"Zen?" asked Naresh getting more confused. "I'm Naresh."

"Naresh. Haven't heard that name before," said Zen. "I'm Zen. Short for Zendaya."

"Ah. Beautiful. Zendaya means beautiful," quipped Naresh with a cheeky grin.

"Does it? You trying to butter me up?" asked Zen.

"I will show you on my iPhone," he said, typing in the name and showing her the Wikipedia entry.

Di looked as well. "It's true," said Di.

Zen pointed to Di. "And that is my friend Di, except when we fight."

"Over cornrows," he said.

Di shook her hair, releasing perfume into the air, jingling her hoop earrings. "What the fuck is going on here? I go away just for a minute and a legless stranger knows me and my best friend's business."

"I'm leg-less, but I am not legless," smiled Naresh.

Zendaya burst out laughing. "True," she said.

"We just started to talk about people's business and what is or isn't," said Naresh.

"Okay," said Zen. "Then I need to be legless to tell you."

"Fine by me," said Naresh, "so long as you get them back later. I can't."

Zen burst out laughing.

"I think you are both mad," said Di, "but I am happy to buy the first round of drinks, which, as Zen knows, is not usual for me."

"True," agreed Zen. "A gin and tonic for me."

Naresh raised his right arm and, within moments, a waiter was with them.

"Three gin and tonics, please."

"Of course."

Zen and Di watched with amazement. There was a pause as the waiter returned with all three drinks on a small wooden tray, together with a bowl of nuts.

"You didn't even ask for that!" said Zen.

"Well, I am a magician," said Naresh. "I made my legs disappear. But I can get metal ones to walk back to my room with. They are called Lance and Roger."

Zen burst out laughing. "Bet your dick has got a name too," she said.

"Dick?" asked Di.

He nodded, coughing over his drink.

"You two ladies are pretty clever."

"Lance, Roger, and Dick," said Zen. "I like it."

Chapter Fourteen

At the coach pick-up stop, Maureen sat on the wooden bench, waiting. She was quite round in shape with flaming red hair, radiating warmth and friendliness with her perpetually beaming smile; a yellow teddy bear was clipped onto her bag teeming with prized objects that threatened to leap out at any moment. Her wheelchair was alongside her. She was on the phone to her carer, Alice.

"I'm not frightened, Alice, because this is my holiday and I am a brave independent woman. Yes. Yes. No-one here yet. Good time-keeper, aren't I, kind Alice? I thank you, Alice. Will have a friend soon. New friend."

Steve and Marion finally arrived at the pick-up point.

"This is the spot for coaches," said the taxi driver. "If it is not here now, it won't be long."

"Thank you, aubergine," Steve said to the driver. They all laughed. Marion took hold of the wheelchair handles as soon as Steve came down the ramp at the back of the cab.

"It looks pretty deserted right now," she said. "But look, the coffee shop is open. That's good if it rains."

And then she saw a big flag. "Marvellous Memories: Wheelchair Wonderland." There was a small red-headed woman with Down's syndrome sitting on the bench. Marion checked her own transit bag next to the two cases. "We clearly are in the right place."

Maureen had noted their arrival and turned off her phone immediately. "Hello," she said loudly to the new man and woman. "Are you going on my wonderful holiday with me?" She pointed to the flag.

Steve nodded.

"What are you called? My name is Maureen."

"Hello Maureen, I am Steve, and my wife is Marion."

Maureen gave an exaggerated smile. Focusing on Marion, she asked her if she was going to be her friend for the holiday. Not waiting for a reply, she smiled sweetly at Marion and Steve in turn. "Are you? Are you my friend, Steve?"

Steve smiled and replied, "So far."

Marion's heart melted. This was why Steve had been so loved by students. He always told the truth in a warm way.

Maureen sat thinking, studying his reply, and asked Marion again.

Marion took a deep breath. Was this going to be a busman's holiday? She still had one pupil with cerebral palsy and a severe learning disability who wanted enough French for her first independent holiday. "Friend means lots of different things, and there are different kinds of friends, aren't there? Perhaps we are holiday friends," she said slowly and cautiously, "because we are all travelling together and being friendly together."

Maureen agreed happily. "Not like my care worker friend Alice, or my friend in my home, or my sisters. They are friends. I used to have brothers too, but they died." Tears welled in her eyes.

Marion felt a pang for her, felt she understood something about her, and wondered how this holiday was going to be. It would be a change for Steve, being with so many people in wheelchairs, but also with those whose brains had never shone in the same way as his.

Suddenly, two more people appeared in the empty coach park. A youngish woman with long brown hair was racing ahead as fast as she could with her Zimmer frame, followed by an older woman pushing the empty wheelchair.

"Hello everybody. My name is Jane Edwards and I am frightened," she said breathlessly, sitting down on the empty wooden seat. "I am going fast because I will be in a wheelchair for the journey and I am stretching my legs, and I am frightened because I have not been away on a holiday for ten years when I went with my mum, who has passed away, bless her. And her name was Janet Edwards, and I am Jane Edwards, because she was my mum, so I have the same last name. They have outings in my home, but I don't want to go away with them because I don't like them so much. But I am frightened I won't make any friends. Won't make any friends."

Before Marion could speak or the older woman could catch up, Maureen was already there.

"Frightened or excited, Jane Edwards?" she asked. "Sometimes it is both, but you can forget."

Jane took a deep breath. Then came a sigh that seemed to flow through her whole body. She smiled genuinely at Maureen. Maureen smiled back.

"Can I sit next to you?" asked Jane, turning her head towards Maureen.

"Of course, you can sit next to me," said Maureen. "Then you won't be so frightened and can be excited."

The older woman caught up and smiled at everyone. "I told you that you would meet new people, didn't I, Jane?"

"That's my carer, Dina," said Jane. "She isn't coming, but she hopes I will meet new people and have a nice time."

"My carer, Alice, isn't coming either," said Maureen.

"Will you be my friend, Maureen?"

"Yes. I will be your friend, Jane Edwards. And I can phone my carer, Alice, and tell her I have already made a good friend at the start of the holiday and before we even got on the coach."

Jane broke into a happy laugh just as a large coach turned into the space next to them. It was painted blue and depicted a deep blue sea and a cobalt sky full of sun. There was a large sandy beach; dotted around the beach were wheelchairs. And in capital letters across the top of the coach, it said WHEELCHAIR WONDERLAND.

"We are going to Wheelchair Wonderland, friend Maureen."

"Yes. Wonderful Wheelchairs. And we will sit next to each other on the coach."

"And can I hold your hand if I get frightened?," asked Jane

"Yes. You can. You can hold this hand, my right hand."

Dina nervously moved towards Steve and Marion, who had been enraptured by the conversation, almost forgetting where they were.

"Hello, I am Dina. I had intended to ask any — any ordinary older people to keep an eye out for Jane, but it looks like they have managed everything all by themselves." She turned away nervously.

The driver stepped down from his high seat. A large burly man in his late 50s, he looked uncomfortable in the blue Wheelchair Wonderland overalls. He wiped his sweating forehead with his hand and took a swig of water from his plastic bottle. "Les here," he said. "We just have to wait half an hour for a few others, and then we will go."

Maureen took out a packet of chocolate biscuits from her crammed bag. "Would you like a biscuit, Les? Hard work driving."

He beamed in surprise at her. "Why thank you, young lady. That is very generous of you, and I will have one even though it is bad for my tummy."

"I am not a young lady," laughed Maureen. "I am a middle-aged lady. Or more than that. Because twice my age is more than a hundred."

"Oooh! I will have to watch this one," said Les.

Maureen laughed happily. She offered a biscuit to Dina, Steve, and Marion, and then to Jane, who had waited anxiously. "Age before beauty," she laughed.

Jane beamed. "You think I am beautiful?"

"Definitely," said Maureen.

Les guffawed. "Well, now I have two beauties to take care of, and that's before I even get to you two," he said, pointing to Steve and Marion.

Maureen turned to Steve and Marion. "Jane Edwards is my new friend and she is a different kind of holiday friend than you two are, because she wants to sit next to me, and you don't want to sit next to me because you are looking after Steve, who is your husband."

Steve smiled back at her. "I don't want her looking after me. But you're right. We're together, even if there isn't room to sit together. It depends on how the wheelchair fits in."

Les looked at his watch. "Well, I can get you set up in there first, so you know where you will be for the journey. You're a no-transfer, aren't you? You have to stay in the chair. Powered, isn't it?"

With a surprising agility for his size, he leapt back into the coach and started a machine going. "We have a lift coming down for you soon, squire. That's what we do here. Your magic carpet to the holiday is my sensational, humungous hydraulic lift."

Marion smiled and Jane and Maureen cheered.

"Come and have a look then — the other side," Les called.

The small group made their way to the other side of the coach where they watched a lift descend to the ground. "And now, ladies and gents — watch this," Les called. He made his way to the bottom of the lift and wheeled Steve into the empty space. "Okay. This is where I make sure you are safely belted up."

"Belt up is rude," chortled Maureen.

"Ah, she's the naughty one that knows all the words," emphasised Len.

Jane laughed. Steve looked nervous, and Marion reminded him that the lift was to take him safely into the coach where he would stay in his wheelchair.

Once Les was satisfied all procedures had been followed, he was back in the coach again. "Peepo," he shouted from the exit, high up in the coach. "We usually have two to do this, but I am a softy and don't like to leave people waiting outside when they could be in comfort."

"Nice softy," agreed Maureen.

"This is where Steve turns into Superman, ladies. Watch him as he flies up the side of the coach."

Steve was frowning, but as the lift went higher a sudden smile covered his face.

"Don't be frightened, friend Steve," called Maureen. "Remember what I said to Jane Edwards. There is fear and excitement. Don't mix them up."

Chapter Fifteen

Lady Hermione Lambton was looking out through the windows of her Rolls Royce Silver Seraph that John was driving. She seemed to have inherited him, like the house, the cars, and everything else. She did not know what he thought about her, or how he felt about James dying. He just stayed there. There was some kind of quiet unspoken agreement that if she said, "I thought I would see the new exhibition at the Royal Academy," then he would drive her there and, when she was ready to go, she just had to phone him and he would pick her up.

All the noise of London and all the quiet of the country were neutralised. In the gracious smoothness of the car, she could stay in her bubble of bereavement. No. Betrayal. "I am in a hearse," she said to herself, "only it is transparent."

It was not for his death, but the death of his sanity and, consequently, of his love for her. It was the death of all their happy years.

She had shown John the pick-up points for Wonderful Wheelchairs. In his quiet voice, he pointed out it would be far quicker to go to Sunville by car in one direct journey, and then she would have more energy for the other events. She found herself breathing a sigh of relief. The moment of aliveness in her studio had faded again. She was an elderly woman who had forgotten how to cross roads and be safe. She wanted to stay in the rich ranks of the permanently chaperoned.

He never spoke except to quietly announce when he needed to stop for petrol and ask if she required the services. Did James find him similarly close but invisible? Did they talk about horses together, or did John just feel the horse-whisperer coming through him?

All those years and she could not even remember a conversation between James and John. Would her memory come back? Or did she have to paint again? To paint, she had to face the wheelchair, the fall, the physical destruction of James. Wonderful Wheelchairs. Oh, please some wonder.

"Nearly there, love," said Dan reassuringly, as Doris drove forward with a jolt and made a jittery right turn. Why couldn't he drive anymore? His poor Doris. She had never liked it, and she liked it even less after their lovely boy had been killed on the road. But she had dutifully taken it up when he couldn't. All the years of driving destroyed. Dan Dare, who couldn't dare any more.

"Well done, love. Thank you. Services in just fifteen minutes and then you don't have to drive anymore."

The car jerked from an anxious gear change. "*Oy gevolt!*" she lapsed into Yiddish, "Can't talk, Dan. You know I can't when I am driving."

He swallowed his anger, his words, his grief. The white Renault Clio, their immaculately polished car, slowly and jerkily took them on their holiday. Had he gone mad? This was never going to work.

Brian could pick up Tom and Gerry. It seemed that almost every planned family visit had someone ill or had to pay attention to in their vulnerable age group. But for this transport, which they could have easily done by Uber, their one and only had insisted on coming to transport them in his people carrier. The journey from London to Sunville was so small. But let him. It was a lovely sight.

"Got everything, dad? Mum? Can I check your suitcases? I always forget something if Marie didn't help and last summer — did I tell you?"

"That little Sam remembered your camera?" interrupted Geraldine. "Darling, you don't have to equalise to make Gerry feel better. He is disabled, and his memory isn't like it was, but you are not."

Brian turned around to hide the big sigh that reverberated through him. Why couldn't they accept help? Look at them. His dear dad with that crude haircut — he had always been so suave and immaculate. There were a few biscuit crumbs on his wine-coloured cardigan. And mum, still in her 60s' beatnik skirts and blouses and obviously preoccupied by something she wouldn't talk about.

Sunville? A dead-end depressed seaside town. Why on Earth? He could have taken them to Brighton at least, not a dead-end hotel. What were they doing? He and Marie had a lovely studio cabin in their garden, with an *en suite* and a clear paved wheelchair route back to their house. He wanted them to come. So did Marie and little Sam. Before it was too late.

"Grendel!" said Tom with sudden great emphasis. "I mustn't forget Grendel!"

"From Beowulf?" asked Brian incredulously.

"Of course! Where else would Grendel be?" asked Tom, a sudden unusual anger in his tone.

Gerry patted Brian's back as they looked at each other, concerned.

"Don't worry, darling," said Gerry, "we have your Grendel notes in the case."

Tom immediately relaxed. "You see, dear boy," said Tom to Brian, "mum is on the case! Gorgeous Gerry herself is going for Grendel! She is my angel."

Brian felt a lump in his throat. Angel. He had never called her that before. Mortality. His lovely parents. His mum knew what his dad needed and look, Tom was restored.

He had done it! He had done it! The first half an hour of "the holiday" and no violence from Roland. As they pulled up at the service station, they all spotted the large Wonderful Wheelchair coach in front of the shopping and restaurant area; Olena and Andrzej looked at each other and sighed in relief. One down and one to go. Would he manage the separation from the driver? How frightened would he be of seeing the other people?

Morris turned round to smile at them. "All here in good time, Roland!" he said.

"Thank you, good driver, Morris," said Roland. "High five, Big A," he called, turning to Andrzej.

Morris was already taking the cases out of the boot, and Olena waited at the side.

"I didn't break the seat or smash the car," said Roland proudly. "Nearly there now?"

Olena touched the cross around her neck.

Chapter Sixteen

Naresh woke up on the carpeted floor of the Guest Suite at the side of his bed. There was a smell of new carpet, cigarette ash, and whisky and a huge smile on his face.

His prosthetic legs lay beside him. He turned his head to the right. There was an empty whisky glass in his right hand and a few drops staining the carpet. He looked at it and smiled. He had christened his room.

He was smiling, really smiling. He had not smiled like this for years. Dick had done him proud, to say nothing of Lance and Roger! They were willingly thrown across the room, landing like the motley shiny collection of C-3PO parts in Star Wars.

Zen. Who would have guessed? Him without his legs and her with her double-D's. Both unclipped and unmasked. She had chucked off her dress to reveal her blue underwear, and he had hurled off his legs and lost his blues. This was him and that was her. At that moment he was ready to marry her.

The sympathetic army doctor had warned him about erection problems and told him most amputees gave up on getting much sex. So, he had given up sexual hope as much as love. He did not want to love anyone while on active service, in case he died and they would have to mourn for him. And now he did not feel he had anything to give a woman.

But she had wanted him. And she hadn't been frightened of him.

His dick — it had done what it was meant to do and he had no thought of disease or protection. It was a miracle. Even if it never happened again. Even if he died from it. He had thrown away his legs and gained a penis.

He turned his head to the left. His mobile was slightly out of reach. Maanika would have been worried. Charlene? Would she have seen him? It didn't matter. He was a single free man.

Light came through the gap in the thick curtains. The sun had finally come out in Sunville.

Chapter Seventeen

The huge motorway cafe was heaving with people. Les pulled up in the large parking bay provided for coaches. Several wooden tables and chairs surrounded it.

"We are here," shouted Maureen in the front right-hand row of the coach. "Thank you, driver Les and well done." She clapped, and the rest of the coach joined in.

"Well done, good driver," shouted Jane Edwards.

"Are we half on the way to the hotel — or is it a quarter?" asked Maureen.

"Any more guesses, ladies and gentlemen?" boomed Les through the loudspeaker system. He turned off the ignition, stood up, and bowed.

"Very good questions," said the lady in the second wheelchair, strapped in behind Steve. She had a smart red cape and a sleek silver bob of hair.

While most of the passengers would be able to be helped from their wheelchairs into an ordinary seat, the left-hand side of the coach had two wheelchair spaces for people who needed to stay in their wheelchairs all the time. They could not be moved to seats, or commodes or other wheelchairs, without large walking aids. It took the most time securing their wheelchairs to the coach floor so all were safe. *Poor bastards*, thought Les. Without his coach and the small number of cabs willing to do the job, they would be stuck inside. The lady in red had a sharp mind, at least.

She pointed to Maureen. "Lady in the front — you are right. We have gone one hundred miles and we have another hundred to go, so this is exactly halfway."

Maureen clapped with delight.

"Am I on Mastermind?" boomed Les. "It is like that Carole Voldemort." He paused theatrically. "Come on you lot — you know who I mean."

Maureen burst out laughing. "Vorderman is the numbers lady and Voldemort is Harry Potter."

"And the brains prize goes to Maureen on the first row," announced Les.

"Hear, hear! You got brains, Maureen!," smiled Jane Edwards. "I haven't got brains, but Maureen is my friend and she says I am beautiful."

"Yes," said Maureen "and you are my new best friend."

"I am Mary," said the woman in the wheelchair. "Dr. Mary Mullins. And I was a mathematician, so well done to you — Maureen, isn't it? — your guess was very good indeed."

Deborah, in the seat adjacent to her, managed to hide her delight. Mary had spoken, been social, been friendly, and to that sweet older woman with a disability.

"Oh, and I am Deborah — Dr. Mullins' companion and carer," she called.

"Oo," called Maureen, "my carer Alice couldn't come. She doesn't come on the holidays with me. She sees me every day but she is not a friend friend. I get the ones that come with the holiday. You must need a lot of help. Doctor Mary must need a lot of help."

Les burst out laughing, and then quickly changed the subject. "Sorry mates and mateys. I forgot to introduce all of you who got on at the last stop, including the two cuties from our care team. I was on my own before. But here we have, applause please, Charlie and Louise." A young man in a David Bowie T-shirt and a spritely older woman waved their hands.

"Within a few minutes, you will all meet one of the other helpers, Muhammid. You see, if Muhammid won't go to the mountain the mountain has to go to Muhammid. And I am the mountain," he laughed tapping his chest. "And then we add Olena, Andrzej, Roland, Hermione, Doris, and Dan, Gerry, and Tom. I think that's it."

Steve's ears perked up. "Hermione? She is more for the winter than a summer holiday."

Marion laughed. "You can't go on holiday without Shakespeare, can you?"

"So," pronounced Les, "before we get out and learn the new names, let us remind ourselves we have, on the very front row, the persevering person who has kept your driver awake — drumroll please — nearest to me: the marvellous —"

"Maureen!" shouted Maureen gleefully.

"And I am Maureen's friend, Jane Edwards, and I met her at the beginning of this journey. And I am a proper friend friend."

"Hello Maureen and Jane, Mary and Les. I am Marion, and that is Steve my husband in the wheelchair on the other side."

"He is asleep, so you can't introduce him. It is a bit rude, really," said Maureen.

Mary burst out laughing. "I like your manners, Maureen!"

There was a confused pause, and then Deborah looked apologetically at Marion and cleared her throat. "Dr. Mary Mullins is the numbers. And I am the letters. Do you realise we have Three Ms here? Maureen, Marion, and Mary."

The distraction worked.

"Never knew this coach was going to be better than Brain of Britain," laughed Les. I hereby announce this coach has arrived at its next pick-up point and toilet break. Your Pee and Tea break! How is that for letters? P and T."

"In my school, when you jumped on the trampoline they called it PT, and then the next year it was called PE," said Maureen.

"Lots of letters," said Jane Edwards.

"And they go in envelopes, too," laughed Les, "but let's clear our heads. Charlie and Louise will get out first. If you look through the windows on the left, you can see lots of wooden picnic tables. They are for us. So just sit on those seats you can see just outside our coach stop. Charlie and Louise will also help with the wheelchairs going down in our humungous hydraulic lift! I will then come down to escort you all to the delectable disabled toilets. And don't joke about the Royal Wee, my fiancée says."

"Ooh," said Maureen, "he has got a fiancée."

"And I've got Royal Wee," laughed Jane Edwards.

Marion burst out laughing. What wonderful travelling companions. She looked across at Steve, who was just opening his eyes. "Hello," she said to him fondly.

"Sleeping beauty is awake," shouted Maureen. "Steve is awake."

Steve stretched his head and looked around. "Hello everyone. I am Steve; and the lovely lady on my right across the gangway is my wife Marion. Are we here yet?"

"Well, we are not *there*, sunshine," joked Les.

"Mathematically, we are halfway there, and Maureen made the best guess," said the other person in the wheelchair.

"Hello, Lady in Red," called Steve.

"Her name is Mary," whispered Marion.

"Hello fellow wheelchair-user," he called.

"I think I prefer Lady in Red," said Mary.

"Okay, coach companions. I will go and get out the manual wheelchairs. You have got twenty minutes to catch a coffee and go to the loo. The coach will be locked, so you can leave all your crown jewels in here, because no-one can get in to nick them. And you will recognise Muhammid when you see me talking to him. So Mary, Lady in Red and key mathematician, you will be the first to go down the lift."

Deborah started to stand. "Don't worry Deborah, you can go out the ordinary door. You can wait for her down there. Follow the coach cuties, Charlie and Louise. They will be awaiting Mary Voldemort first, and then Sleeping Beauty Steve."

"Vorderman," laughed Maureen.

Charlie and Louise waved at everyone as they walked down the coach gangway and down the stairs to the outside.

"Time for a Royal Wee," said Jane Edwards.

"P and T," agreed Maureen.

"Do you realise?" said Jane Edwards, laughing, "that if Wonderful Wheelchair Company was just the Wheelchair Company, it would be WC."

Chapter Eighteen

Charlene was sitting on the adjustable bed in Room 1. It was still covered with polythene. Brand new. She breathed in the smell of newness. Hotel Mirabelle was about to be christened.

Well, she thought, *being christened with urine was inevitable.* She had a cupboard in each room filled with bed protectors and incontinence sheets. Bags for stowing waste. Aprons and gloves. Disinfectant. Creams.

Her mother would have laughed. "If you want to know about the ageing process of anyone, look in their bathroom cabinet, love, all those beautiful, smelly creams turn into disinfectants and barrier creams, as if a wicked fairy had walked in!"

She walked into the pristine bathroom with its safety cord and throne toilet and shower with its safe seat. "*But look, mum,*" she thought. Inside the mirror cabinet were beautiful-smelling soaps, and fragrant hand and body creams. "*It is not just disinfectant!*"

Back in the bedroom, her eyes went to the bedside cabinet and the bowl of fruit and chocolates. She wanted this to be a holiday. A luxurious place. Not a rigid local authority care home with all the old folks dying silently in front of a talking television in a beige boring room with a few old pictures. At least that wasn't her parents' fate. They were slowly swept away together on their side-by-side recliners, bolstered by daily visits from Della, and her, and a team of community nurses and neighbours.

She wiped her eyes as she looked around. It was all clean, all fresh and bright. How she wished Bert and Betty were here to see it. A restaurant named after Betty, a bar for Bert. *Please God, say she was a good daughter.* But they weren't here to enjoy it, were they?

Was this all mad? Guilt? That all their hard-earned money and time had been to help her and Della? No. They loved her. But if she hadn't picked Bob or been picked by him (who knows how it had worked), then none of this would have happened. And what was that bastard doing now? Chatting up the rich widows in the expat bars? Who knows? And she hadn't searched. Twenty-two years. Della had never shown any curiosity. Nor did she seem troubled in any way. She had such lovely, loving grandparents. Well, the two she knew. Who knew what Bob's were like, or if they were alive even?

Room 1. She suddenly didn't like that. What about a name? Supposing the rooms had the name of the resident on the door? She started phoning Della before she could stop herself. It was engaged, so she hung up. Then, suddenly her phone rang.

"How are you, Charlene?" came Irene's delightfully blunt tone.

"How did you know?" asked Charlene.

"I have been around the block, you know! Fifty years doesn't change much though! An afternoon prosecco?"

Charlene replied, "Done. See you here". Then, just a moment later, Della phoned back.

"Hi mum — everything okay?"

"What do you think of the idea of each room having the name of the guest on the door? To make people feel seen and not just be a number?"

"Mum, what about privacy and data protection? This means exposing their name and where they are geographically."

Della paused, then continued. "On the other hand, they are all in one travelling party, and no-one else will be up there. Let's think about it. We can ask the carers."

Charlene sighed with relief. "You know Della, you really are good at this work."

Chapter Nineteen

The bald, middle-aged man was looking worriedly at his mother, while the elderly man in the wheelchair he was pushing happily drank his cappuccino.

"Why don't you sit down outside while I take dad to the loo? I won't be a minute."

"No. I am just a bit tired from the early start," said his mother, clutching her Tibetan shawl around her small frame.

There was a small queue of people outside the disabled loo, most noticeable of which was a very large young man with a huge afro, accompanied by what appeared to be his two carers.

"It won't be a moment," said one of them in an Eastern European accent.

"Will miss the coach, Big A," said the young man.

"No, you won't. Wonderful Wheelchairs know we are here, and they are waiting for us."

"Wonderful Wheelchairs?" said the man in the wheelchair, suddenly looking around vividly. "That's what we are here for. Going to Hotel Mirabelle."

"So, we aren't too late?" asked the young man.

"No," said the man pushing the wheelchair. "By the way, my name is Brian. And it is my dad here, Tom, and my mum, Gerry, who are going."

"Tom and Gerry," laughed the young man. "You are a cat and a mouse."

"That's what our grandson says," smiled Gerry, faintly.

The toilet door opened and out came a smart woman in a red cape sitting in her wheelchair, pushed by a younger woman. "Sorry to have kept you waiting."

"Tom and Gerry, Tom and Gerry," shrieked Roland building up into a crescendo, as his two carers wheeled him into the toilet.

"Look at that!" said Maureen.

"Look at it. It is like a film star's car," said Jane Edwards.

Les put his coffee down on the wooden table and turned around to see what they were looking at. "Cor blimey! A Rolls Royce Seraph!" he shouted. "What a beaut! 1998 to 2002, they were made."

"You know a lot about cars," said Maureen.

"I know a lot about lots of things!" he chuckled.

Deborah turned Dr. Mullins' wheelchair so she could see what was happening.

"She walks in beauty like the night," recited Steve, as he watched a beautiful woman being helped out of the car by a rather imposing man.

"Of cloudless climes and starry skies," added a beautiful tenor male voice coming from a wheelchair further back, pushed by a bald man in his 50s, and a rather frail elderly woman in bright bohemian clothes.

"The name's Tom."

"Steve."

There was a small, surprised pause before the group all focused their eyes on the couple from the Rolls Royce.

"Is she a princess?" asked Jane Edwards.

Les picked up his clipboard and looked through his list. "Bingo! She is one of ours. Lady Hermione."

Standing up, he walked towards the beautiful tall elderly woman, noting her long silver hair almost down to her waist and a silver shawl around her shoulders.

"Wonderful Wheelchairs?" he asked.

She nodded shyly.

"Come aboard, my lady. And welcome." He took her suitcase from John and went to put it in the hold. "We are about to board in five minutes. Here are some of our merry crew, and just a few more are due."

"Hello, everyone," said Hermione, nodding seriously at them all.

Steve made an elaborate bow with his hands. "The silence often of pure innocence," he began.

"... persuades when speaking fails," completed Tom.

The two men looked at each other and laughed heartily.

"We have got twins here," pronounced Maureen.

Hermione smiled at them both. "I see you both know A Winter's Tale. Paulina – Act 2, Scene 2!"

"And you must know it very well, being the fortunate, or unfortunate, bearer of the name," said Tom.

"Absolutely. Both, I think. My mother fell in love with Winter's Tale when she was pregnant with me. I have had rather a lifetime of it!"

Lady Hermione looked round at the small group who had joined together to see her. Their faces looked most confused. "Sorry, everyone. Where are my manners? My name is Hermione, and your companions here," she pointed to Steve and Tom, "know a famous play by Shakespeare which is all about a woman called Hermione."

"And my name is Steve," said Steve, and "my lovely wife, Marion, is just there."

"He always calls her his lovely wife," said Maureen. "That means he loves her, even if she isn't lovely."

Les burst out laughing. Dr. Mullins grinned, while Deborah looked over anxiously, hoping that Marion had not heard that. The woman next to Tom smiled nervously.

"Then she is lovely," she added.

"Maureen is our group compère," explained Les, "She has something important to say about everyone."

"And I am Jane Edwards, the new friend of Maureen, and she thinks I am beautiful."

"Well, you are," said Les. "What a load of beauties in the coach. My goodness me."

John had been standing silently. Once he saw Hermione was settled, he bowed his head and turned to go. "See you here on your return, my lady."

"Thank you, John," said Hermione, oblivious to the whole group taking in her title.

"Do I call you princess or lady?" asked Jane Edwards. "I haven't spoken to a lady before."

"Yes, you have. You have been talking to me," laughed Maureen.

Dr. Mullins wiped away the crumbs from her egg and tomato sandwich and smiled for the first time. "Yes. We have a lot of ladies here."

"And doctor ladies and lady ladies," added Deborah pointedly, a comment that caused Dr. Mullins to smile even more.

Charlie and Louise started helping with the suitcases while the rest finished their drinks.

"Are we nearly there, Big A? I want some chocolate! I want some Cadbury's. I won't punch anyone." Roland's loud voice reached the group minutes before they saw him.

Olena and Andrzej both instantly tensed up. "Sorry. This is Roland. Roland, say hello to everyone."

Maureen stood up and walked towards him. "Now look here. This is a nice coach for nice people, and you don't have to go shouting like that. And you are not allowed to punch anyone. So be nice on this coach, and I will give you a chocolate biscuit."

Roland looked at her, dumbfounded. Dr. Mullins clapped her hands and said,"Well done, Maureen."

Maureen smiled. "You are the maths lady, and you like me."

"I certainly do," said Dr. Mullins.

Maureen turned to face Roland and his carers, who were also in a shocked silence. "And carers, you don't just come and introduce Roland. He is a big boy and can introduce himself. And you didn't say your names."

Hermione felt a strange warmth go right through her. This was going to work. It had to.

Olena blushed and looked at Roland. He was completely silent, staring at Maureen.

"Okay," called Louise. "I am going to help Steve and Marion up first so their wheelchairs are nice and secure."

"And I will be at the top," called Charlie, "to help them off the lift into their places."

"You watch the wheelchair going up in the lift. It is very clever," said Maureen to Roland.

"Come on. You carers push him nearer, so he can see. It is great fun. We don't go up in it, though, if we can get out of our wheelchairs onto a seat."

"Thank you," said Andrzej. "My name is Andrzej everyone, and I am a carer for Roland here, and so is Olena. And your name?" he asked.

"Maureen."

"Let's go round with names," said Les, "we can even do it here before we are in the coach."

Roland started shouting, "Tom and Gerry! Tom and Gerry. We have a cat and a mouse." Everyone turned to look at him.

Smiling, Brian explained. "I am Brian, and I drove my parents here for the journey with you. Their names are Tom and Gerry. Geraldine."

The frail-looking woman turned to Hermione. "We all suffer for our names. I think my mother must have spent her childhood watching cartoons."

"Well now, well now," said Les, clearing his throat, "and I am Les your driver, comedian, and master of ceremonies. I declare we are almost all here, except for Muhammid and the Ricksteins. And I thought I had brought the mountain to Muhammid."

"He texted to say he is in a cab that is just pulling up," called Charlie.

There was a sudden honk as a small white Renault suddenly braked and a short round elderly couple emerged. The man had a walking stick, and his wife was opening the boot to get the suitcases out and the fold-up wheelchair.

"Doris and Dan," he completed.

"Greetings Mr. and Mrs. Rickstein," he said loudly. "Allow me, Madam, to take the suitcases and wheelchair. You can go and park in the long-stay, just round there, and we will have him in the coach all ready for you to sit next to him."

"Thank you. Thank you," stammered Doris, breathlessly. "It has been difficult."

A stunning young man leapt out of a cab, like a male Aphrodite, fully formed, coming out of a shell. "No. It is for me to help, Madam. I am Muhammid. Hello everyone. Hello Louise. Hello Les. I am here to help."

Doris's right hand went to the Star of David around her neck.

"He is helping, love," said Dan. "It is all alright."

Marion burst out laughing. "Just look. Two kind men all fighting to help you. Is it Doris or Mrs. Rickstein?"

Doris, red-faced, turned to her husband.

"It sounds like it is first names here — so let's keep it that way. Dan and Doris," said her husband. "Very pleased to meet you. We had a difficult journey."

The rest of the group introduced themselves. To everyone's surprise, Roland looked up and said, "I am Roland and I am with two carers: Olena and Andrzej. You had two people helping you and I have two. And we have a Tom and Jerry."

Maureen beamed at him. "You are good at numbers. You are right. You have two people and so did they." Then, turning to Dr. Mullins, she asked, "Isn't that right, numbers lady?"

"Right as usual, Maureen. And we have not even got there yet."

Chapter Twenty

Susan Moreau could not contain her delight. In her sea-view room at Hotel Mirabelle, she was dancing and catching her smile in the full-length mirror. She adored the fragrant smell of newness, the smart kettle, the tray of miniature teas and coffees, the bowl of fruit and biscuits — it was so luxurious. All the bedrooms were double-sized to have room for disability equipment, and this room felt as large as her whole flat at home. And it had her name on the door next to the number, as she had chosen: "Susan, Room 12."

She would have her own room while she worked there and had been given the hint more work would come her way if she liked it. She didn't have to pay. It came with the job. Okay, it was minimum wage, but that was on top of the room and board. Lots of places deducted room and lodgings, and she was getting proper hotel food, too. And everything was sparkly and new.

She had met Ibrahim, who was very straightforward and helpful, and he had said she was a natural. He had clarified she would be assisting Steve and Marion, and that Marion was a French lecturer. He thought her love of French, which was in the notes, would be an asset in that work. Steve was the main client, but supporting Marion was also important. She had minor issues in one leg and suffered from stress incontinence. Both clients had a PhD.

She would not have to do the transfers. Whichever man was free would help her. Drs. S. and M. Baker. They would be older than her mum — maybe they would be like her lovely grandparents, Bess and Maurice. Whatever they were, they wouldn't be like her dad and just run away.

Maanika had been lovely. So busy, but still she managed to spend more than ten minutes with her today and even gave her such a warm and welcoming hug. Irene gave her some more training on the commodes and walking aids and told her she had been really quick to learn it.

She would meet Charlene, the hotel owner, later. Coming in at the start of such an ambitious project meant she was meeting everyone who mattered straight up. Where else would a lowly new staff member get all these privileges? How clever her mother had been to realise all of this.

But in the meantime, she was overcome with amazement. Mirrorland — she had never seen a cloakroom like it! It was like being in Hollywood. She had even sneaked in there for half an hour. She had never looked at herself in the mirror for so long. She had the whole amazing room to herself. She could not really look at herself in any mirror in the flat without her mother appearing and saying how lovely she was, what a strong sturdy body with child-bearing hips. Not what she wanted to hear! She pulled her long jumper further over her jeans to hide her stomach. That was better. Her mother had just been about to give birth at her age, and she looked pregnant but from fat.

She liked her eyes, though. And her long eyelashes. Her dark Moreau eyes she had from her grandfather's side of the family, unless they were her biological father's. There. She had said it. Perhaps it was only possible to say it to herself when she wasn't with her mother. Winston, she thought. How strange that was. Only a name. That was all. Like the word Susan on her door. A name — Prime Minister Winston Churchill. An American cigarette. From the old English, meaning joy and stone, used in the Caribbean.

Poor mum. She said she had got all the joy she needed from having her, and so did her parents. But stone? A stonewall? Half her inheritance, a mahogany man, a name and a colour. Susan — and what colour? Bess always said she looked as if she had just gone to Spain for a summer holiday. Maurice, bless him, said she would never need face powder because her skin was such a lovely colour. And her hair, her black bush of hair, tamed and stifled in a ponytail.

Enough of that. She would never have a child in such circumstances — if she ever had a child anyway. Enough of that. Her mum was already a mother at her age, but she wasn't. But she was going to be a single free young woman with a job. And this was the start of the rest of her life.

How proud her mother was that she had got this job. At one level it was crazy — a first-class French degree to do a care assistant job only just above minimum wage. But this was a chance to be independent, to learn new skills to help her on her way. It was her key to the door. She did not have to take it further now.

There was a sudden knock on her door.

"Hello," she called.

"It's Della. I am Charlene's daughter," said the voice, "She told me to look in on you."

Chapter Twenty-one

Geraldine put her hand on her heart. She could feel it beating through her T-shirt, kaftan, and shawl like a drum. But this was not a friendly drum. Why couldn't she tell Tom? His same old lovely self would find something from literature to help her. Mary Coleridge perhaps.

Be still my beating heart, be still
There is no hope for thee tonight

Or better still — *The Odyssey*. "Be still my heart, thou hast known worse than this."

But had her heart known worse? Childbirth had been joyful. Brian was born to a smiling, ecstatic mother. Loving Tom had been joyful. They were so, so lucky. Even his dementia was lucky. The same man she had always loved still smiled out at her each morning.

It was her panic. She could not conceive of herself being ill — if she was. What would happen to Tom? How would they live? They didn't want to move from town to live in Brian's rural house, though he genuinely wanted them to be there. Alzheimer's. It might be slow at first, but then she would not know how to look after him or how to be. How had she let this happen? But, of course, she hadn't. Time and illness were not under control. They were ageing.

No-one would know the treasures that would unfurl from little Sam's treasure chest of being. And then for them, everything happened in reverse — the treasures got sucked back in and lost forever. No-one knew how their end was going to be. How powerful a reversal it would be. Why couldn't she tell him? The secret was crippling her. Tom would be sensible, lovely. "Poor old girl. Well, it happens to all of us — even to you. Golden girls and boys all must as chimney sweepers come to dust." He would kiss her, and that would be that.

But she couldn't tell him yet. Why? Was the secret to herself? If she said it, spoke it, then it was really true that she had an appointment to be told the results. And if she said nothing, then it was a dream, a nonentity. "We are such stuff as dreams are made on; and our little life is rounded with a sleep." Goodness. She was turning into Tom. And both their memories of Shakespeare were still pretty good.

She smiled to herself and sat back in her seat, letting her mind get drawn in to the banter between numbers and letters.

Act 3
Arrival

Chapter Twenty-Two

Sunville was doing its best. It was a grey day where the sea and sky were hard to separate. But the shingly beach was spotless: Charlene had organised the local Brownies in an anti-plastic drive to clean it. The Grand Parade was lit up like an apology for the gloom, and Hotel Mirabelle shone, all its lights blazing across the terrace and around the beach road.

"Honestly," said one of the waiters, "we are better than a lighthouse. I bet they can see us from far out at sea."

An attendant in a black sparkly Hotel Mirabelle T-shirt and white nautical trousers stood on the steps, ready to greet the coach, while others were ready to help with suitcases. Della, Maanika, Ibrahim, Susan, and Irene stood to attention on the adjacent ramp near Charlene with excited smiles on their faces.

"Naresh texted to say he would be here soon," said Maanika apologetically.

"Don't worry. He will come when he can come," said Charlene. "Without him, we would not be here like this. He can come when and if he feels okay."

Maanika ran to hug her. "Thank you."

Charlene smiled. "Who would have thought we would be here, like this?"

"Grandma and grandad would be overflowing with joy if they could see us," said Della.

"And I am so proud to be here as part of this," said Ibrahim, solemnly.

"Ladies, doctors, numbers, and letters. We are here," shouted Les as he opened the door. "This is where you stay sitting until the helpers and I get you comfortable and transferred to the hotel. Those of you who can come down the stairs with assistance will be given your wheelchairs when down, and those of you needing to stay in your wheelchairs will come down the lift. You know the drill by now."

The welcoming group at the top of the ramp heard his words but could not understand them. "Those will be Les's jokes. It will be something he can explain later," smiled Irene.

Their own staff came out first — Charley, Louise and Muhammid — who then stood to help others out. Ibrahim breathed a sigh of relief at seeing his brother there. It was not just Maanika who felt like her brother's keeper!

A frail lady in bohemian clothes came out first with a tentative smile on her face. Then came a rather short, round couple, the man smiling and the woman looking down nervously. A striking elderly woman came next with long silver hair. She was followed by a huge young man with two carers, two middle-aged women giggling together, and a slightly older woman with a walking stick. Coming down in the hydraulic lift in her wheelchair was a woman, smartly dressed in red, who was then expertly wheeled to the side by her companion, a much younger woman. And then another man in a wheelchair came down, instantly wheeled to the side by the woman with the walking stick. And finally, a rather distinguished man with a shock of white silver hair was wheeled next to the rather frail, beatnik-looking woman.

Their guests. Their first guests. And all here and ready for their holiday.

Just as Charlene stepped forward ready to welcome them, there was a loud ripping noise coming from the gravel pathway. Naresh, in his self-operating wheelchair, raced towards them, ignoring the smooth tarmac path running parallel. He was hooting his horn loudly.

Hermione stared transfixed, suddenly thinking of her painting.

"Welcome," Naresh shouted. "Before I hand over to Charlene, the wonderful owner of Hotel Mirabelle, I have just a few words to say, and since those of us who most need a seat are already sitting, I am going to say this before you come inside and get warm!"

There was a ripple of laughter. Maanika crossed her fingers anxiously.

"I am Naresh. A man who lost his legs fighting with the British army."

Doris squeezed Dan's hand. She never thought of soldiers as rescuers, only as a threat.

"Well, you shouldn't have been fighting them," shouted Les. "You should have been on their side."

Another ripple of laughter swept through the group.

"Hello Les," said Naresh. "And good to see you again. Les gives us his coach wheels that allow us to travel together. Wheels are everywhere — on cars, bikes, wheelchairs. To be honest, I would prefer to have normal legs instead of this chariot, I admit that. But since I can't, I want to make sure that I and all of you can have the best holiday possible."

"Yes! Yes!" shouted Maureen happily.

"Me too," said Jane Edwards.

"And to make this break even better — and when I say break I don't mean your legs or arms — I mean a little holiday."

"Break!" said Maureen. "Isn't that funny it means two things."

"There's my numbers' girl," called Dr. Mullins.

"To make this break better," continued Naresh, "Charlene has put a lot of hard work into getting this hotel all ready for us. You can go anywhere in the hotel in your wheelchair. Well, not down the stairs or into my room, but you can go to the restaurant, the bar, the hair salon, the cloakrooms — just you wait and see. Thank you, Charlene."

Charlene stood forward. "This is my dream. A hotel where anyone in a wheelchair can go and explore easily, and which provides a huge friendly welcome to everyone who stays with us, whatever their circumstances. Enjoy your room, the bar, the restaurant — we will see you all for supper in Betty's Restaurant in half an hour. We will help you get refreshed and settled first. Betty, my mother, loved this hotel, but when she was in a wheelchair she could not come here. So I have called the restaurant Betty's in her honour."

"That is lovely," said the tall woman with long silver hair.

"Hear, hear," said Les. "A round of applause for Naresh and Charlene."

Chapter Twenty-Three

Hermione looked out of her window at the grey view beyond. The kind young man from the coach, Muhammid, had brought her cases up. She pulled down the blinds. A little stiff with newness. A nice touch — her name on the door.

She sat on the edge of the bed and slowly lifted her legs up. With a little swivel she was lying down, a soft pillow under her head still smelling of the plastic covering it had been wrapped in. Looking through the wide open doors to the *en suite* wet room, she could see the tab on the toilet paper on top of the throne toilet to show no-one else had touched it. There were unusually large, mirrored cupboards for medication, not for make-up. She could almost feel the NHS quality non-trip floor covering in the wet room just by looking at it. All the better not to slip on. Oh, but where was the marble, the statues, where were her holidays with James?

But look — a bowl filled with fruit and chocolate biscuits. That was a nice touch, especially as this wasn't a hotel of the kind she and James would have stayed in. She closed her eyes. She wanted to savour the moment. A good moment. Naresh, the founder of Wonderful Wheelchairs, driving like a madman across the gravel in his wheelchair — like a wild stallion, she suddenly thought. She wanted to paint him. She had to paint him.

"Look!" said Roland. "My name!"

He pointed to the front of his door. "R – O – L – A – N – D," he spelt out.

"That's good," said Olena.

"Here is the key, Roly," said Andrzej. "Do you want to open the door?"

"Yes. My room." Roland opened the door and gasped. "Look. Look. Beautiful room."

The extra-large double room had an alcove with an ordinary bed intended for a carer who was sleeping in or having a waking night with their client. Roland understood it immediately. "You sleeping there, Big A," he pointed.

"Yes," said Andrzej, "and when it is morning, I have another room to go and rest in. And one of us will always be with you, and some of the time two of us, as well as Charlie or Louise or Muhammid."

Roland looked round the room. A tension was building in the air. His eyes fell on the bowl of fruit. "You are going away from me," he screamed, and before anything could be done he had spun his chair forward, picked up the fruit bowl, and smashed it on the ground, its grapes rolling across the floor like a muttered afterthought.

Olena sighed and walked out of the room. "I will get Ibrahim."

Roland's shrieks could be heard along the wide corridor of the first floor, and Maureen was quite annoyed. "I am not giving him any more chocolate biscuits if he behaves like this."

"No. He doesn't deserve them," said Jane.

"Look," said Maureen, "I am room number 1, and you are number 2."

"We are next to each other!" agreed Jane.

Louise smiled at them both. "And I will help you both with the cases. Do you want to open the doors yourselves, or would you like me to?"

"Can you open my door and put my case in, Louise? I am going to knock on Roly's door," said Maureen.

"Be careful," said Jane

"Yes," added Louise. "When people suddenly get angry, they find it hard to stop themselves."

"I know all about that," said Maureen, "but there will be a carer there."

Louise gasped at Maureen's perception. She had been feeling too frightened to go and try to sort things out.

The wide corridor had room for two wheelchairs to be side by side and Maureen went fast, ringing her bell, in memory of Naresh in his wheelchair. "Out of my way! Crisis," she called.

The noise was getting loud as she went further down the corridor. She stopped outside the door that said "Roland" and knocked loudly. "Roland," she called.

The noise inside was too loud. No-one in that room would be able to hear her. Marion was walking towards her with a walking stick, while Charlie pushed Steve.

"Your walking stick needed, please, Marion," said Maureen. "I need to get Roland to behave."

Marion moved her right hand to the side of the wheelchair and worriedly handed over the walking stick.

"Watch, everyone." Maureen picked up the stick and rapped forcefully on the door. The noise behind the door quietened. Confidently, she handed the stick back to Marion.

"Shut up, Roland!" she called. "Apologies for the bad language, but you are upsetting everyone just as we arrive to start our holiday. Be a good boy and I will give you a chocolate biscuit after supper, but if you carry on that will be it for the whole holiday."

There was a silence, and then Olena broke the quiet by running breathlessly along the corridor with Ibrahim.

"Calm down, Olena. He is being a good boy now."

Andrzej opened the door. He looked exhausted, but smiled warmly at Maureen. "Thank you, Maureen."

Roland looked nervously at Maureen. "Sorry, Maureen."

The corridor suddenly seemed to be full of people applauding Maureen. Even Dr. Mullins appeared in her wheelchair, followed by Deborah.

"I am so proud of you, Maureen," she said.

"Good boy, Roland," said Maureen warmly. "I always keep my promises, so I will bring you a chocolate biscuit for after supper. I am very pleased with you." She proudly turned her chair around and slowly propelled it back to her room, calling out the numbers on the doors on the way.

Dan poked his head outside his bedroom door. "Everything okay?" he asked.

Louise quickly walked to his door. "So sorry about that. It was Roland. Beginnings are hard. But he had his own carers with him, Olena and Andrzej, and Olena went to get Ibrahim to help. But it was Maureen who saved the day by telling Rowland to 'shut up.'"

"That must have been horrible for your wife. Would it help if I came in and explained, or will you?"

"That's okay," smiled Dan gratefully. "It sounded so close and it could have been anything."

Tom and Steve smiled at each other, while their wives pushed their chairs down the corridor next to each other.

"Well, Shakespeare twins?" asked Marion, smiling at Geraldine. "Do we have a quote?"

"It will have blood, they say; blood will have blood," pronounced Tom, "*Macbeth*."

"Violent fires soon burn out themselves," replied Gerry. "Small showers last long, but sudden storms are short; he tires betimes that spurs too hard. Richard III."

"Ah, we are at our door," said Gerry, pointing.

"Well," wondered Marion, "Susan has already brought our cases in. Once we are all unpacked, what do you say that whoever is down for supper first saves seats at their table for the other couple? Or is that too pushy of me?"

"Lovely lady, it is excellent of you," said Tom.

"Done," said Steve.

They all looked at Gerry. "That is wonderful," she said, mustering a smile and pulling her shawl more tightly around her.

Chapter Twenty-Four

Susan had not taken a breath. Her usual pragmatic calm had deserted her, and she felt like a naïve teenager. She couldn't believe it. A room of her own, with all the modern conveniences of a hotel, including the food — and she had a new friend. Really — already? And not just any friend. Della was the daughter of Charlene, who owned the hotel. And Della was an only child, and did not know who her father was, either. Della worked as a temporary classroom assistant, but she hadn't decided what she wanted to do yet, although she could always find work at Mirabelle. Although she had always done well at school, it was the teachers she had a relationship with. She had never had a close friend in school or university. Somehow, her sense of illegitimacy impacted her, even though she had such a supportive family. To find friendship and a first job in the same place was totally unexpected.

Susan was humming to herself. She grinned. Yes. She was humming "To Moreau," the family song. Her mum would be pleased! She was longing to call her, but wanted to savour this rare sense of privacy. The first meeting with Drs. Marion and Steve Baker had been fine. They were lovely. It had not been necessary to mention the French connection at this first meeting. All of that would follow. She had gone to check that Ibrahim was okay after he had been rushed off to calm Roland down — everything was fine there. A guest with a disability, Maureen, had done the calming work better than any professional. Then, she had popped in on Tom and Gerry. What wonderful names. They were a lovely couple, too, who were clearly going to join up with the Bakers, so Ibrahim thought it would be sensible for her to check on them as well.

Her group were all able to feed themselves, so she was free to accept Della's invitation and have supper in her room. Della only had a single name for her father — Bob — and she only had the name Winston.

One name. And she had a colour. Mahogany. Bob was white. They met in Marbella. Both men had left, and maybe never even knew they had a child. Left their mothers, not them. But it felt like they had been left, even though their mothers were both sure it hadn't bothered them.

And they both had loving grandparents who worked hard to give them a strong family around them. Both were watched all the time as if they were tiny and fragile. And both were at a major crossroads in their lives and didn't know how best to use their qualifications.

Della looked around her studio room. She hadn't wanted one of the "owner suites" her mother had offered—they were almost hidden on the ground floor. That was wasteful. Nor was she sure if she wanted to live in where she was working, especially as her mum would be her boss. However, she decided in the end to accept a large studio room with a separate bathroom and kitchenette.

There was a glorious smell coming from her coffee machine with its range of fairtrade capsules and shining chrome — a present from her mother to celebrate the upgrade of Hotel Mirabelle. She loved the smell even though the look wasn't one she appreciated. She had resisted all the steel and grey and chrome of the refurbishment and had insisted on wooden floors, natural materials, and textures. The walls now seemed to sprout timber shelves everywhere, with Indian and Thai silks and plants hanging from them. A fold-up wooden table had been placed in front of the windows, with her computer in pride of place, and wooden in-trays on each side. The table could be extended by opening it up for entertaining as well as studying, and she was thrilled to have rescued four fold-up wooden chairs. The double bed was covered with Indonesian coverings, and, with huge cushions, it doubled as a luxurious Eastern sofa. The walls were like an indoor forest with all the tiny shelves on which the plants sat, their leaves hanging down from them like a green waterfall between her books, posters, postcards, and prints.

It now felt more like her space and somewhere she could feel at home.

She went into her galley kitchen to get a bottle of wine and two glasses. The bottle was already opened, so it didn't feel rude to drink a bit more. She needed to check her feelings.

She had been so pleased with the way her mother had been asking her advice. It had pushed away those inconvenient worries about Bob. Bob's your uncle! Except he was her father. The idea that a man could be walking about, carrying on with his life, with no idea he had a grown-up daughter. And all from a one-night, one-week stand? How could it happen?

And Susan had the same. Winston. A brown man. And that was it. So, two pieces of madness. Two men, who didn't even know they had a daughter. Maybe sons, too, or other daughters. A woman at each port not saying she was pregnant. The whole world is full of bastards. Her mum never said the B word — thank God she had not been born earlier, when attitudes had been so appalling. Bert and Betty had been so all-encompassing it never felt like she was missing anyone. But she knew deep down her relationships were with the teachers and then the lecturers. She had superficial polite exchanges with some of the other girls, but nothing serious.

But just looking at Susan, she could see all the missing pieces. All the missing pieces of her life, her soul, her DNA. She just wanted to see her face again. It was better than her reflection in the Mirrorland mirrors. It was like having a twin.

Chapter Twenty-Five

Betty's Restaurant was all aglow with light and noise. Charlene stood shyly in the corner, hardly believing the beauty of it all. Her dream had become real. Despite dressing up for the occasion, her black bob all glossy and immaculate, she was wearing dark glasses — but she didn't know why. Irene had helped, and so had the prosecco, but she had never expected such waves of pleasure and fear.

Opening night. Excited locals mixed with the hotel's first residents. Mirrorland was buzzing with excited women. Wheelchairs and pushchairs sat resplendent in the special ground floor parking zone. Bert's Bar was utterly filled, and a satisfactory number were already walking into Betty's Restaurant, all in Hotel Mirabelle.

The space between the tables was perfect for the range of wheelchairs that made their way through. This was how it should be. They did not stand out. They fit. Her breathing relaxed now, she focused on the hotel and not herself. Her eyes were drawn to the vast young man in the wheelchair who was being accompanied by Ibrahim. She had, of course, been informed of the earlier crisis. Poor kid. So young, and all his pain turned to fat.

She patted her stomach almost unconsciously. Damn "Bob the Bastard!" How dare he pop up in her mind again on the day of her biggest triumph.

All that practising was behind them. This was it. It was real. The Wonderful Wheelchair Company at Hotel Mirabelle. Huge glowing chandeliers and small amber lamps shone their luminous circles on the round wooden tables, sending sparkles into the tiny glass vases; red velvet chairs added to the glamour. There was the buzz of conversation and people relishing the freshly decorated atmosphere of their night out. Even a local reporter had managed to come. Launch-night drinks in the restaurant and Bert's Bar were all organised, and special reductions on the full menu.

It was real. It had happened.

Charlene was checking and troubleshooting. Irene seemed to be everywhere as eyes and ears for her and Maanika. Della, to her surprise, was having supper in her room. She would have liked her there with her, but the kid was tired out. Naresh had also not yet been seen. But everything was running fine. She had been waiting for this her whole life.

She had just come from the busy kitchen, which was filled with nervous excitement. Cliff, the main chef, had everything under control. This was his day, too. It was the moment he had been waiting for ever since Seaspray, the new Brighton restaurant he had started working at, had been closed due to Covid. He had another chef from Seaspray and four school-leavers from Sunville. He also had two impeccable French waiters, who, despite Brexit, wanted to improve their language skills. Gaston, the more senior, was also able to work in Bert's Bar.

"Thank you, Cliff," she repeated to herself. He had managed to bring Justin, the other senior chef, from Seaspray just before he was due to disappear to the furthest point of Cornwall. What timing and what luck. No. Not luck. It was her decision-making; her excellent choices. She had not been let down by anyone — except Bob.

An angry sound rose in her throat mingled with an unexpected tearfulness. One man; one mistake. That was all it took to transform a life. How could she have? But perhaps it wasn't surprising. An orphan, she suddenly chuckled to herself. It was odd to think someone of her age was nevertheless an orphan. She did all this as a woman on her own.

She had scooped up a couple of receptionists from the cinema, too. Hotel Mirabelle was no longer a Last Chance Saloon for performers, but it certainly was for staff. *Oh mother,* if only she was here in person. "Betty's," just look at it: red, brown, and green, and such a shimmering quality of light. She knew the food would be good. *Oh, mother.* She would have loved to have come here.

Olena was exhausted. "I don't know if I can do this much longer," she said to Andrzej. "I need a drink, and you know I stopped."

He put a protective arm around her. To their amazement, Roland had allowed Ibrahim to take him down to dinner. There he was, a little ahead of them, but out of earshot. With Ibrahim pushing the wheelchair, they entered Betty's Restaurant. Behind them, keeping a distance, was that nervous little woman Doris and her husband Dan.

Olena slowed down. There was always a period of apology and peace from Roland after an outburst, but it might not last long. A crowded restaurant. She could not bear the shame if he had an outburst here!

Andrzej was torn. He felt it was too much to expect Ibrahim to manage the supper shift, but Olena was in danger of leaving, and that would devastate Roland—and him—even more.

"It is not the right client for you when your country is at war," said Andrzej.

"Tell me!" said Olena. "I would feel better in Kyiv than here."

The short man with the nervous wife turned round. "Sorry for intruding. You would not want to be in Kyiv. One man's tragic war with his own poor brain is not the same as living with bombs falling, buildings collapsing, and other atrocities."

Olena was struck dumb. Andrzej took a deep breath. He did not know what to do.

"I am sorry," he said in a calm voice. "This was a private conversation."

"War is not a private conversation," said Dan, with an unusual air of authority.

Doris squeezed his arm and they walked on ahead, right past Roland who was happily chatting with Ibrahim.

Tom, Gerry, Steve, and Marion had chosen a table for four by the window, as far from the main noise as possible.

"Thank you," said Marion. "My ears aren't so good, and it matters I hear what Steve wants."

"Hark you, Guildenstern, and you too at each ear a hearer," smiled Tom.

"Give every man thine ear, but few thy voice," added Steve.

"My goodness," said the surprisingly quiet Geraldine, a rare smile lighting up her face. "You have got me on it now. Friends. Romans. Countrymen, lend me your ears."

"Ear, ear!" shouted a loud familiar voice. It was Les on his way to claim his free meal.

"Well, you wouldn't want mine, I guess; I do better than a queen bee for wax," said Marion.

Geraldine was in a beautiful and long velvet dress with another shawl around her. But she looked so sad despite the beauty of her clothes. Tom and Steve, on the other hand, looked so happy to have found each other. She could manage this.

Maureen and Jane proudly walked into the restaurant. Maureen had decided to leave her wheelchair and use her walking stick for exercise. She looked around with a big sigh.

"This is a proper holiday, Jane Edwards. Proper hotel."

"Yes," said Jane Edwards. "Look at the big lights."

Louise caught up with them. "It is lovely, isn't it?"

"Well, shall we find a table you would like us to sit at? The waiters and waitresses will come to the table to take your orders and explain the menu."

"I know about restaurants," said Maureen briskly. "I did not ask for help, and I will choose my table with Jane Edwards," she added.

Louise stood uncertainly.

"Hello, my numbers woman," said a sharp voice.

Maureen broke into a big smile. Dr. Mullins was there with Deborah at her side. Deborah smiled reassuringly at Louise.

"It is the numbers doctor," said Maureen happily. "Numbers doctor and carer. Would you like to have dinner with me and my friend Jane Edwards?"

"That is what I was coming to ask you. And well done for calming Roland."

"And I am coming because I am Maureen's best friend," said Jane Edwards.

"Well, enjoy your dinner, everyone, and you have my mobile so call me if there is anything useful I can do."

Maureen smiled at her. "Thank you, carer Louise. I'm not wanting to teach you your job, but I am good at restaurants."

"You are a good teacher, Maureen," said Louise awkwardly.

"And it can be hard to be a pupil," said Dr. Mullins sharply.

Deborah winced and smiled sympathetically at Louise, who gave a nervous laugh and walked quickly away.

Deborah began to push the wheelchair. "No," said Dr. Mullins. "I am learning from my number's woman here. I didn't ask to be pushed and in fact I will do it myself."

Pushing the forward button, she sailed ahead followed by Maureen with her walking stick, Jane Edwards, and a bewildered Deborah.

Chapter Twenty-Six

Naresh was sitting in Bert's Bar, his favourite place in Hotel Mirabelle. He had never been much of a pub man before the explosion, but after his injuries he had found them welcoming places. So long as he had enough money to pay for a drink, pubs wanted his custom and didn't care about his legs.

His favourite sport seemed to be ordering a drink, sitting down, and removing his legs. Leg masks. That would give the racists something to deal with. He had an answer for anything.

So, he was there in a sparkling new T-shirt and black leather jacket. Looking like a TV show host. You never saw their legs, because you never saw them below their waist. His mind was not on the launch of Hotel Mirabelle and Wonderful Wheelchairs. All he could think about was Zen, hoping she would come back to the scene of the crime.

Maanika and Sunil had popped in, and so had Irene, but he was staying put. He felt like a stupid teenager. All his years of army and warfare hadn't let this part of him grow up. Why hadn't he asked for her number? Why hadn't she asked for his? It was ridiculous. The bar staff had been told not to identify him by surname or association, but that he was happy to be presented with free drinks. Another bottle of beer was already making its way over.

He checked his phone. He felt like he was going insane: she still didn't have his number. Messages from Ibrahim, Irene, Maanika, and even Charlene were of no interest to him. Not even messages from Invictus or fellow amputees from Afghanistan.

So, I'm a bloody teenager, he thought, reaching out for the next bottle.

Zen was in Mirrorland, but she no longer had it to herself. It was filled with women. She was in green tonight, wearing her favourite push-up, push-over, and push-away bras. But she didn't want to call it a push-away bra tonight. She wanted a hello-come-and-meet-me bra. An enjoy the beauty of my body bra.

What the fuck had she been doing? No surname or address. Only the hotel room. But she wasn't going to go to a snotty receptionist and ask for a message to go to an anonymous room number. She had been there before, treated like trash.

No. This was different. She wanted to see him. Mr. Legless. But to go into the bar. To be seen to be looking. What a bitch Di was. She needed her to walk into the bar with her. Then she wouldn't look like a loser. A woman who couldn't even get the attention of a legless man.

She reached for her mobile and texted: WHERE ARE YOU BITCH? NEED YOU AT MIRRORLAND. YOU SAID YOU WANTED TO BE AT THE LAUNCH SO DON'T PLAY GAMES WITH ME.

Hermione stood naked in front of the mirror. She had been wrong about the bathroom. There were some lovely creams there. She scanned her face, her body, feeling her skin take in the cream as if it had been parched.

Naresh. She needed time to process that thrill. Her longing to paint him was growing unbearable. The man on his custom-made bike, screaming his disability to the world. The man in the wheelchair in her painting. What rage James had. The rage against his disability, his hatred for his horse, himself, and, of course, for her.

"Do not go gentle into that good night," Dylan Thomas had said. Should age rage or just surrender? Or both?

She brushed her hair, watching it fall against her body. How James had loved her hair. Undoing it when pinned up, seizing it in his hands when making love, and sometimes just brushing it. How untouched she was. So long since James had touched her. Now, it was only a pedicure or a massage. But the bathroom was not just medical — it had fragrant face and body creams too — and that eased something that had been long silent.

And Maureen — that marvellous woman. What a way she celebrated her difference. She knew who she was so strongly. She was an inspiration. She was going to do that painting even if it was from memory. And she would take a photo. This holiday was going to be the turning point.

Chapter Twenty-Seven

We really wanted to meet other people with this mixed dementia," said Marion, squeezing some tomato ketchup onto her scampi. This was the first day of a first break in a long time, and she was going to enjoy it.

Steve nodded. "Nearly every dementia meeting we went to, there were people with Alzheimer's but not with the cerebral vascular dementia."

Tom listened intently. "Gerry, love, tell her about the — you know — room — with taps. No use on a journey."

Gerry looked at Tom intently. "You mean when you can't transfer to a toilet without a walking aid, it means a disability toilet is useless when travelling!"

Steve banged his fist on the table in applause. "Good translator there! That was very quick ,Gerry. Well done."

Marion agreed. "Absolutely! All those otherwise wonderful day trips that could happen! Steve is so brave. I would be petrified of managing a soiled pad for hours because they wouldn't be able to clean him up, either."

After a pause, Gerry asked, softly, "Have you always been so open about it?"

"No other way, Gerry angel," said Tom, brushing crumbs off his bib.

"This above all to thine own self be true," added Steve.

Marion watched Gerry wince and pull her shawl around her. "Gerry, how about we have a little seafront walk while Susan and — will it be Charlie or Muhammid — get you two literati comfortable?"

"Good idea, angel," said Tom. "You could do with some female relaxing time."

"And Tom and I can have some literary time without boring you before it is dark," laughed Steve.

Gerry's eyes filled with tears. "I get relaxing time with you, Tom — but it would be nice to get to know Marion better."

"And you can talk quicker without us," said Steve.

"Although we will do some good talk together. Tell her about the R, Marion."

"Oh yes — the DNR," said Marion. "The Do Not Resuscitate."

Again, that flinch from Gerry. "But before we go into that, we have to tell you the lovely joke we had last night. It is literary."

"Steve — do you want to say it — the Miller play?"

Steve and Tom both looked up.

"Aha, yes," said Steve. "This may have happened to you, too. I wanted to remember the title of *The Night of the Iguana*."

"As you do," laughed Gerry, a glimpse of her former self.

"And — what I called it instead, I have forgotten. Say it, Marion."

"The Night of the Artichoke," said Marion, bursting out laughing and soon joined by the others.

"Ah, it is Charlie and Louise who will help you both. It is on the rota. They will come to the table looking for you if we are not back by then," said Marion in her official voice.

"And you can always phone me," added Gerry to Tom.

"Do you realise, Steve, we could make a night of it? Get the carers to wheel us to Bert's Bar. We already have our safe ride home!"

They all left, the two men with utter joy and the two women feeling slightly unsettled in this new world.

Chapter Twenty-Eight

My poor lady," said Muhammid. "You have had a worrying time." He sat on her left side while Dan was on her right. With her serviette, she was already sweeping the crumbs on the table around Dan's plate into her hand. Dan watched her protectively.

She could never stop cleaning. At home, he saw it as a strength. He loved the way crumbs disappeared, a raisin on the carpet, weeds, dying plants. He felt she could make the world ordered. But outside of the home, outside of family and a few friends and shops, she shrunk. He had not realised how frail and tiny she looked. She was weak from carrying her family trauma and the loss of their son — and, he admitted, the loss of how he used to be. He used to be her chauffeur, and he had not properly taken on board what she had lost.

He reached for her hand and squeezed it.

"It was the car drive," she replied, just before Dan was going to say it.

"Our son — our Dan Junior — was killed by a drunken driver. 18 years old. His whole life was in front of him. But he died. But not as bad as if we were still in Kyiv, where my grandparents died. There is dying in a mad terrible accident and there is deliberate genocide and murder. They are not the same. I really don't like driving."

Doris's left hand started shaking, and Muhammid held it gently.

The two men, each holding one of Doris's hands, looked at each other seriously.

"And it is because of my condition. I can't drive anymore," said Dan. "I loved driving and Doris hated it because of — because of our boy."

Doris couldn't stop shaking. Olena and Andrzej walked past on their way to the desert trolley, wrapped in conversation, and Doris flinched.

"So you, brave lady, you drove here to help your husband, because you love him even though it was terrible for you, and it brought out all your ghosts: your loved son with all his life in front of him, and your grandparents who died in terror in Ukraine."

Dan looked at him with amazement. "Sorry. I didn't think you would understand. It is not your background. Your religion. Your name."

"Mr. Rickstein, what do you think I am with my name and religion?"

But Dan could not reply. Doris had carried on speaking. All her worries were pouring out. "And the violent young man shouting. And then the woman said she would prefer to be in Kyiv. Kyiv. I didn't know what generation's life I was living."

"Of course, my poor lady. The loss of your son is terrible. And to have someone appearing to dismiss this by wishing they were somewhere that was terrible for your family — that is all too much so close together. Violence, noise, mention of Kyiv, driving: all too much."

Doris took a huge breath and sat bolt upright. "What am I doing, Dan? Talking to an Arab like this? He might hurt me." She let go of Muhammid's hand sharply.

Muhammid smiled calmly at the frightened couple. " I am an Arab from Egypt, yes. There are Christians there and Jews and Muslims. Are you frightened that my skin is a different colour? Jews in Egypt are the same colour as me."

He paused, and then continued, "Now I will go and get you both a dessert. The dessert is self-service. Then coffee or tea will come to the table. I will then ask you if you would like a different carer. You do not have to have me, if the sight of me frightens you. You have enough worries in your head."

He stood up gently and walked away.

"Oh, Dan — *oy gevolt*," Doris moaned, holding her head in her hands. "What have I done? I have been rude to a good man."

Dan hugged her tightly. "Yes. He is a good man. But he will come back, and you will say sorry. You are frightened, and you only do things that aren't like you when you are frightened. And you are frightened of me getting ill and dying and not being able to look after me. But we can talk about it."

Muhammid made his way to the overflowing dessert trolleys. Andrzej and Olena were just in front of him.

"Your brother is wonderful," said Andrzej to him. "Olena and I really needed a break."

"And that is why we are here. You deserve one," said Muhammid. He looked earnestly at them. "But I also am here to tell you of something sensitive. It is the poor Ricksteins."

"Oh, those rude people!" said Olena angrily.

"Yes. It was rudeness. But not out of wanting to be rude. I am afraid they have a history in Kyiv as well as you. Bad history. It is why they are here."

"Ah," said Andrzej. "The Pogroms."

"Yes," said Muhammid.

Olena shrugged her shoulders. "Everyone is a walking history of badness in the world. We cannot take account of all of it. I am exhausted."

"Of course, of course," said Muhammid. "I just wished to help you know why you got that rude response. It was trauma. She is an old, frightened lady with a husband who is ill, and I tell you in confidence, as carers, that her son was killed by a drunk driver at only 18. This break is a very big deal for them."

Olena looked down embarrassedly. "I understand," she said and quickly served herself a dessert. Andrzej and Muhammid nodded at each other.

"Allo, allo," called Les, holding out an empty bowl, "Hello, mountain. Decided I would have seconds before going back to the missus. Well, my Almost-Missus."

"Mountain?" asked Muhammid with a confused smile.

Olena looked up. "It is a very old saying. "If Mohammed won't go to the mountain, then the mountain must come to the Mohammed." She fingered her cross. "I don't know where it comes from. My background is Christian."

"So is mine," said Muhammid.

Olena looked shocked.

"My, oh my," said Les, wiping his brow with mock seriousness, "all we need is Maureen and numbers woman and I am back on Mastermind." Taking an extra portion of ice cream and chocolate cake, he made his noisy way back to the tables, high-fiving on the way.

"Well," said Andrzej, "somehow, his jokes don't work as well in here as they did on the coach."

Olena laughed. "Sorry, Muhammid," said Olena, "you must get it as both a Muslim and a Christian then."

"And an Indian," added Andrzej thoughtfully.

"I am actually Egyptian," corrected Muhammid.

"Poles, Ukrainians, Egyptians, Christians, Jews — a good old British melting pot," said Andrzej.

"And I don't want your ice cream to melt," said Muhammid, "and I must bring back some dessert for the Ricksteins."

Olena and Andrzej looked at each other.

"I would like to help," said Olena.

Muhammid sighed and turned his head. If only another staff member was here. Perhaps someone more experienced might understand how to deal with all this. Another fifteen minutes and he promised himself that, unless there was a dangerous accident, he would go and play the piano in Bert's Bar. Irene had cleared it with Charlene and it would help him relax.

Chapter Twenty-Nine

Sunil was concerned. He had entered Bert's Bar at Maanika's request to see how his brother-in-law was. He didn't want dessert; he just wanted an early night. Maanika had spent so much time on all of this and, he worried, some money too. They planned to try to start a family next year. So tiny their family was now. Just the three of them. No grandparents to babysit, even if he and Maanika were able to get pregnant. How would they know anyway? Infertile people had parents who had managed to have a child. Just three of them. No-one to help out, provide money, promise a pram or a cot.

That is why they worked all hours. He wanted Naresh to be well, to be an uncle. To be a good uncle. He was not likely to want a child now. Although you could never tell. Getting drunk with promiscuous women is not what he wanted for Naresh. No legs. How would he manage?

He loved Naresh and, to be honest, wished he was not there sometimes. He had brought such pain into their lives. But Maanika loved him, needed him. Even though she was a younger sister by so many years, she had always looked after him. He must not be selfish. He loved him too. He had to. The only relative.

The bar was filling up. There was laughter and a hum of enjoyment. It did not feel like a dangerous, immoral place. A young man was tinkling on the piano. He played quite well, and it was more tasteful than muzak blasting through loudspeakers.

Sunil saw Naresh sitting at the furthest end, with empty bottles and glasses on the table in front of him. And then, looking back, he could see the prosthetics lying on the Chesterfield next to the wing chair.

Sunil moved to the bar counter. Naresh was clearly saving the place. Perhaps for the woman Maanika had told him about. Sitting with no legs. No cover-up. Was it brave, or was it reckless? He swallowed, and moved swiftly towards Naresh. "Can I get you another drink?" he asked.

Naresh looked up, shocked at the sound of his voice. "Sit down," he said and clicked his fingers. A waiter appeared almost immediately. "A drink for my brother-in-law, please. What will you have, Sunil?"

"Orange juice."

Naresh laughed. "You haven't turned Hindu, have you?"

"No. Just tired," said Sunil.

"Then you can imagine how tired I am today. All the preparations and work."

"Well done to you. We are so proud of you," said Sunil.

Naresh wiped his eyes. His voice broke. "Thank you, brother. Thank you. Sorry. Sorry."

Sunil sat down next to him, carefully moving the prosthetic legs.

"Don't worry about that," said Naresh, still wiping his eyes. "It won't break. I am the Tin Man from the Wizard of Oz."

Sunil spontaneously put an arm around him. "But you do have a heart, brother. A very big one and a brave one and maybe it feels broken right now."

A huge sigh broke through Naresh's body.

Chapter Thirty

Gerry had changed into comfortable walking shoes and a warm thick shawl, and Marion now wore a leather jacket as they walked together along the grey shingle of Sunville beach.

Marion turned around to look back at Hotel Mirabelle. "I hate leaving him — even when I want to."

"Me, too," sighed Gerry. "It is like a giant umbilical cord, even though we are over 80."

"Goodness," said Marion. "You give me hope. You are fifteen years ahead, and I thought we were the same age."

Gerry laughed. "But you know they are so happy together. They will quote to each other all night."

Marion took a deep breath. "I wonder how long they could go on for?"

"It could be a fundraiser for Wonderful Wheelchair Company."

They both looked back at the Mirabelle. "What a lovely hotel," added Marion, "and what a lovely light it casts on this —"

"Depressing UK seaside?" finished Gerry.

Both women laughed. Their shoes made a satisfying crunch on the gravel as they followed the curve of the beach. "I would never have come to a place like this for a day out before, let alone a few days," confided Marion.

Gerry nodded. "It was Tom who found it. It is so rare now for him to find what he thinks he is looking for, so I thought this really mattered. But there is no retail therapy to be had along the seafront, which is one of my guilty pleasures."

"No, so let's hope it isn't down on the itinerary as an exciting day trip," echoed Marion.

The thought amused her and took over. "Special Quiz: How Many Betting Shops, Charity Shops, Poundlands?"

They both laughed, and then a quiet took over. "Sorry," said Marion. "That was thoughtless of me. I am glad there are Poundlands and charity shops. It is just not where I would choose for a holiday!"

"We are entitled to what we expect in terms of forking out for a holiday," said Gerry gently. "I'd have said it if you hadn't."

They carried on walking in their own silence, listening instead to the sounds of their feet on the shingle and the gentle lapping of the sea. Pulling her shawl tighter around her, Gerry said, suddenly: "It still matters, doesn't it! This. Sea. Air. New friendships, laying new memories. Do you know, this is the first time I have not been in the same place as Tom for a few years?" Her voice appeared to break.

"You okay?" asked Maureen.

"No," said Gerry, simply. "I was a receptionist, typist, did freelance editing. Anything to fit around Tom's work. He was an English Literature lecturer, as you can hear. He specialised in Anglo-Saxon. We worked around his job. I saw you had a PhD. You were down on the list as Dr. Baker, so you have a career like your husband did. I am not used to talking to anyone who isn't a carer, or part of a medical team, or children worrying about us, or friends dying. But perhaps it is the age difference, too."

"Yes," agreed Marion. "It is the new busy social life of the impaired elderly. Nose, feet, ears, feet, chest, lungs, brain — in no particular order. That part is true for me, too. Yes. My PhD was in French literature, but I loved being an interpreter. Now, because of Steve, it is just a few students. I had to retire. As you can probably imagine, it was Anglo-Saxon literature he was most interested in outside of Shakespeare."

"So, Wonderful Wheelchairs have done something different for both of us," said Gerry. "Do you mind, Marion? I feel a need to go back and check on Tom. I feel my umbilical cord is pulling whenever I have the prospect of enjoying something that is not attached to him."

"Well, let's see what our Shakespeare twins are up to. If we had had Doris with us, we could have out-Shakespeared them with 'When shall we three meet again?'"

Gerry laughed as they turned to go back. "Thank you. You knew there was something worrying me, didn't you?"

"Yes."

"Would it feel intrusive if I asked whether we could be together for breakfast?" asked Gerry.

"No. I would have asked you," responded Marion. "Wherever we go, there is never anyone else who has a wheelchair and Alzheimer's. It has been so good to meet you both.

"8 AM?"

"Fine."

"Unless they suddenly hate each other," added Gerry with a smile.

"I can't see that happening. Not with the literary desert he has been existing in," responded Marion.

"It feels disloyal to say this, but if he starts on Grendel, it means he is confused. It is a paper he is obsessed with, and it is always a sign he is feeling vulnerable," she sighed.

"Grendel," repeated Gerry. "I suppose my equivalent is when he calls me angel. He never used to."

"You mean he is worrying about mortality."

"Yes." There was a sudden crunch of shingle as Gerry lost her footing and slid against Marion, who held onto her tightly.

"Are you alright, Gerry? I've got you. Don't worry."

"I suddenly felt dizzy," said Gerry and burst into tears.

Marion carefully steered her to a wooden bench. "Let's sit down a moment. There is something else wrong, isn't there?"

Gerry held a piece of her shawl to her mouth. "I didn't want anyone to notice."

"Well, I'm not anyone," smiled Marion. "You can tell me. I won't speak if you don't want me to. And you don't have to tell me if you don't want to. But something has been affecting you on the trip, and I could see something was wrong."

And so, on the wooden bench with a brass plaque in honour of a local resident who had loved sitting there, Geraldine was finally able to pour out her worries. She was concerned, as she kept having dizzy spells and seemed to be forgetting things she wouldn't normally. She was scared that, as Tom's main carer, she was now going to be found impaired. The hospital had sent her an appointment for just after they returned, and she didn't want to know the results of the tests they had done. She knew if she was impaired it would mean living with their son, daughter-in-law, and grandson. They had never wanted that.

And so, they talked until wisps of dark cloud spread across the grey sky, and a full moon slowly rolled in to join them.

Chapter Thirty-One

Maanika felt her mobile vibrate. It was heaving in Mirrorland, too noisy to hear notifications.Sunil. It was a text from Sunil. I LOVE YOU. HAVING A DRINK WITH YOUR BROTHER IN BERT'S BAR. CONGRATULATIONS!

She looked up. In front of the giant mirrors were women of all shapes and sizes. The counters were gleaming with potions, jars, bottles, sprays, lipsticks, eyeshadow palettes, and brushes. She must photograph this happy buzz, scattered with laughter and exclamations. Moving around to the dressing-room area, she gasped at the realisation. Charlene's dream had worked here, too. Women in various states of undress happily trying on new dresses with friends or family members sitting around, making comments. It was camaraderie. It felt safe. Women in wheelchairs. Women perched on stools like exotic birds. It was alive.

Catching her breath, she made her way around to the unfinished area of the salon and beauty parlour. Strange that Charlene, as a former hairdresser, hadn't sorted that first. If she had met her earlier, she would have offered help. It was only for a couple of years that she had worked as a salon junior while sorting out her office management studies. But she had loved making women feel beautiful and happy, so it was well worth the sweeping and cleaning and long hours. But there was only one poor young stylist there in My-Lights, on her own, blow-drying a young woman's fine long hair. No-one was yet in the unopened beauty parlour extension. But it would happen. It would become what it was dreamt to be. It could have a dressmaker on-site, a clothes shop, lingerie; the possibilities were endless.

"Looks a bit sad, dunnit," said a loud voice behind her. Maanika turned round, startled from her reverie.

The woman, in her late 50s or early 60s, wore a luminous green velvet dress with a very low top revealing ample breasts. Manila looked at her, and then answered, "It does really. But I am sure it will happen. Rome wasn't built in a day."

"What's Rome got to do with it?" asked the woman with a puzzled frown.

"It's one of those phrases," said Maanika. "It means you can't do everything at once."

"True," said the woman. "And that Mirrorland is a bloody marvel, excuse my language. Haven't seen anything like it anywhere. It is better than a five-star."

Manika warmed to the woman. "Agreed," she said.

"But this hairdo place, My-Lights, it needs a lot more to be as good as Mirrorland."

"Yes," agreed Maanika, "What do you think it needs?"

"Well," said the woman, thinking seriously. "For me to go there, it would need to do Black hair. African hair. It is a big deal for us Black women to find a place that can do our hair properly. Even in Brighton. And then there could be Indian hair, oils, and wedding makeovers. Your hair is lovely — quite like Indian hair."

"Thank you," said Maanika. "I am from India."

"See, it should be for women of the world — Hair Today!" she burst out laughing.

"Hair Today! I like that! Like 'here today.' How do you know so much about hair?" asked Maanika.

"What I used to do a long, long time ago. Probably when you were born. But things happened, lots of things since then."

"It is good to be free to change, to not be stuck in what you once did," pronounced Maanika.

The woman frowned and then smiled. "Well, see you around. My friend was supposed to meet me here to go to Bert's Bar, but she hasn't turned up, the bitch, so I will totter there on my own."

"Great," said Maanika with a sudden energy, "I am going there, too. So why don't we walk there together. My name's Maanika."

"Zendaya," said the woman. "You can call me Zen."

Chapter Thirty-Two

Scampi! I haven't eaten scampi before," said Maureen. "I was in Cornwall, and I had a Cornish pasty. That is food just for Cornwall."

"She was in Cornwall but she did not have corn!" laughed Jane Edwards. "I had scampi and chips once at the seaside in Margate when my mum was alive. She paid for it because it cost a lot of money and she said it was because it was a holiday."

"Food is interesting for the memories we get from it," said Dr. Mullins.

"Even when we have eaten it," added Maureen.

A waitress came up to take their empty plates away. "Wait," said Maureen. "The food has been eaten but it is not finished yet in my memory."

"You want the plate a bit longer?" asked the waitress, incredulously.

"Me, too," said Jane Edwards. "We are making food memories."

Deborah looked guiltily at the waitress. "Do you mind coming back in a few minutes?"

"Of course not. But keep an eye over there on those trolleys. All the desserts are there, and tonight it's self-service. I wouldn't want you to find that all the ones you like best have already been taken. Those will be new memories."

Deborah smiled at her. "Thank you. Please congratulate the chef. We have really enjoyed our food so far."

The waitress smiled and nodded before walking quickly away.

"Do you think she will thank him?" asked Maureen. "Will it be just a chef — one person — or do you think there are lots of people making the desserts who should be thanked? What do you think, numbers lady?"

Dr. Mullins beamed at her. "You are a very good person to be on holiday with, Maureen. You ask very interesting questions."

"Alice says that, too," said Maureen seriously. "She is my worker at home who I see more than anyone else."

"You see me all day," protested Jane Edwards.

"But this is only for a few days, and Alice has known me for years," argued Maureen.

"This is where it isn't about numbers, Maureen. Jane is telling you that you are very important to her even though when counting days it is not for long," said Deborah gently.

"Yes. You are my best friend, Jane Edwards, and she is my best care worker."

Jane smiled and let out a big sigh. She turned to look at Deborah. "Is numbers lady your best friend?"

Deborah looked confused. Dr. Mullins grinned at her. "We need total honesty here, Deborah."

They all looked at her. "Very interesting question and a very difficult one," she began.

"Oooh, ooh, she is not your bestie," laughed Maureen.

"No. It is not like that," said Deborah. "It is like what you said about Alice. I care deeply for numbers lady, but she is my boss. She pays me to be a carer. That is different to being a friend. It doesn't mean you care less for someone, but it is a different relationship."

"Well put!" smiled Dr. Mullins. "And I am very happy sitting here, making new food memories and new friendship memories. In fact, I now feel ready to make some more food memories. I am ready to go to the trolleys and scoop up something luscious and creamy."

Maureen clapped her hands loudly. Jane followed, and their waitress, right by the desert trolleys, came to take their plates away.

"Can you see anyone else from our coach?" asked Maureen, picking up her walking stick from the side of her chair, while Dr. Mullins turned the motor on her wheelchair back on.

Betty's Restaurant had high ceilings and wheelchair space around all the tables. It was a packed opening evening. Table lamps, chandeliers, waiters and waitresses either in sparkly black and white or white and blue.

"This is like a film," said Jane Edwards, walking with Deborah behind Maureen and Dr. Mullins.

"Ooh, there's the Shakespeare twins," called Maureen, pointing out the two men in animated conversation, with Charlie sitting on the edge of the table, looking confused.

"They are still eating their scampi. Bet they have been too busy talking," said Jane Edwards.

"Hello, Shakespeares," called Maureen. Some people turned their heads to see who was calling. Deborah was aware of a delicious feeling of relaxation. It was all right. It was safe, whatever they said. Dr. Mullins was happier than she had seen her for months, and this hotel was just right for her.

Tom and Steve turned round from their animated conversation and smiled at the four women. "If music be the food of love, play on," called Tom.

"Oh look! There's your good boy," said Jane Edwards, turning to look at Roland. Roland was sitting at the table with Andrzej, Olena, and Ibrahim. He beamed when he saw Maureen.

"Look. Good boy, Roland. Going to eat roly-poly pudding," he called.

"Good boy, Roland. Don't eat too much roly-poly pudding and don't eat yourself," Maureen, Jane, and Roland burst out laughing.

"Enjoy your desserts, ladies," said Ibrahim warmly.

"He called me a lady," said Jane Edwards,

"Well, you are a lady," said Maureen.

"But not a *lady* lady," said Jane.

"Lady, ladies, ladies, doctors, and good boy," decided Maureen.

"Heh, are you having a guided tour?" called Les, sitting at another table with three men. "You seem to be making a stop at everyone who was on our coach."

"Who are you with, Les?" asked Maureen.

"Well trust you to ask, brainbox. These are the drivers from other coaches or minicabs," said Les. "I am just having these nom-nom desserts and putting on weight, and then I will go back to my Almost-Missus."

"Don't eat too much, Almost-Fiancée," laughed Maureen, "Or you won't be able to walk to your coach."

"See what I get from these brainboxes?" laughed Les, turning to the men at his table.

Dr. Mullins made a slight detour, having spotted the Ricksteins. "Lovely meal, don't you think?"

"Yes," smiled Dan. "We don't eat scampi, but they kindly made us a lovely roast chicken," he added. Doris looked up shyly.

"Excellent," said Mary.

"Looks like I am the only one with a carer here," smiled Mary as Deborah walked up beside her.

"We sent Louise away, as we have all managed together."

"We had that lovely Muhammid, but he has gone to play the piano in Bert's Bar," offered Doris.

"What a talented young man," said Deborah.

"He is. A really kind young man," added Doris.

"Well, we might try Bert's Bar tomorrow," said Mary. "After dessert, I might have an early night and watch something on TV."

"See you tomorrow."

"Night," added Deborah. She looked affectionately at the brimming silver trolleys. Maureen and Jane were happily filling their bowls and that kind waitress was ready with her tray to return them to the table.

Chapter Thirty-Three

"My goodness — I can't believe how crowded it is," said Maanika, as she and Zen edged their way out.

"That's why I came here for the last few days," confided Zen. "I wanted a space that I knew before I came back."

She slipped slightly, and Maanika held her arm tightly. "Are you okay?" asked Maanika, worriedly.

"It's my heels. My own fault," said Zen in a jocular tone. She took a pair of sunglasses out of her bag and put them on. "If you can't see the stupid thing you just done, it won't hurt you."

Maanika burst out laughing. "Whatever helps you?"

"Too right, girl," endorsed Zen.

Around the corner there was slightly more space, and the noises from Bert's Bar could now be distinctly heard. Together with the hum of voices and laughter, and the clink of glasses, there was also faint tinkling from the piano.

"That must be Muhammid," said Maanika.

"The young, coloured guy with the brother?" asked Zen.

Maanika paused.

"I'm not up to date with the PC stuff and all that," laughed Zen. "Whatever you call him, I am Black."

She started walking confidently again.

Maanika cleared her throat. "Everyone is so —," but just as they reached the outside of Bert's Bar, Zendaya suddenly interrupted.

"Sorry Maanika — sorry sister — I can't go in now. I have to go." Letting go of Maanika's arm, she rushed back to Mirrorland.

Taking off her dark glasses, Zendaya hobbled on her high heels back to the welcoming home of Mirrorland. She couldn't face seeing him if he was there, or not seeing him if he wasn't. She felt like a bloody teenager:

50 years old wearing dark glasses. She didn't need it. If ever she needed Di, and the bitch was never there when she wanted her.

"Zen," shouted a loud voice, recognisable amidst all the buzz.

She ran blindly towards it.

"Zen! I'm here."

A pair of large white arms encircled her, and there, in the comfort of Mirrorland, she found herself shaking and shaking.

Maanika stood still for a moment, shocked by the sudden hasty departure of Zendaya. Had she frightened her? The woman was a contradiction. She had seemed such a confident, outgoing woman, ready to face the world, and then she had covered her face, hiding behind dark glasses, had tripped and worried about the things she was saying. Was she a retired pop star?

Lots to think about for My-Lights, but right now, she wanted to celebrate with Naresh and Sunil. She pushed her way through the open door that was rammed with revellers. Even though it was wide enough to allow two wheelchairs to go through at the same time, it was filled.

Once she was through, a whole new wall of noise met her. All around the bar were happy customers holding up their glasses for more drinks. Beyond the bar was Muhammid, bless him, playing songs on request. A small group were arranged around him singing "Summertime."

"There, there," said a beaming Di. "I never knew you cared so much. I'm not cross."

Zendaya burst out laughing, her mood changing dramatically. "I wasn't crying over you, deluded bitch. I was scared of seeing him."

Di let go of her arm savagely. "Okay, then I'll go."

"Fuck it! Can't you ever do the right thing? You weren't here when you said you would be. We don't do late for each other."

"Sorry," acknowledged Di. "I was having a last go at Ted. But I think I will have to give up on him."

They squeezed onto the end of a chaise longue. A young woman loaded with shopping bags reluctantly moved off, and they spread out.

"Since when do you have a last try with a dead guy walking when we have made an arrangement? His willy has been in hibernation for so long it won't even come up for air."

Di struggled against laughing. "Yes, he is a sleepy scrotum, but just because you did the deed with a new guy! Remember: Ted has legs."

They both burst out laughing. "Look at my face," said Zen pointing to her reflection. She wiped her eyes savagely.

"You look really good. I love your velvets with the matching high heels," said Di to distract her from the inevitable self-pity.

"Look. I'll tell you," said Zen, " I wanted to go to Bert's Bar to see if he is there, and I freaked out, so I went to look at the salon they have here. And this pretty coloured woman — Indian — started up a conversation and then I said I was waiting for you, but she was going to Bert's Bar and said I could go with her. And I wanted to. I really did, but I freaked out when we got to the door."

"And rushed to Mother Di," concluded Di.

"So, what do we do?" asked Zen.

"We?"

"Yes. Are we going to Bert's Bar?"

Act 4
Coming Together

Chapter Thirty-Four

Charlene and Irene walked wearily to her office. Quietly placed in the owner's flat, it felt cushioned from the noise and the crowds. Charlene threw off he shoes and sank into a welcoming sofa.

"We have lift-off! Cliff is wonderful. The waiters did well. No disasters," she pronounced.

"Prosecco?" asked Irene, moving to the sparkling new bar.

"I don't even have to say, 'one for the road,'" laughed Charlene.

"Yes, and I will take you up on your offer and stay here tonight too," pronounced Irene. "What a success! And even the Sunville Herald managed to come. Your Della called them, I believe."

Della. Where was she? "Do you know," said Charlene, trying to sound casual, "Della has disappeared on me this evening. She decided to have supper in her room. That is very unusual for her. And she has been out of communication since."

"It must be quite a thing for her to take on board. Her mum doing this, and it being about her grandparents, too," wondered Irene.

Charlene sighed. "Am I expecting too much thinking she would be beside me on this?"

"A mother's place is in the wrong," said Irene, laughing and handing over the glass of sparkly. "Cheers!"

"I will drink to that," said Charlene. "How are you so wise about this stuff, Irene, when you haven't got any kids?"

"Well, that's why I am so wise," laughed Irene.

"Do you think you missed out by not having children?"

"Not often," said Irene. "And it makes my relationships with younger people much more enjoyable. I feel maternal to them. Well, not all of them. Charlie and Louise are sweet, but I find the two brothers, Ibrahim and Muhammid, very considerate and hard-working, and that new young girl, Susan." She took a few more sips. "In fact, although it is so relatively new, I have really taken to Maanika and, in fact, your Della."

Charlene smiled gratefully.

"What a time to re-find a best friend." Irene put her empty glass down on the glass coffee table.

"More?"

"No, I need a brain," said Charlene. "What is it? You're looking very thoughtful."

"Does Della have friends?"

"Well, she goes out regularly."

"No. I mean a good friend, like we used to be, like we are again now."

"Oh my God — I am a bad mother. I don't know. I have been so obsessed with my own parents, I haven't thought. Why?"

"Well, I wondered if she wasn't with you right now because she needed to talk it all over with a friend. Maybe even a new friend."

Charlene sat bolt upright. She reached for her phone and immediately texted Della.

"It's my mother," said Della, raising an eyebrow as she looked at her mobile. They were sitting on her sofa with the coffee table tray loaded with their dinner remains. Della had made clear staff would be collecting it and they didn't have to wash up.

"Well, she gave you longer than mine did," laughed Susan, checking hers. Her mother had tried three times in the last eight hours. On the other hand, she had found the job for her.

"Oh. It is different from usual," said Della. "She is thanking me for my help in all of this. And inviting me and a friend to Bert's Bar in half an hour, if I feel like it. That is different. A bit of mental space."

"That must still be heavy going into your grandfather's bar."

"Yes. Fucking hell, the hotel feels a bit like a Disney cemetery! Walk inside granny, a drink with grandad. It is a bit late. And there I am, waiting with all the children whose parents are late."

They both burst out laughing.

"I can't believe how much it has been affecting me without me realising," said Della

Susan nodded, knocking her white wine onto the pristine sofa. "Oh, so sorry," she said, leaping up. Taking a wad of tissues out of her bag, she immediately dabbed at the stain, taking up as much of the liquid as possible. Rushing into the kitchenette, she poured some kitchen liquid soap into a small bowl of hot water. She then rubbed at the fabric with a brand-new dishcloth.

Della watched with amazement. "Gosh, you are an expert."

"Well, as I told you," said Susan, "my mother is an expert cleaner, and that is why I was so unhappy leaving the plates for someone else to wash. Every so often, it rubs off on me. White and champagne are much easier than red wine. Mum uses hairspray on top of that after sponging up what she can."

They were both silent for a moment after that, and then Susan said, "I hadn't realised how much it had all got to me either, and then I make a mess."

They sat in a warming silence. "They have done a lot, haven't they," mused Della.

"Shall we reply then?" asked Susan, her finger already poised.

Chapter Thirty-Five

Well, why not?" smiled Tom. "I haven't been inside a hotel bar for years. A lifetime, it feels like."

"And let my liver rather heat with wine than cool with mortifying groans," backed Steve.

"Will they know how to find us? This is the first time angel has gone out on her own — not on her own, I mean without me," asked Tom.

"Don't worry, we will let all the staff know so when they come back they will be directed to the bar," said Charlie, tapping quickly on his phone.

"We will take you there first and get you settled, and then come back to check if your ladies have returned," added Louise. With both men comfortably ensconced, they wheeled them out of Betty's, side by side.

"I hope I didn't sound selfish," said Tom, "when I said she had not been out without me. I am glad to see her talk to Marion, and she does need someone outside of family and doctors to talk to."

"We have to be, oh — what's the word — self-actualising?"

"Centred."

"Yes. Self-centred, because that is what we are, a self, and if we don't look after it we won't have anything. Marion has a leg problem. Nothing much, and not serious, but it frightened me because she has been my carer."

Their conversation paused as a wave of merrymakers swept along the wide corridor to the restaurant. Tom listened to the waves of sound rising and falling. How beautiful it was to see so many people, but how frightening, too. He knew Gerry had packed masks and he wished he was wearing one. He watched the people going to and fro. Such a buzz of excitement and hope. People who gave no thought to mortality, even though death lay curled and brittle inside them like tiny autumnal leaves. Not like him. Not like the other people on this holiday. He too was falling, falling. Grendel. He must hold onto Grendel. Grendel and Cain.

"Hello, hello, hello!" shouted a familiar voice distracting all of them.

Les was coming out of Bert's Bar just as they were going in. Louise and Charlie moved the wheelchairs back into the hall so they could talk.

"Hello, Shakespeare twins," said Les. "I am off home to my Almost-Missus. I will find out how many more things she has bought for our wedding festivities and how many more coach drives I have to go on before I will have paid for it."

"Well, good you are not spending more on drink, then," joked Steve. "Congratulations."

"Oh, it was free, thanks to this gig! Very special here. I have cut down on everything. It is what the women spend at weddings."

"Weddings are very different now," said Tom. "The women treat it like a reality show they are going to win. What they spend on a dress would pay a mortgage."

Les took a big sigh. "That's the one thing I did do, and all by myself. I got a mortgage; I have a home of my own."

"And that's the most important," said Charlie. "I am still living with my parents."

"Good luck, Les," said Louise.

"Well, you will still see me a few times before then," said Les. "But thanks."

As he turned away, Steve felt as if the sun was disappearing behind a cloud. What a lovely mountain of a man. Mountain. Look how the Muhammid quip had entered his psyche.

"Look at this! A good set for Falstaff, don't you think?" smiled Tom.

Inside Bert's Bar there was the sound of laughter, talking, and the tinkle of a piano in the corner where Muhammid was playing with a group all stationed around him singing. All clean and new and bright, people around the counter, all dressed up. And wheelchairs: he could see three others. It was like Christmas, like graduation, like a wedding. Men and women in sparkly black and white or blue and white Hotel Mirabelle T-shirts moved around gracefully, taking orders.

Tom felt in his pocket. "I think I will put my mask on. This is the largest group I have been near for years, it feels!"

Steve felt a burst of excitement inside himself. A spark. A small smile beginning to unfold. This was him, in his wheelchair, in a beautiful hotel bar without Marion. He could link up with his pre-disabled self. He could enjoy it.

"Darling," called a voice near him.

"Tomcat," said the other voice.

Marion and Gerry, bringing a blast of cold sea air with them, had rushed up to their two husbands with grateful and guilty expressions of love.

"Look, there is room for you there," called Charlie. "Luckily, you already have two chairs, and there are two lovely wing chairs for the ladies. I will pass on your orders and then leave you to relax for a while. Text me if you want help going back to your room."

Gerry hastened to sit on the red wing chair, relaxing into the warmth and comfort.

"You are freezing, angel," said Tom. "Do you want me to go up and get you another shawl?"

Gerry wiped her eyes with the edge of her shawl. "It's okay, darling. I will go and get it. I just wanted to see you as quickly as possible."

There was no point telling him he could not go and get it. He had forgotten he could not propel the wheelchair himself. The cerebral vascular issues had stopped that possibility.

"Oh, let me," said Louise cheerfully. "I have just been sitting and eating, and so I need some exercise."

"Oh, thank you," said Gerry with a deep sigh. "That is really kind." She handed over the key.

"If you are sure, angel. I hate to see you shivering."

Marion squeezed her arm. "What a lovely husband you are, Tom," she said warmly, as Louise quickly turned and left.

Steve smiled at her. "Was that a good walk? Did you remember the way back?"

Marion sat down next to Gerry. "We both forgot the time and the way back," she laughed. "It was really cold and dark out there. But good. Really good. And how have you two been?"

"Well, we had our quote-athon — what is it? Words. Competition. Shakespeare marathon!" exclaimed Tom.

"We expected that," said Gerry.

"Are you Shakespeared out?"

"We just need breath for a second round," laughed Steve. "Or we could go to Hopkins, or Thomas, or Browning."

"Okay," laughed Marion, "I will keep my walking shoes at hand."

Chapter Thirty-Six

Naresh was talking, *really* talking. Sunil had never heard him like this. Naresh described his life, how he had escaped to England after violence in India. They moved to Leicester and then to London when Maanika was only a baby. Naresh had joined the army, because so many of his family members had been killed by neighbours. This was cruelty. India and then Afghanistan. And disability. What a cruel judge he had been to Naresh.

Charlene and Irene arrived in the midst of the conversation. They sat silently, Charlene miming a drink request to the nearest waiter.

Naresh hardly noticed them, but he felt more heard tonight than he had ever felt before, outside of that miracle night with Zen.

"It is why Afghanistan, Syria, and Palestine fill me with dread. A civil war is totally different from facing an outside enemy. Neighbours against neighbours. It is also like when your body fights against you with cancer or dementia. Everything about it is different, except for the pain and loss."

Maanika looked intently at him. "Thank you for looking after me, big brother, when you had all the terrible memories and I have none."

He stretched a hand out to touch her. "Looking after you gave me a purpose. And you had no memory of our mother and father, how they loved you."

"I know they must have loved you, Maanika," Sunil added, "because of the way you are so loving."

As the server returned with the drinks for her and Irene, Charlene added, "And Wonderful Wheelchairs says we can turn a civil war of the body and stigma and lack of resources into something different. Slowly, slowly, but we will make a difference." Then, raising her drink, she said, "To Hotel Mirabelle and the Wonderful Wheelchair Company."

"Seconded," called Irene.

Just at that moment, Della and Susan appeared.

"Maanika!" said Susan quietly, but with emotion.

Maanika beamed broadly. "Aha. Yes. It is the French graduate who wants a non-holiday-holiday. It feels like ages since we spoke. Are you okay?"

Susan nodded reticently and stepped back.

Naresh looked up, rather confused and suddenly dislocated from what he had been saying. He did not move his prosthesis, which took up a whole Chesterfield. The girls were unsure where to sit.

Della smiled comfortably at them all. "Have we come just in time for a toast?" she asked.

"Definitely," said Irene, frowning imperceptibly at Charlene who was ready to say "no."

Charlene smiled and clicked her fingers, and the next round of glasses and bottles and bowls of nuts began to appear. Susan and Della squeezed together on a wing chair that suddenly appeared.

"Thank you for talking about India, Naresh, when we have not had that conversation before," said Charlene seriously. She had so wanted her daughter to join her to celebrate, but now she wished she was not there, and especially not with a new staff member, however well-vetted and nice.

Naresh had lost the spirit that had sparkled in him just a moment earlier. Charlene looked at Irene, Sunil, and Maanika. To her surprise, Maanika looked comfortable, while Sunil and Naresh looked deep in thought. "Sunil, Naresh — sorry, Irene and I appeared just when you were having an important discussion. Would you like us to go? We can go elsewhere."

"Oh," said Della, "Have we gooseberried?" She looked at her mother for clarification. "Susan and I can go elsewhere," she added.

Naresh seemed unable to speak. Maanika lay a gentle hand on his arm. "Brother, do you want us to stay or do you need quiet?"

Naresh suddenly turned his head to look at the entrance to the bar. He moved his prosthetic legs and waved. His face flushed. Two women in their 50s were making their way towards them.

Like middle-aged Barbies, thought Della.

Aren't they marvellous, thought Susan.

Charlene and Irene grinned at each other.

"It's Zen," said Maanika, happily waving.

"Zen, Z–Zen—you know her?" stammered Naresh.

"She had some really good ideas for My-Lights," said Maanika.

"I bet she did," grinned Irene.

Maanika looked at her bewildered, and then turned to sign for more chairs to be brought up.

"It's all right," said Naresh, suddenly recovering. "We don't need more chairs. She can have my legs."

Smiling, Zen sashayed towards them in a cloud of perfume and cleavage. She happily moved onto the Chesterfield, lifting the prosthetic legs casually, as if they were a handbag.

"Hi Maanika, good to see you again. Love how you've done your hair. Hi, Naresh. I'll put them under the sofa—then you can stay legless."

Naresh and Zen burst out laughing, while Charlene, Irene, Maanika, Sunil, Della, and Susan stared, each lost in their own thoughts.

"Well, what you looking at? We're not from outer space," said Di, following close behind her. "Introduce me!"

"Well, here's to you, sister," smiled Della, coming out of her momentary shock. "I am Della."

"And I am Susan," added Susan.

Di hoisted her bra strap and smiled all around. "Okay, then. I am Di, a friend of Zen, and the big question is who is going to get me a drink."

"Cool it, Di," said Zendaya. "We weren't invited to meet them all."

"Just me," said Naresh, smiling helplessly.

A waiter appeared to clear away bottles and take drink orders.

Zen giggled. "Look. It's happened again! Whenever I am with you, drinks appear like magic."

Charlene and Irene looked at each other. "Well, we are going on to a meeting," said Charlene. "Sunil, Maanika, Susan, and Della. Would you like to join us in my room, or will you be staying down here a bit?"

"Whatever you want," said Susan, turning to Della.

"Well, that's quite a dangerous thing to say," laughed Di, flicking her blonde curls.

Zen laughed too, looking intently at Naresh.

"Well, now we have had introductions, I would like to catch-up with Zen. We missed each other earlier," said Naresh, beaming at the others.

Maanika felt tearful seeing the joy on his face. "Okay, brother! But make sure you have her contact number. She had some really good ideas about My-Lights."

"Your sister?" asked Zen, looking intently from one to the other. "I'd like that." She breathed a deep sigh, hand touching her cornrows and then her cross.

Maanika smiled and stood up to leave, and Sunil turned briefly back to Naresh. "Well, really good to have had our conversation, Naresh," said Sunil. "Can I talk about it with the others?"

"Whatever you want," said Naresh.

"Ooh, that sentence again — can I have that sentence too!" laughed Zen, all her spirit returning to her.

"Whatever you want," said Naresh joyously.

"Oh, get a room!" muttered Della to Susan as they made their good-byes.

"Spread out then, Di. I don't need you on my lap," Zen said, as Di re-arranged herself on a freed-up chair.

"So what happened?" asked Naresh. "Why didn't I have your number?"

"Because you never asked," said Zen. "I have been waiting all day to hear from you, but you couldn't call me, so I couldn't get cross with you, but I was so fucked off."

"And I have been waiting all my life," said Naresh smiling at her.

"Okay, I have had enough," shouted Di. "You used me to come into the bar, bitch, and now you don't need me because he is here and you both ignore me. I am not staying just to watch you two." Standing up, she strutted through the bar. "I'm too old to be a gooseberry," she called back.

"Let her go," said Zen, "It doesn't matter. And before we do anything else, let's swap numbers."

As they took out their phones, an elderly man near the bar door stood up to intercept Di. "I like gooseberries. In fact, I am one sitting here by myself. Could I invite you to have a drink with an elderly gooseberry?" He took a leather wallet out of his jacket pocket to flash his cards.

"Don't mind if I do," said Di, mollified.

With old-fashioned courtesy, he pulled a chair back for Di to take a seat and watched with pleasure while she looked at the bar menu.

Chapter Thirty-Seven

Mary had pointed to her favourite tartan pyjamas which Deborah laid out on the bed, ready for the carer — Louise, would it be? It didn't matter. All was well.

Deborah looked happily round the bright two-bedroomed apartment. Room 4. She and Mary were used to sharing for holidays or breaks, and this room was one of the nicest. It was the space, the newness. Although she would not admit it, Mary looked happier than she had seen her for ages, too. *Numbers lady*.

"What are you looking so pleased about, Deborah? Don't think I don't notice," came Mary's sharp but kindly voice.

"Wouldn't you like to know!" grinned Deborah.

"Well, now," said Mary, "I think I know you enough to consider you are assuming that the happiness you feel must be linked to a happiness I am feeling. You are doing your Pollyanna act."

Deborah burst out laughing. "Bingo!"

Mary smiled.

"Well, I am not unhappy," she said grudgingly, and then could not help smiling. "It is that Maureen. She is a wonder. My books were never for children with a learning disability, but she makes me wish I had written one."

Deborah held her breath with excitement. She knew it was not safe to speak.

"You are probably thinking I should," said Mary sharply.

"'Should' is an ugly word," said Deborah, on safer ground. "You know I don't believe in shoulds."

Mary took a deep breath. "I like her. I really like her."

"Yes," agreed Deborah. "There really is something special about her."

"Deborah," said Mary nervously, "Before a carer comes. I need you to know that I want to swim when we go to Brighton, but I am rather frightened. Would you swim with me?"

Deborah struggled to keep her face still. Mary hated to ask for anything, even though she was the employee. Better not to draw attention to it. "I would love that," she said simply and then asked Mary if she would like a cup of tea.

~

Maureen was sitting on her bed, hands clasped in prayer.

"Dear God, I am sorry I cannot kneel down, but my knees hurt and I am sure you don't mind. It is the prayer that matters and I am still praying like I do on Sundays. I have good news to tell you. I am on holiday by myself. I came without Alice. My legs and brain are working as well as they can as you made me.

"I want to tell you there is a numbers lady who is a brainbox and she really likes me. She made me think of Mr. Grass whose middle name was Anders, you remember, and I am Anderson. She sees I have a brain like he did. But then he got that thing and forgot me, so that means she will too.

"Do I have to go through this again? Is this because I wished Miss Jenkins was dead because she was horrible to me, and I told you? I know you don't answer questions. You have the world asking you things. But that is the problem I am sharing.

"Thank you. And be nice to Alice and numbers lady, and Jane Edwards," she hurriedly added. "Oh, and good driver Les."

Maureen then unclasped her hands, sighed, and reached for her yellow teddy bear. "I wish Alice was here, Teddy. But we will be all right."

~

Hermione was lying in her large double bed, her mind a fever of excitement. On her lap was her last sketch pad, a helter-skelter of wheelchairs and horses charging page after page.

And now she was drawing Naresh's face. She had used his photo from the advertising material to base the sketch and then added to it. Some body. No body. No thing. What was a human? What was she? James mocking her golden walking stick. Her powerful phallic man, an Icarus on horseback. Going too high and collapsing. And then hating her. His wife. Why couldn't she bypass that back to their beginning and enjoy all the moments of joy and love? But his hatred of her and his disability seared her still. What was she looking for in her painting? It could be a fool's quest. But something inside her felt she was ready for an answer.

Her right hand was aching for her brushes, her paint, the sweep of plain canvas. Without her painting she was incomplete. It was her wheelchair.

Les finally allowed himself to leave Hotel Mirabelle. Unlike his other jobs, this was practically local for him. So, he didn't need to be back to make sure of an early night.

It was always hard saying goodbye, even since his Tracey had moved in. Before, the work was his only friendship besides the Hen and Horse. Oh, what a popular clown he was: bookings kept coming in. Popular Les, who had no-one. And now, there was Tracey. Unbelievable Tracey.

And that was the worry. Could he believe it? Was it just a wedding she wanted? Was he the irrelevant appendage that came with a glittering wedding and a house? Why would anyone want him? Only homeless Gwyne and cruelly-dumped Trace. And there she was, his lovely Trace, sitting in his home, queen of it, with all her wedding magazines and bride magazines. Where was he? Was he anywhere? Yes — she did understand him. She knew how much this work meant to him and how much he meant to them. But did she love him, or was she only marrying him?

Les was walking to the inland cab place. He needed the night air. He was exhausted from the journey and its aftermath. Where else did they expect the driver to be a comedian, group therapist, encyclopaedia? Keeping up with Maureen and all the other tos and fros was exhausting while watching the road. He could have gone home as soon as he had unloaded them all. Why did he carry on being helpful when he had done his job? Why push his jokes beyond their sell-by date? Wasting his energy, for what? No answers there. Brief trips that all looked like friendships and then they were over. Who would remember the driver?

And now the driver had someone wonderful to go home to, but was she even waiting for him? Or was she sitting, surrounded by magazines, not even thinking of him or knowing that time he could have been back? Suddenly overtaken by a fit of anger, he kicked at stray bottles. How did he even know she would not dump him on their wedding day the same way she had been?

The lights from Colin's Cabs welcomed him. Only because he was paying, he thought. No-one wanted him, unless it was for money.

Chapter Thirty-Eight

Ibrahim was surprised and exhausted. The guests were less dependent than usual, and even those who could not transfer themselves from a wheelchair to a toilet were able to help. Roland, poor young man, was of concern, but Maureen had been a godsend. That was why Ibrahim was surprised. He was exhausted, though, from worrying about Muhammid.

Perhaps he hadn't needed to worry. Irene had made sure to compliment Ibrahim on how he had subtly helped his brother and had thanked him for it. She also said Muhammid was a natural for this work. Charlene had even said he could play the piano which, he knew, would have relaxed Muhammid. But Ibrahim still felt like he needed to be his brother's keeper.

Ibrahim had come to the UK first, doing jobs English people did not want to do. People did not look after their families. He worked hours in cold care homes, watching the slow deterioration of the unloved. He wanted to change it. After five years, he gained his right to remain and then helped Muhammid to come when the job with Wonderful Wheelchair Company came up. A large double room instead of his damp studio. The two of them together making a new life.

Realising his uncle would never accept the truth of who Ibrahim was meant Ibrahim had spent years planning his escape. Only his love for his little brother had delayed him, but he had a plan to bring him, too. He went first by boat to Tobruk, paying nearly all his savings to the people smugglers. And then to Italy, and finally to the UK. He would never go on a boat again. Never had he felt closer to death. But it was death to his soul to not to accept he was gay, even though he had no partner.

Muhammid, on the other hand, came to the UK the proper way, with papers already signed and a job already arranged. Ibrahim had risked his life, his home, and his job in bringing his brother here, and now he had worried whether Muhammid would manage, or if he'd do something to ruin his own reputation.

Muhammid, though, was a natural carer. He had their mother's sweetness. And he had learned the piano!

After completing the paperwork for the guests, Ibrahim decided to go to Bert's Bar to collect his brother. Hotel staff smiled at him as they walked past, recognising him. This hotel was like a new country he had walked into. A country that had almost decided to accept him. He took a deep breath and slowed down his step.

The buzz of the noise in Bert's Bar reached him before he walked in. It was still packed, but there, in the corner, was Charlene beckoning a waiter with orange juice to his brother. And her daughter, Della, with Susan. Irene was there, too. And the co-director of Wonderful Wheelchairs, Maanika.

His heart was pounding. Everyone who had power over him, who could sack him, who could leave him: all there with his brother.

His footsteps slowed. A wave rose in his heart, from the journey to Tobruk. It was in danger of drowning him.

"Ibrahim!" called Irene warmly. She held up a glass of champagne and toasted him. "And here are two good brothers!" she added, smiling at Maanika.

"Thank you for bringing him here," said Maanika. "His piano-playing has been a delight."

Muhammid's face broke into a huge smile. "I did not disgrace you brother, and I did know a lot of the songs they liked."

Charlene smiled at him. "We have really christened Hotel Mirabelle now. And that was my favourite version of 'Summertime' that I have ever heard."

"Thank you, thank you," beamed Muhammid. "You see, brother, it was a good use of my education."

"The best," agreed Della.

The wave melted into the warm air. He was dry and home. He walked forward formally and held his brother in a hug.

Chapter Thirty-Nine

Doris had folded their clothes away and stowed them in the large wardrobes. "Look," she called, "They even have enough hangars. Usually you only get three or four."

Dan smiled lovingly at her. She had already calmed down. "And I will try not to eat all the chocolates in the welcome bowl," he said.

"Please try," she said earnestly. "I couldn't cope with anything more happening to you."

He pulled himself into a sitting position. "Now, look here, Doris, you have seen Steve, Marion, and Tom — they're all worse off than me. Are they complaining?"

She put a hand against her heart. "My heart! It is beating so fast and hard."

"Because you are frightened. Even though you realised you were being prejudiced. And I am so proud of you for saying sorry."

She stopped fussing and sat on the bed. "He was so nice. The world is so difficult. There are good and bad in all groups."

"You are just frightened coming out into the uncontrolled world. Not just the people you know in our street, our synagogue, our family, our food."

"This is not a kosher hotel, Daniel," she nodded. "How can you be so calm? Your parents went through the Battle of Cable Street same as mine, had the swastikas on the door, the Mosleyites, the fascists."

"Yes. But goodness won, didn't it?" he enforced.

"Did it? I think I must have the soul of my Buba inside me. Whenever she went out to buy anything, she was in danger from Cossacks. I know that is not just Jews. Think of the girls going to get water from a well in India, Afghanistan, Syria, and risk dying of thirst or being raped."

"Exactly," he said. "Now you are being a wise woman. There is only racism. Words like antisemitism don't help. And racism comes from fear. You being frightened of Muhammid could have really hurt him."

"Don't say it again. I know. I am too ashamed to hear," she whispered. "What I only sounded like."

"Yes. But you said sorry and you said you were frightened. And it is my fault you are frightened, as I made you drive out of your comfort zone for me and you did it because you are a lovely woman. I bless the day I set my eyes on you. You drove to get me here, to make me happy, even though you hated it. And especially after Danny's death. And look how you managed the food. You knew it wouldn't be kosher, but you didn't make a song and dance about it."

"Well, because Dan dared," she said.

"Desperate Dan," he added. He held out his hand, and she fell back into the comforting arc of his arms.

Chapter Forty

Tracey was waiting. The bungalow, Les's house, was immaculate. The table was clear and all the wedding magazines had been piled neatly on a side table. There was an empty plate on the table that had been scraped clean. She could not wait any longer and had finished her tandoori chicken. She hadn't made it; that honour belonged to Mr. Sainsbury's around the corner. Les's portion was on a plate in the cold microwave, waiting to be heated.

He had never been this late.

She reached for the open bottle of red wine. One glass more wouldn't hurt. He was probably drinking. Perhaps at the Chicken and Horse — whatever it was called — with his friends. Or perhaps he was drinking at Hotel Mirabelle. It was their launch night, so the bar would have been flowing with freebies. Her fiancée. He called her his "Almost-Missus."

She liked that. She was "almost." Almost married, and he was almost her husband. He wasn't anything like her ex. He would never let her down like that. That was how they met, after all. He knew what she had gone through.

She checked her phone. No text and no messages. Should she phone him? He had never been this late before, not without phoning her. Would that be intrusive? Was he wanting to check he would still have his freedom as a married man? Was he checking out how she managed him being late? Oh God — this was not how it was supposed to be. Was he fed up with her being deep in her bride magazines? Had she ignored him?

She paced up and down the lounge, the hallway, and the kitchen. She would send a text message. That was the way to do it.

She sat down on the edge of the sofa, trying not to smoke a cigarette. She had stopped. For the wedding. She looked at the biscuit tin. No, she had stopped that for the wedding. Everything was the wedding. Was she mad? Was she one of those bridezillas? Was that why he was late? Was he going to dump her because he could not bear it? She reached for a chocolate digestive. Better than her lungs being damaged.

Cool it, she ordered herself. She picked up her mobile.

JUST CHECKING YOU ARE OKAY. LOVE YOU AND MISS YOU.

She wanted to sign it Almost-Missus, but then felt that would be dangerous. It was still about the wedding. But why shouldn't it be? Wasn't it the biggest thing in their lives?

She opened the front door. All was quiet and darkening. No sound of a car coming. He would be in a cab. When he did these jobs the coach stayed near the hotel and he had to get a cab there and back.

Could he have had an accident? Should she phone the police, or the local hospital? Should she phone the Mirabelle? Would they know if he had gone? If she phoned to ask, would he be angry? But if he had had an accident, he might be pleased she had cared. Who was he? Who was she? She was a woman who was dumped at the altar. He was a man who had picked up desperate waifs and dumped brides because no one else would have him. Is that all they were? Leftovers?

Perhaps, she shouldn't have a dress. Perhaps it would remind both of them of how they met.

Still no reply. She would just go up to bed.

Chapter Forty-One

Olena and Andrzej held their breath as they made their way from Roland's room. The moment they were out of earshot, they burst out laughing.

"I feel like a wicked schoolgirl," said Olena.

They stood still to listen. There were no screams. Good for Roland. He had adapted to the schedule. Charlie and Louise were getting him washed and into pyjamas. Then he could watch his favourite television programmes, and Andrzej would return.

Silently, they tiptoed down the wide corridor until they came to the stairs, which they spontaneously took instead of the lift.

"Yes," agreed Andrzej. "I am feeling such relief with the wide lifts and corridors but it also makes me grateful I am not disabled, and I can speak two languages and can walk freely walk up these stairs. I do feel a bit guilty leaving. Even though Charlie and Louise are there to help tonight, I still feel it is my job. But, of course, I can't be with him twenty-four hours a day. It is hard enough I am having to sleep there or do a waking night."

"Yes," said Olena. "That, at least, was one thing they could not put on me. I have a room of my own. And it is a big one."

"Shall we go to the bar?" asked Andrzej.

"Or the seafront?" suggested Olena. "I don't feel like doing anything that will take too much time," she added. " I just want to put my feet up and watch the television. It is a lovely big television and I have a lovely big double bed."

"Double bed?" asked Andrzej, "You mean not a small adjustable one, like in a hospital?"

"No. I am — how do they say here? Ableist! I have a normal double bed, and I want to feel normal tonight. It was exhausting, even though Roly did well."

"Yes. He did do well," said Andrzej as they just missed bumping into Muhammid and Ibrahim outside the bar.

"Cześć!" said Ibrahim, carefully moving to the side.

Andrzej looked at him in amazement. "You speak Polish?"

"No," said Ibrahim sadly. "But I had a Polish friend."

"Well, it was nice to hear. Thank you," said Andrzej. He rubbed his nose, and Olena took a quick worried look at him.

"I think you made him homesick," said Olena, turning to Muhammid. "If you are leaving, does that mean the piano-playing is over?"

"For today," said Muhammid. "But I will play again tomorrow evening."

They all moved to the side of the wide corridor to let other people go in and out.

"Do you know, Ibrahim," said Andrzej, "I do feel homesick. But perhaps all of us do, us four," he wondered reflectively. "Strange word — homesick. Sick in English is like nausea, like seasickness. Homesickness is more a longing." He coughed. "Where are you from?" he asked, looking intently at Ibrahim.

"Egypt."

"So we are Egypt, Poland, and Ukraine," said Olena.

"Wonderful Wheelchairs is a mini-United Nations."

"It seems English people don't care about looking after the old and disabled," Muhammid sighed. "But that is good for me, because I love looking after people, and I love England."

The others smiled at him, as if he were a little child.

"Egypt is beautiful," said Andrzej. "I have seen the pyramids. But what shocked me most is that Egyptian people look like their gods and goddesses. That must be very different, to look like your deities. Jesus, after all, was a Jew, but all of Europe made him blonde-haired and blue-eyed with a blonde Mary, too. It seems we can't bear to have a god who does not look like us. It makes us feel like orphans."

Olena touched her crucifix nervously. "In England, they say don't talk about religion, money, and politics."

Ibrahim smiled at her. "Yes. And now it is more dangerous. You can get 'cancelled.' But it is still safer than most countries. Yes. This is not a religious comment. Our people are beautiful and do look like our gods and goddesses. Well, some of them do. I feel the same about Indians and their deities. Every country has something beautiful to make up for the ugliness."

Olena frowned. "And I am too raw and tired to answer questions on Ukraine when the ugliness is going on right now. I would like to change the conversation, or I can leave you to it."

"Heh," said Muhammid, "to move away from that ugliness, would you both like to join us for tea or coffee? Is that all right, brother, me asking in your name too?"

Ibrahim beamed at him. "Yes indeed. They can come to the staff room with us as they are staff too. Or to our room?"

"Or mine?" laughed Olena. "I have a double room, but poor Andrzej may need to be in the same room as Roland, although he has a small dayroom, too, and you two have a room."

"Oh, wouldn't Maureen and numbers lady like this conversation," laughed Muhammid. "Wherever we go, can we go now? I need to sit down."

"Then please come to our room," said Ibrahim formally. And off they went, Ibrahim and Andrzej, leading the way while Muhammid and an amused Olena followed.

Chapter Forty-Two

There was an uneasy silence once drinks had been poured and nibbles magically appeared in tiny pottery bowls — olives, crisps, chocolate, and ginger balls. Candles were also lit, and a sweet smell of vanilla drifted between them.

"Okay, I will say it, if no-one else will," said Irene, pouring more prosecco into her glass. "It seems that Naresh is celebrating something really important tonight. Zen has done something to make him forget his wounds. No. Not forget. They just don't matter as much as the new feelings."

Maanika looked uncomfortable. "Am I being a baby here? Did I not understand? Are you trying to tell me my brother was intimate with Zen, had sex with her, when he has only just met her? Before she had been introduced to me by him?"

Della raised her eyebrows at Susan conspiratorially.

"Wasn't that obvious?" asked Charlene, winking at Irene.

Sunil looked at all of them. He held his hand out to Maanika.

"Naresh is a braver man than I ever realised. He told me today for the first time what he and his family went through in the anti-Christian riots in India. They were murdered. They helped the Dalit people, the untouchables. They tried to educate them so they would not be exploited. And they were murdered. He and his little sister, Maanika, and their grandfather came to England. Everyone else was murdered. And so he joined the British army as soon as he was old enough and went to Afghanistan.

"Think about it. He slaves and slaves with no personal joy. He has no girlfriends, because he does not want anyone to have to weep for him. He does not want to lose anyone else. He decided to leave the army eventually, after some awful battles and minor wounds, and he decided, with Maanika, to set up Wonderful Wheelchairs. But then he gets blown up and look what more he loses — half his body! He could have committed suicide. He could have lost his soul in drink and drugs and —"

"Loose women?" interrupted Maanika, distraught. "But isn't that what he is doing now?"

"You liked her," said Della sharply. "You have taste, and you liked her. So why can't he like her."

"But Charlene and Irene told me there were easy women who came here to find old men with money," said Maanika.

"So?" asked Della. "There are also women of all kinds who would not go near a disabled man."

Irene took a deep breath. "It is easy to be judgemental about a group of people when you don't know them. I know Naresh. He hasn't been right lately, even though he is thrilled we are now launched. It is literally almost over his dead body. Maanika has been overloaded lately, because he has not been able to work. He is depressed. And he has plenty to be depressed about. So, I am really glad something or someone is making him happy, and we will see what happens. It might be a real long-term relationship; it might be a one-night stand — or whatever it is called for someone in his condition, you know, because he can't."

She and Charlene laughed. Maanika looked around anxiously. "I did like her, though. She seemed real. But that was just from one meeting."

Susan gave a nervous cough. These were her bosses and she was the most junior employee there. "I am sorry. Forgive my intrusion. We all come from different cultures, even when we look the same. My mother got pregnant with a man after a one-night stand, and he never even knew she was pregnant with me. She was white and he was dark-skinned. So you see how someone's looks can be misleading."

Charlene's eyes filled with tears. Maanika sighed and a smile lit up her tired face. "I chose well in giving you the job from one conversation, Susan. You are right. Sometimes it is only one meeting and a link is made. Whatever happens later. My Dadaji found Sunil for me. And we got engaged and then married." She smiled shyly at Sunil. "So yes. I am lucky. He found me a wonderful man."

Irene held up a glass. "Okay, okay. That is deep enough for one night. I am a woman who had a one-night stand and whose mother followed useless blokes all over the country. But I did not get any lovely kids out of it. Susan and Della are a credit to their mothers."

Irene and Charlene hugged each other. "Okay, okay, okay," said Charlene, slightly tipsy. "Hotel Mirabelle and the Wonderful Wheelchair Company are now truly launched in Sunville."

Chapter Forty-Three

I missed you," said Naresh.

"I really fucking missed you." Zen had stretched her legs across him.

"Was that all you missed?" she asked with a raised eyebrow.

They grinned at each other.

"No. But I missed that, too. Did you miss me?" he asked.

"Course, I fucking missed you," she replied. "I missed Dick, Lance, and Roger, and not just Dick," she added.

"I have been going mad looking at my phone and realising you couldn't phone me because you didn't have my number. And I couldn't find a personal phone number under Hotel Mirabelle. "

He smiled happily. "You really missed me!"

"Yes, and what's worse, I couldn't blame you either! Yes, you got the point, Mister. How many times do I have to say it?"

"Oh, again and again and again," smiled Naresh.

"Did you miss me?" he asked again.

"Yes. I bloody well did. I fucking did. Don't do that to me again."

"But I didn't do it. We both forgot the most important thing of all."

"How could we have done it?" asked Zen.

"I don't know," wondered Naresh.

"You know. I will always love you for coming back to the bar today," he said seriously.

Tears came into her eyes. "What did you say, Legless? Don't play with me."

"But I like playing with you," said Naresh. "In fact, I can't think of anyone in the whole world I would rather be with."

"So, we are together," she said in a suddenly shy soft voice.

"You bet we are," he laughed with joy.

"If I was like I was, I would lift you up and carry you to my room."

"If you were like you was, you probably wouldn't notice me," she grinned.

"How could anyone not notice you?" he asked. "You are just gorgeous." His hand stroked her legs lovingly. "And you are all there."

"And all here," she added.

She looked around Bert's Bar. "I'm here with you, innit?"

"Of course you are here with me."

"I mean, I know we are in the same bar. I didn't mean that. I mean I am not getting it wrong; I am here with you. You know what I mean?"

He looked intently at her. "You are here with me, and I have been waiting for you all my life. So I am quite happy staying down here until the bar closes, so that everyone knows you are with me."

"I like that," she said with an unusual smile spreading inside her.

"So do I," he replied. "You have met my sister now, and brother-in-law and my co-directors, and I am too old to have parents alive, and they were killed anyway in India. So you have met everyone."

"Directors?"

"Yes. The Wonderful Wheelchair Company. It is joining up with Hotel Mirabelle."

Zen sat up abruptly. "Really? So that's why they kept bringing the drinks. You are a real posh one I have caught."

"Sounds posh, but we don't know if it will pick up."

"Course it will, and especially if Maanika makes My-Lights more Afro and Indian."

Naresh looked curiously at Zendaya.

"You didn't know I had a business brain," said Zendaya, laughing, "and I didn't know you were an even bigger catch."

She looked round Bert's Bar and saw Di at the table nearest the door. She was with an old fellow who had his hand on her thigh. Perhaps it was a good night for her, too.

"And Di is the only close friend I have, which tells you a lot about me," she added.

"So that's it," laughed Naresh. "We only need a wedding space to accommodate you and me, Di, Maanika, and Sunil, Charlene and Irene, Susan and Della, and maybe a waiter or two or some care workers. But I am a cheap wedding date. Not more than a dozen."

She sat up abruptly, moving her legs off him.

"Ouch!" he said.

"Sorry. Sorry. Was that a proposal?"

"No, it is a repeat of the fact of a proposal. I said I wanted to marry you within a few minutes of meeting you."

"But do I get a proposal? A real proposal?"

"I can't get down on my knees," he laughed, "although, for you, I have done all sorts of things I didn't know I could do."

"Naresh, is this Naresh proposing to me, Zendaya, even if you are drunk and will say you never said it tomorrow?"

Naresh pushed himself into a more comfortable position on the Chesterfield. He took a ring-pull from one of the empty cans. With great solemnity, he put it on her little finger. "Zendaya, will you do me the honour of becoming my wife? In sickness and — probably more sickness?

"Yes. Yes," said Zendaya, kissing his hand.

"I never asked you," said Naresh. "Are you married? Are you free to marry me?"

"I was married. To a bastard. He died of cancer, and I nursed him even though he kicked me in the stomach when I was young. I lost my baby."

She turned to him, happy to move on. "Are you free?"

"Yes. Free, or you could say abandoned, as I did not feel free. I have never had a girlfriend. And even though you may laugh at me — I had never had sex before."

"So, no kids?"

"No. Unless I was a male Virgin Mary somehow impregnating women through my mere presence."

"So we are both free to marry," she said.

They looked at each other and held hands.

"I need to tell my sister before we announce it," he said.

"Yes, and I will tell Di."

"So now we are engaged," said Naresh. "You are my fiancée."

"Fiancée," said Zen, savouring the word.

They both looked at each other.

"We have saved a lot of time," said Naresh.

"And money," said Zendaya.

"We haven't done the fancy restaurants, the films, the presents."

"No, and I didn't have to pay for the hotel room, either!"

"And all the hairdos and dresses and everything I haven't had to do! Just two dresses I wore, but I had already bought them. No more old frogs to kiss."

He looked at her. "And you don't have to sow any wild oats because you have already done it."

"And you are not jealous?"

"No. That was before me and that was why you could be like you were with me."

She looked at him lovingly. "Any criminal record I need to know about?"

"No. Just drunk. And you? Any drugs, porn films, blackmail?"

"Possibly. But I'd tell you. Not really a problem. I don't care about it. Di and I have tried having girls' nights out to find us a rich old man and there was a lot worse than kissing frogs."

They both burst out laughing. "This is a Guinness Book of Records catch-up!" laughed Zen.

"My prosthesis can make me more sore at times and then I prefer to go out in the world as handicapped as I really am — a cut-down man."

"Fine with me. Whatever feels true to you," said Zen blithely. "And I wear my breasts up to show I have got them. My mother had breast cancer and lost them, and she felt the men lost interest after that, including my dad. And I do my face up like this before I go out."

"And whatever feels true to you is good with me," said Naresh.

"Work commitments?" asked Zen. "Your company?"

"Well, I run it with my sister, who has done lots of the heavy work because I was mentally occupied. If it works here at Hotel Mirabelle, we might base it here and stop all the other tours. You?"

"Hairdresser, masseuse, that was before. Then after my husband's — my first husband's death — I went downhill and got desperate and did more of the call girl escort stuff."

"Ah, like me after Afghanistan. Downhill, and too much drink. But no women."

"I am too old to have a baby," said Zen, "I should be a grandma, but you still could have a child. Is that a problem?"

"Not after being in a war and my parents murdered for being Christians in India."

"And I never even asked about religion," said Zen, fingering her crucifix. "I am Christian, too. Not that I go to church much outside of Christmas, weddings, and funerals. But it matters to me."

"Well," said Naresh happily, "we started off with sex and we have done religion, families, past sexual experience, problems, work — anything we have missed? I think we have covered a few years of dating now."

"Well, I have thought of two more things," said Zen.

"Go ahead, my bride-to-be."

"Can we have a church wedding? I would like that. And where do we live?" She looked down rather shamefacedly. "I only have a studio room I rent. My ex was a gambler. I had to pay off his debts after he died. Ex. I prefer that to my first husband."

Naresh picked up her hand joyfully. "I am only doing it once and I haven't done it before, so I definitely want it to be in church. And you move in with me now. Right away. I don't want another day without you. And, of course, we will hold the wedding party for our twelve people here."

And they kissed, unaware of a small group of waiters and bar staff clapping.

"Ouch," said Naresh as her body pressed against his left upper thigh, sore from the prosthesis.

"Sorry, fiancée," said Zen, kissing him again.

"So it wasn't just a one-night stand," she added seriously.

"Well it is hard for me to stand," he joked. But then he lifted her hands and kissed them. "It is a one-life stand."

Act 5
Being There

Chapter Forty-Four

Outside of a couple of smartly dressed waiters, Maureen was the first in Betty's for breakfast from Wonderful Wheelchairs. As she stood holding onto her walking frame and looking through at the vast emptiness, Charlie came to join her.

"That's good that you are using your walking frame," said Charlie, "it gives your bottom a break from sitting down in the wheelchair all the time."

"That is what Alice said to me," agreed Maureen. She stopped and looked around the huge silent restaurant. "Look how tidy it is. Hundreds of people were here last night with all the food and crumbs and mess and look, it is only a few hours later, really, and it is all clean."

A young waiter smiled broadly as he walked past. "Thanks, love! Can I tell my mates what you said?"

"Of course," said Maureen regally. "It is a very good job. Ten out of ten."

"That was very nice of you, Maureen. People often don't think to say thank you," said Charlie warmly. "Jane still asleep?" he then asked.

"Probably. She hasn't texted me yet. But I am good at restaurants. I know what to do by myself. It is a buffet, isn't it? So they will come to the table to see if I want tea or coffee, and then I go to the buffet. I am going to have bacon and egg and mushrooms and tomatoes, if they have all that, and toast, and — what's it called — croissant? I like a holiday breakfast."

"You are making me hungry," laughed Charlie.

"I am making myself hungry! That's funny!" She stood still again. "Listen to how quiet! Just us talking. But my clock tells me the right time and it is breakfast, if you are awake and want it now."

"Quite right, Maureen. Breakfast is served from 7 am to 10 pm and it is 7 am."

"So people who went to bed at midnight have had seven hours of sleep now."

Before Charlie could reply, they heard the gentle whirring of an electric wheelchair: Mary, accompanied by a worried-looking Deborah.

"Did I hear numbers?" asked Mary in a pantomime villain voice. But her face was pale, despite the spark of pleasure.

"Numbers lady," said Maureen delightedly. "I gave the waiter ten out of ten for how tidy the restaurant is this morning, and I worked out how much sleep people have who went to bed at midnight and come to breakfast at 7am."

"Well, I give you ten out of ten, as well, Maureen. It is lovely for me to meet someone who cares for numbers like I do."

"You going to sit next to me for breakfast?" asked Maureen shyly.

"Absolutely, if you are not fed up with me," said Mary.

"How could I get fed up with you?" asked Maureen.

"Well, bless you, Maureen. It is part of why everyone likes you so much that you can ask a question like that."

Deborah and Charlie smiled at each other, but Maureen continued to look confused. She looked carefully into Mary's face. "Something is wrong, isn't it?"

Then it was Charlie's turn to be confused. He was just about to explain things to Maureen when, to his surprise, Mary spoke up.

"Yes. I will tell you about it when we are sitting down."

"You are sitting down," said Maureen, "but if we all get our breakfast then we will all be sitting down. Because I came down with my frame this morning and not my wheelchair."

Charlie led the way to the gleaming chrome serving platters.

"Oh, beautiful bacon and sausages," called Maureen in delight. "I will have to be very careful, or I will be as big as a balloon."

"Shall I get your food, Mary?" asked Deborah "and then you can save all our places for us."

"You mean, I might as well do something useful," said Mary with a self-deprecating grin.

"Saving places is useful," said Maureen. "Because we don't have nameplates on the table. Anyone can sit anywhere. It is empty, so we won't have a problem, but it will be nice to know our same table as last night is ours again."

Mary nodded and speedily turned her wheelchair around.

"She had a bad sleep," said Maureen decisively. "Alice says you don't sleep if you don't talk about your worries. Ooh, baked beans, too. This is truly delicious. If Jane comes too late, it will all be gobbled up."

"Don't worry," said Charlie, "they have lots more in the kitchen. They don't put it all out at once, because then it would get cold."

"I didn't think of that," reflected Maureen. "Lots of things to learn here. Charlie, will you carry my plate; I can't do the plate and the Zimmer frame. And I want everything!"

Charlie nodded. "Now I can be useful."

"And I can go and sit with numbers lady and be useful," smiled Maureen. She turned herself round to go back to their table. A few more early people were making their way in, but they were not from Wonderful Wheelchairs. And they were settling at the opposite end of the restaurant.

Maureen sat down next to Mary. "Now, Mary, it is time for you to say what is worrying you."

"It sounds really stupid," said Mary. "I feel quite shy to say it. But it is a sunny day, and we will be going to Brighton, and I have brought my swimming costume, but the thing is: I am a bit frightened of the water."

Maureen's eyes were round and wide open. "You can do all those numbers things, but the water frightens you? Well, goodness me, that is a surprise. I thought you were going to say you had forgotten to bring your cozzie, or you didn't like it. Well, I have brought mine, and I like going in. Sometimes, I only paddle. I get frightened if the waves could knock me over, but not if it is nice and still; and with sunny weather today, it should be lovely and still."

"Maureen!" shouted a loud voice. Maureen looked round. It was Jane Edwards, waving heartily as she entered the room. She came quickly to the table. "You are very early, but I am not so late. Good morning, Maureen, good morning, Dr. Mary."

"Jane Edwards, we are having an important discussion here. Numbers lady wants to swim in the sea at Brighton but she is frightened. Can you swim?" asked Maureen.

Jane sat herself down on a chair and breathed heavily.

"Well?"

"Well, I got a certificate for swimming in the shallow end in junior school, but I don't think I have swum in the sea since. Maybe I put my toe in the water in Bognor. But no."

"Did you bring your swimming costume?"

"Yes. I don't know if it is the right size. It is what I had in my cupboard. It has got a picture of fish on it and is blue and yellow. The sand is yellow and the sea is blue and there are little fishes on it."

"Well," said Maureen, summing up the situation. "It seems to me we are going to be a supported swimming group. I can swim. So we will walk into the sea with me in the middle, and I will hold both your hands. How is that?"

"That sounds wonderful," said Deborah, putting a tray of food down in front of Mary, while Charlie put the tray down for Maureen.

"And what about you Deborah? Will you swim?"

"Sorry. I can swim, but I don't like swimming in a cold sea. I can watch and call for help if anyone is in danger."

"I'll come in," said Charlie. "I haven't swum at Brighton before, and I would like that. Who knows, Roland might feel brave enough, too."

"Only if he doesn't splash us," said Maureen sternly. "But if he is a good boy, he can come with us."

Mary sat quietly, lifting her knife and fork, and a little sigh of hope came out of her.

"Look," said Maureen, commandingly, "Look at the water." She pointed to the huge floor-to-ceiling windows through which the shingle disappearing into the sea could be seen.

"Wait a minute," said Charlie, worriedly, "We didn't have swimming in the brochure because, although it has got the pier and the Royal Pavilion, which are fine with wheelchairs, and the art gallery and museum, they have not got boardwalks here. It is really sad. Now, I know there is a beach just a few yards to the right of the Winged Angel of Peace statue where there is a small slope, and then you are on the beach, and we can carry wheelchairs over. But I don't know if we can push a wheelchair down the shingle beach to the sea."

"It should have said in the brochure," said Mary sharply.

"But a brochure can't say all the things you can't do," said Deborah.

Jane Edwards burst out laughing. "Come to Sunville. You can't swim and there isn't a proper pier. Come to Brighton, you can't swim in the sea if you are handicapped."

Maureen was frowning. "A boy in my Cherry Tree sheltered housing wanted to be brave and go on a bus. But he didn't know the bus had a sign saying, "Only come on with the right change." He couldn't read so he couldn't read it. And when he gave the driver a five-pound note the diver shouted, 'Can't you read?' He should have been warned."

Charlie looked at her with admiration. "Thank you, Maureen and Mary. I will pass that back to the directors. But let's see what we can do. Perhaps Muhammid and I could carry you into the water, Mary, if that didn't frighten you."

Mary grinned. "That sounds like a plan. The birth of Venus."

"What's that?" asked Maureen.

"It is a famous painting. I will tell you all about it."

Chapter Forty-Five

Naresh and Zendaya made their way from his suite to Betty's. They had hardly slept, yet they looked and felt refreshed and alive. He was wearing Lance and Roger and an elegant dark blue suit. Zen had put on a dark blue dress which covered her cleavage. They had gone to her studio flat with a couple of the hotel staff to parcel up what she most needed, and she said she wanted him to see her "invisible and undercover." The dark blue dress was shyly removed from the back of her wardrobe. Her one dress, he said, that was not a Black Barbie outfit. She nodded. She had already looked through his clothes and chose the one smart suit that was there. They had considered having breakfast in his hotel suite, but Naresh wanted everyone to see them and know they were a couple.

"The people travelling here with Wonderful Wheelchairs don't know anything about me, except I have no legs and my sister does the work with me. So it will be easy for them to meet you."

"Going like this, I am asking you, are we masking or unmasking?" asked Zen.

"You know you really are zen with ace points like that," said Naresh kissing her cheek. "Sometimes I feel unmasked showing my body as it is without extras and other times, I feel more myself with Lance and Roger and even a smart suit."

"And don't forget Dick," laughed Zen.

"Oh, he is just fine!" said Naresh, kissing her again.

"Same with my boobs. Perhaps they should have names, too."

"Lorelai and Regina," suggested Naresh.

"Vagina — are you getting your zones mixed up?" laughed Zen.

"Regina," said Naresh. "It is the formal word for queen."

"Blimey," said Zen

"Perhaps the right one should be Regina then. Then we'd have a Roger and a Regina. Don't you know? Gina is the informal word for cunt."

Laughing loudly, and arm in arm, they made their way to Betty's.

"Heh," she said as they reached the grand open doors.

"You never told me what my surname will be."

"Singh," said Naresh. "With an 'H' at the end."

"You'd have a sore throat if you sang with an 'H' at the end," laughed Zen.

"And what's yours?" asked Naresh.

"Brown," said Zen. "Slave name. I'll be glad to lose it."

"Then, Zen Singh, please do me the honour of accompanying me to breakfast."

"I do," said Zen.

Chapter Forty-Six

Gerry watched Tom. He was still asleep. A tuft of white hair peeped up, surrounded by twisted sheets, with his face fully covered. He was slowly sleeping more and more, for longer and longer. "Little deaths" she called them. When he was asleep she did not have to worry about him; but as he slept so long, she was anxious whether he was still alive. Sometimes, this brought on thoughts of her own mortality.

A little snore came from under the sheets. She leapt forward to watch. Was he about to wake? It reminded her of when their Brian was a baby. She was considered as an older mother at that time. Over 40. It was normal now, but then she had been seen as a real risk. And baby Brian was watched over by the medical staff as if his birth was a miracle. That was her feeling, too. Waking at night to check he was still breathing, the little body in the beautiful white cot, the reassuring rise and fall of his tiny chest.

"Don't leave me," she whispered. She rubbed her eyes fiercely. But he would have to leave her, because it would be even worse if she had to leave him by dying first. She had to sort it out. She had to organise care. That is what this strange "holiday" was about. Yes. Why hadn't she realised? It was a way of accepting full-time care without having to admit it, because it was called a holiday.

She sat down on the armchair, energised in a way she had not felt for ages. It was her dear Tom who had spotted the holiday advert; out of love she had followed it up. What it offered was more important than she had ever realised. They needed full-time care, and they had room for it. Then she could go to her hospital appointment without worrying about how he was. And if she was not all right, if there was something really wrong, then they would already have someone in place for Tom. If she was all right, she had support.

The letter from the hospital wanted to discuss the results of her blood tests. It did not say she was dying from cancer. It might be all right. But past 80, any small health scare was alarming. She had not thought it would be like this. Tom was dying from hundreds of small attacks stopping blood from getting to his brain adequately. Each day he was losing more of himself—or gaining his truest self. Which was it? Sometimes, it felt like both. He was so kind, so appreciative. He bore his disability with such courage.

If she had a live-in-carer, then her shortcomings would be catered for. They would have someone who could drive and pick up shopping and dry cleaning, who could do some light housework and cooking. They would both prefer that, rather than moving in with Brian and his family.

At this age, they were regularly receiving invitations to funerals. At a recent one, a widowed friend said something that stuck with Gerry. She'd said, "If he dies quickly now, you and his family will still remember the man he was, but the longer he stays with dementia, the more peoples' memories will be of the non-talking, non-walking man."

But there was no choice, even if he had wanted one. It would be whatever it was, and regardless, it would end with death. Gerry could feel the abyss into which she would fall without him there. What would she do with their flat? Sell it and buy something smaller? Rent out rooms cheaply in exchange for companionship? Why hadn't she had this discussion with herself before?

A sob broke out of her mouth. It would have been Tom she told all this to. And she did. They had discussed it all in their 40s, and then in their 50s when they made wills, but she could not remember what he said. She needed to know, but he could not answer. And suppose she forgot all his words, and suppose she had dementia and lost all the memory she had now. How would she be?

Wringing her hands together, she stood up and paced around the room. She needed to distract herself from these fears. She would make a cup of tea and would then call for a carer to come.

A ping came on her phone. A text. A welcome distraction. It was Brian.

HELLO MUM, HOPE THIS ISN'T AN INTRUSION. JUST WANTED TO SAY HOW BRAVE WE THINK YOU ARE DOING THIS FOR DAD. IT REALLY WILL

GET SOME NEW MEMORIES FOR HIM. AND DON'T WEAR YOURSELF OUT. USE THE HELP THAT IS OFFERED. WE ALL LOVE YOU VERY MUCH.

She reached for the tissue box, but the tears that came were not of fear but of relief.

"Angel?" came a voice from the bed. "Is it night-time or morning?"

A rush of love sped her onto her feet. "Good morning darling, my handsome man, it is the perfect time for us to get help and go to breakfast. Would you like a cup of tea first?"

"Yes. And if you are, too."

Smiling happily, she went to fill the kettle.

Chapter Forty-Seven

Les had woken up just minutes away from his house. He rubbed his head and then bent over a knee-high bush to vomit. Every bit of him felt stinking. He felt like a tramp. Dirty, drunk, cold, homeless. There was his home, and he was outside of it, and she was inside. He could see a light in the lounge — his lounge, his front room that she had turned into a bridal shop.

All his life he had been waiting for someone, the right one. And she had just walked past him to get to a wedding. What an idiot to think it was him she was after. No-one was after him, except the old bill, and that was decades ago. Wonderful fucking Wheelchairs — he had a Brighton trip to do later. They had booked him properly. They paid him. It wasn't their fault he was with a bitch hooked on weddings.

A piss. He needed a piss. But where? And then there wasn't a choice. Warm liquid gushed down the inside of his trousers.

What to do now? Creep in? No. It was his bloody house, and she better not say anything about the state he was in. He had put up with her wedding nonsense for months.

Head down, he made his way to his house. He had the key in his hand, he wasn't going to make any noise with them at the front door. He would go in quiet. He didn't want her to see him like this or even at all. He just wanted to shower and lie on his bed and put the TV on and have a beer. No. No drink. He had had too much. No. A coffee. A black, strong coffee.

The key slid into the lock. Why was he being so fucking quiet? It was his house. He could come in as noisy as he liked. "I'm back — in my home," he suddenly shouted, distracted by the calm gentle warmth of his tidy hallway. There was no reply. He went into the kitchen. Everything was washed up and put away. His heart started racing.

He rushed into the lounge — the Bridal Bazaar. It was empty, everything where it should be. No sign of her. He raced into the bedroom. Her side of the wardrobe was empty. Everything gone.

There was a large envelope on the bed addressed to him.

Chapter Forty-Eight

"You fancy him," said Olena.

"Who fancies who?" asked Roland excitedly. "Me? Does someone fancy me?"

"I would not be surprised," said Olena, "because when you are nice and polite and you are an interesting single man."

"I have been good in the night, haven't I, Big A?" asked Roland.

"Yes. I was able to have some sleep too, so I am very happy," said Andrzej. He could not keep a smile off his face.

"Is that why you are smiling?" asked Roland.

"You are good at noticing things," said Andrzej.

"I heard some nice news from someone last night," he added.

Olena frowned. "What T-shirt would you like this morning, Roland? The weather forecast says it will be sunny, and in the afternoon we will go to a beach in a place called Brighton; we will see a palace and go up high in the sky."

Andrzej nodded at her, thankful for her distraction. His mind was racing. Nothing had been said, by him or Ibrahim. But they both knew. He liked Ibrahim. He really liked him. Maybe something would happen.

"Shall I have stripes like a sailor? Mummy says stripes are like a sailor."

"That's right, Roland. And you could have your navy blue shorts if you like. We can put your swimming trunks under them, so after lunch when we go if you feel like putting your toes in the water it will be easier for you."

"Toes in the water? Ouch. It will be cold," said Roland. "And Maureen said there were jellyfish in the sea in Brighton."

Olena and Andrzej smiled at him, and Olena explained, "There are jellyfish all around the coast, but they are not dangerous; these ones are scared of our feet."

"Really?" asked Roland.

"Yes," said Olena, lost in the moment, "and that's when they nip your feet if you accidentally step on them."

Roland kicked off his slippers and punted the side of the bed. "Don't get near me jellyfish. I will kill you," he shouted, still booting the side of the bed.

Andrzej raised an eyebrow at Olena. "It's okay, Roland. I will be there with you if you go in."

Roland's kicking diminished a little, and Andrzej asked, "Shall we get you down to breakfast and see if Maureen is there?"

"Yes — chocolate biscuit," said Roland.

Olena smiled at them both. "I will phone Ibrahim for help with going down to breakfast," she said.

Andrzej felt heat coming out of his face. "If you think we need help. If you don't think we can manage together," he added.

"I just think it makes it nicer," she said.

"Is Ibrahim coming?" asked Roland

"We don't know if he is in his room at the moment," said Andrzej, watching Olena intently as she texted.

A notification sounded. "He is coming immediately," Olena said.

"That is quick. But I am not being bad, am I?" asked Roland.

"No. You are not. But sometimes, a change can happen quickly and it makes it nice and calm much more quickly if there is someone else here. And you liked him, didn't you?" She grinned at Andrzej while asking the question, and he turned his face away.

Roland put his arms through the striped T-shirt. "Yes. I do like him. Nice quiet man. Doesn't laugh at people."

"And that matters," said Olena pointedly.

Andrzej looked at Olena. "You've cheered up today."

"Yes. I enjoyed the conversation last night. Made me feel not so alone and not English, and I like seeing you happy, too."

"You happy, Big A?" asked Roland, looking at his reflection in the mirror.

Just then, Ibrahim knocked on the door and gently called outside it. As he walked in, Roland let out a heartbreaking wail. "No-one fancies me!" he shouted and threw a shoe at the mirror.

Ibrahim gently sat on the armchair a little distant from Roland and turned to him. “Is that what you would like in your life now, Roland? You are a man and you would like a partner. But it is hard to find a partner when you throw shoes at the mirror.” He smiled, and Roland stopped shouting.

“I am a man,” he said. “A man.”

“Yes. You are,” said Olena.

“And you must be a hungry man, because it is time for breakfast now, and we can all go together,” said Andrzej, trying not to look too intently at Ibrahim.(^pkghdfss

Chapter Forty-Nine

Hermione decided to go to breakfast. She had missed all the social events of the evening, but now felt ready to deal with them. She went down to Betty's at 8am; she didn't like to be the first one there. She did not want to be the object of attention. Hotels like this were not used to titles. She had thought of removing it, but it felt part of her. It came from her parents, not from James. It was part of her identity. They could trace themselves back to William the Conqueror.

After a broken night filled with images of ancient mythic skies, she wanted to see the sea, and not just look at it. She wanted to swim and to have her hands shaping the waves before she picked up her brushes. The female goddesses were more earth- or sea-based, like Botticelli's Venus rising from a scallop shell. The men always pushed too far from their element. Poor Icarus, flying too high. No wonder she was drawn to paint him. And how did she know in her painting that a wheelchair was the shadow-side of his flight? Was James an Icarus? Trying to be as swift and successful as his father, a highly decorated colonel. No. She could not feel sorry for Icarus. He was warned by his father and ignored the warning.

What a strange hotel to find herself in. What a strange idea for a holiday. But she felt ready to face her fellow guests. None of them seemed like anyone or anything she knew. Except for Naresh on his motorbike — she recognised him. His psyche. And the lovely young man and his brother who helped her: like twin Egyptian gods. Such beautiful faces, both of them. It wasn't class that was the issue. That was the outer-wrapping that made for easy assumptions. It was whether she recognised them through her eyes.

There was an excited atmosphere in the hotel, with people talking as they walked along the wide corridors. She would have to look at Mirrorland later. Right now, it brought back memories of excited boarding school dressing up, as well as bullying. She relished her own bedroom. She could smell the breakfast aromas before entering the restaurant; all the usual British focus on fry-ups, but there was also fruit and cheese and a range of pastries.

She stood in the entrance looking around at the bustling groups of people moving onto their tables and then going to the long tempting buffet display.

"It's the lady lady," said a loud voice. Getting ready to leave were Maureen, Jane, Mary, and Deborah.

"Hello, Lady Hermione," said Deborah gently. "It really is a surprisingly good breakfast. We were in the very early group."

"Just call me Hermione, please," said Hermione. "I am glad it is good!"

"Why surprisingly?" asked Maureen.

Deborah looked awkward.

"Because this hotel is not a top hotel so you don't usually expect the best breakfast," said Mary, tartly.

"I'm Mary Mullins. Dr. Mary Mullins. But call me Mary, please."

"We have lady ladies and doctor ladies here," said Jane Edwards proudly, "and I am Jane Edwards."

"Well, thank you, and don't let me keep you," said Hermione, spying Naresh out of the corner of her eye sitting at a table with a rather radiant woman.

"You don't keep me," said Maureen, feeling confused. "Goodbye."

Hermione moved over to the table where Naresh sat. He was deep in conversation with his companion, and she hovered for a moment before a waiter suddenly rushed to the table, giving a discreet cough and pulling out a chair for Hermione.

"Hello," she said. "I am from Wonderful Wheelchairs, too. May I join you?"

"Certainly," said Naresh. "Lady Lambton, let me introduce you to my fiancée Zendaya. In fact, you are the first person to be told this morning that I proposed to her last night and she has accepted me."

"Please call me Hermione," she smiled. "I am honoured to be the first person to hear your lovely news, and that you remembered my name."

"How long have you been together?" she asked.

"Since the day before yesterday," said Zen proudly.

"Really?" said Hermione. "You have got engaged in just two days? You are quick!"

"Well, I have waited all my life," said Naresh simply.

"And I have waited until now," echoed Zen.

"Well," said Hermione, "it is known that when we meet new people we decide unconsciously within twenty seconds if we like them, and the rest of the time is just building up more knowledge."

"That is it, innit?" endorsed Zendaya. "We saw each other and that was it. I have spent my life kissing frogs, and this is my first prince."

"Well, it seems a rather major realisation. Congratulations!" She looked at Naresh closely. "You look different," she said.

"To when?" he asked.

"From when you roared up on your motorbike-wheelchair like a stallion to greet us all from the coach."

"You noticed!" he laughed.

"Yes. It was like a moment from a film. I am an artist, so things affect me visually and, in fact, I wanted to ask if you would allow me to have a photograph of you to paint from or, even better, to sit for a painting."

"Blimey," said Zendaya. "I thought I was a fast, but you are some fast woman. What does sitting for you mean? Clothes on or off?"

"Like we have all said, ideas come in seconds when you meet the right people," laughed Hermione. She raised the empty cup of coffee to toast them both.

"So what kind of paintings do you paint?" asked Zendaya.

"Large canvases. Usually with oil paints. I used to paint my late husband—he died after injuries sustained when he fell from his horse."

"So, he was the stallion that needed to be a motorbike and not a wheelchair," said Zen seriously.

Hermione looked at her with shock. "How did you know?" She paused. "Sorry, that sounded rude. I am rather shell-shocked. That is exactly it, everything, and about my art, too."

Naresh looked at them both. "You mean, seeing me do my Hell's Angels bit made you think of your husband giving up when he fell off his horse and not fighting it."

"Yes," said Hermione. "And I have not been able to paint since, and when I saw this holiday I just wanted to face it."

"Like us?" asked Zendaya.

"Yes. Yes. Because in loving him, you are facing it."

"Are we interrupting?" came a gentle voice. "Sounds like a very serious conversation for early in the morning."

Maanika and Sunil were standing there. "Can we join you, big brother? Hello, Zen."

"Hello, Maanika. Good to see you. It is a very serious morning and a very beautiful one, too."

Zendaya looked at Naresh.

Naresh looked at his sister and brother-in-law, their dear faces, his only relatives. "I am sorry you are not the first to know as you should have been."

"First to know what?" asked Maanika worriedly. "Are you all right?"

"He is very all right if I may presume to say — sorry, I am Lady Hermione Lambton."

"Yes! Yes," smiled Maanika, "I remember your application."

"Well," said Naresh. He took Zendaya's hand and lifted it up. "We are engaged."

Sunil and Maanika looked at each other with great confusion "Engaged?"

"Yes. Engaged to be married — as opposed to being engaged like a toilet," said Zendaya.

Hermione laughed. "It is rather sudden news after a very sudden courtship."

Sunil sat down, while Maanika stood holding onto the edge of the table.

"Engaged?" she repeated.

"Yes. It happened last night. That is why I needed you and the others to leave. We needed to catch-up."

"Well, yes," said Sunil worriedly, "a lifetime to catch-up with after knowing each other—"

"Two days," prompted Naresh.

"Two days," repeated Maanika.

"Sit down, Maanika — take the load off your feet and head," smiled Zendaya. "I liked you within twenty seconds of meeting you, and now you will be my sister-in-law; I never had a sister or a sister-in-law before."

Maanika took a deep breath and looked apologetically at Zen. "Sorry. Sorry. I am not wanting to — what is it? Rain on your parade. It is just so sudden. Sunil and I went out together for two years before we got engaged, and then we were engaged for a year before we got married." She paused.

"Yes," said Naresh, "and if we had wanted an arranged marriage, it could have been very quick, just a few meetings."

"I wish I had known before," said Maanika feebly.

"Before this morning? But it only happened last night, little sister. I knew when I met her the first time, just the day before, that something major had happened. I felt happiness for the first time in my life. It was a one-life stand, not a one-night stand."

Maanika looked at him deeply. "Yes. You do look happy. And no, it does not look mad. It does look really happy." She burst into tears. "Dearest older brother, you have been in such pain for so much of your life, and the first time you have joy the circumstances turn me into a robot. Zen, sorry. Please know we wish you the greatest happiness."

He opened his arms and she rushed into them. He opened his arms wider for Zen to enter their hug and then Sunil.

"It couldn't have happened without Wonderful Wheelchairs, and it was you, Maanika, who said I should come on the first holiday here to experience it. And I did, and I met Zen in Bert's Bar."

Hermione dabbed her eyes with a serviette. "I know it is only 8am, but please do not think me intrusive — as a guest — I am asking the waiter to bring a bottle of champagne to toast you both, and I am hungry, too, so then I will get some breakfast."

Chapter Fifty

After another scrub, hair wash, and rigorous dry, Les rinsed the shower and threw his dirty clothes into the washing machine. Then he put on a warm jumper on top of his T-shirt and blue jeans. It was a glorious sunny day, but he had dressed for deepest winter.

Sitting at his spotless kitchen table with a hot mug of strong coffee, he looked through his phone. His home had never felt so sterile and empty.

She had phoned and texted all through the night with a few gaps and apologies for intruding. She only gave up at dawn when he had not replied. She had left just before he finally came home. She could not stand it any longer. She had phoned all the hospitals, so she had given him the benefit of the doubt. She had phoned the local minicab place and heard he was drunk. And she had phoned the Mirabelle to check if he was there. She had done everything right.

And now the wedding train had left him. The beautiful magazines with their forever-after promises had gone. The silks, the serviettes, the menus. All these things for their big day had gone as if it had never happened—and it was because of him.

Looking through her messages had him in tears again. She had apologised if she was too obsessed. She had said she was tidying all the magazines up. She had apologised if he was sick of the subject. She apologised that she had got more frightened of a repeat as it got nearer. She had worried she had driven him away with it all, when all that really mattered was that she loved him. And then the messages stopped.

Of course, the messages had bloody stopped. Who would want to carry on with a drunk who didn't come home when he said and stayed out all night?

He would go to Hotel Mirabelle to get ready for the Brighton ride. Sodding Brighton. Who wanted to do another coach trip? It had only been to raise money for the wedding. He wanted to run to the Hen and Horse and scream his life out.

Chapter Fifty-One

Zen had gone for another look at Mirrorland and My-Lights, while Naresh made his own preparations. He was going to buy her a ring in Brighton that afternoon. People were still asleep or at breakfast, so there was still room in front of the vast mirrors.

Zendaya Brown, about to be married, looked at her hair. She had been told by her grandmother that cornrows showed you were fighting slavery. Rice seeds could be braided into the hair, so could maps and information. And the geometric lines could also represent growing lines. Your hair could save you, and so could your breasts — even if it meant sexual slavery.

Naresh had known about cornrows! And her sexual self had made it safe for him. So why was she wearing her only dress that didn't show off her cleavage? What was she masking, and what was she unmasking?

Inside, she felt like a tremulous teenager about to make the biggest step in life, while in the mirror she saw a curvy woman of a certain age, one of those women other women didn't like. But that wasn't true. Maanika did like her, and they had taken to each other.

As she walked to the changing room, she heard faint sobs, and speeding up her pace she saw a woman in a white slip holding up a white wedding dress. Mascara-stained tears poured down her face.

"Heh," she called, "Heh, sister. What's the bastard done?"

The woman burst out laughing in the midst of her sobs, clutching the dress to her breasts. "That's just what I needed. You don't know what has happened, but you were on my side with no questions asked."

"Absolutely — we women must stick together, innit," said Zen, walking towards her and handing her a tissue from her bag. She sat down, gesturing to the other woman to take a deep breath and sit down, too.

"I'm Trace," she said. "I'm engaged to Les; he is the coach driver for Wonderful Wheelchairs. You may have heard of it?"

"Yes," grinned Zen, "I think I have."

"Well, we are getting married in a month or so, or we were! This might be the only time I can wear it."

Sobbing loudly, she pulled it over her head and Zen smoothed out the flowing layers of the skirt.

"We met when he was the driver of the car to my wedding, when I was dumped at the altar."

"Dumped you?" interjected Zen.

"Yes. And Les felt so sorry for me. He drove me to his place and looked after me and now we are getting married. Or we were!"

"So you have been pushing the big M, and now he feels he is only wanted as a wedding and you are scared he is going to dump you again."

Trace stared at Zen. "You got it in one." Why were people surprised she had a brain? She had been around the block a fair few times, she knew lots of things.

"So. Now we come to the interesting bit. Very simple."

"Really?" asked Trace, blowing her nose and sighing deeply.

"Yes. Two questions only. Do you love him? Do you want to marry him?"

"Yes," shouted Trace without any pause. "He is the kindest man. He cares so deeply, and for the people with disabilities here. He puts up a bluff with his bad language and jokes, but he has a heart of gold; he has just been lonely for most of his life."

"Enough of the violins," said Zen authoritatively. "The thing is, you love him. He is now petrified you have left him and you are terrified he will leave you. So, someone has got to face their fears. Maybe he will, but the only person you can control is you. So, tell me, have you arranged the marriage venue yet?"

"No," said Trace, "we have looked at three church halls already, but they weren't quite right as we don't have many people between us and we don't have much money. He is driving the coach to Brighton after lunch today to help pay for the venue."

"Okay," said Zen. "It is looking beautifully easy. I am your wedding angel, you see. Just sit there while I text my sister-in-law and someone else."

Both women sat in silence while Zen typed on her phone. Not long after, a notification bell sounded, and Zen read the message intently.

"All sorted. You are going to be married in Betty's Restaurant on Sunday next week, with drinks first in Bert's Bar, and you will be the first marriage for Hotel Mirabelle. What's more, as Les is a driver for the Wonderful Wheelchair Company, you won't have to pay for the venue."

Trace sat dumbstruck. "What is going on? Is this a scam? A nightmare? What is happening? Please don't tell me this is a trick."

Zen held her hand. "Sister — you are going to have a wedding. And do you know, I just engaged today myself. And it is my fiancée who founded Wonderful Wheelchair Company."

Trace stared at her. A huge smile covered her face, and then she looked terrified. "He won't sack him because I told you he got drunk last night?"

"Of course not. So long as he doesn't turn up here drunk in charge of a coach."

"Congratulations," said Trace to Zen.

"Thank you," said Zen happily.

"You're a right bit of posh, aren't you?"

"Suppose I am," said Zen. Standing Trace up and opening her own large bag, Zen took out make-up remover and tissues and gently started repairing Trace's face. "And I've got an idea," she said. "What time is he supposed to be coming here?"

While the Wonderful Wheelchair guests enjoyed their lunch, Les carefully parked the coach at the large entrance. He had finally dared to text her. He sent his true apologies, no excuses — but there was no reply.

He sat inside the coach, his eyes slightly blurred with tears. Coming out of the terrace's double doors, holding a heavy bag of holiday leaflets, he suddenly saw a woman in a white wedding dress walking towards him, her dress flowing in the gentle breeze. Was this the Ghost of Weddings come to punish him and haunt him? He gave a cry of pain.

As the figure came nearer he could see it was Trace. His Trace, with a big smile on her face. She was looking at him, waving to him. He got out of the coach and ran towards her, scooping her up in his arms.

"My bride, my beautiful bride, please forgive me."

After they let go of each other he looked at her, really looked into her eyes. Then he knelt on the gravel and, looking up, he said, "My darling Trace, will you marry me?"

"Yes," she replied. "Yes. And you still want to marry me?"

"Yes!" he shouted, throwing his carrier bag of leaflets up in the air. the coloured photos of swimming pools and seas poured over them like confetti.

"Really?" she asked, hugging him so tightly they nearly both fell down.

"Yes. Really. Really you," he shouted.

"The wedding," she mumbled, in between kisses and tears, "will be here and it will all be free." And kissing and hugging each other, she told him all about Zen and what had happened.

Chapter Fifty-Two

"So, what have you got there?" asked Naresh curiously, as Zen disappeared ever more deeply into her battered old leather trunk. As well as all her dresses in polythene covers, there were mysterious small compartments.

"Every minute, I am catching up on the years I did not know you! I never knew you were such a careful packer and that you looked after your clothes so well. Today, I also learnt you can look after a despairing about-to-be-jilted bride and make her look beautiful, as well as keep me in this happy mood that I am not used to."

She ran to kiss him. "I'm just a battered old trunk, aren't I? You are just a trunk, as well," she laughed, as he began to tickle her.

"Now no-one worked that out before," laughed Naresh. "A trunk! I like that. A trunk and a Dick," he added, reaching forward to pull her towards him.

"And Lance and Reginald," she added, reaching for his prosthesis.

"Ouch, careful!" he laughed, "And you've got Regina — and I have forgotten your left boob."

"Lorelai — she's left out," giggled Zen. "Look," she said, reaching for a packet of confetti. " It is for when the coach starts."

"How did you have that in your emergency store cupboard?" he asked.

"Very handy for surprise weddings."

"But they are not married yet."

"No, but it can be their rehearsal," said Zen.

"I thought we could give the coach a send-off before we go in the taxi. I don't want to share you with everyone." Another hug. "Seriously, Zen, I still haven't heard about your conversation with Maanika before you knew we were related."

"Ah, now that was another life, innit, when I did hairdressing — before my ex died. And a bit of care assistant work." She sat down and faced him seriously. "Everything we did is in the past, it is what we do now," she said.

"I haven't been pulling my weight with WW — Maanika has done most of it. But I do care about it," said Naresh.

"So do I," said Zen. "Just think — in My-Lights, you could do Black hair, Indian hair, wedding make-up. You could have a dress shop down here, too. And you could do trips to Black places of interest. There's enough Black people in wheelchairs."

Naresh took a deep breath. "Yes. We will see Les and Trace off and we can always bump into them in Brighton. I want to show you The Lanes where you can buy some real unique rings."

After closing the trunk and buckling it, and with the confetti bag in her hand, Zen and Naresh made their way to the lift. She smiled at her face in the lift mirror. She liked the brightness of her eyes. She was not sure if she really recognised herself any more.

"Gorgeous," said Naresh, watching her actions. "My fiancée. After you, Ms. Brown."

"After you, Mr. Singh."

Making their way from the lift through to the terrace and outside parking, every visitor and staff member nodded to say hello to Naresh. Zendaya was getting used to it. She was the mate, the missus, the wife, the queen. She deserved the looks. She had the authority. Zendaya Brown — she felt legitimate for the first time in her life.

Outside, there was a huge commotion around the coach. Trace was outside in her wedding dress, and it seemed almost every guest was holding up their phone to photograph Trace on her own and then Trace with Les. Lady Hermione was there with her expensive camera, and there was a whole crowd of people in wheelchairs. Les looked especially happy in Charlene's photograph of him and Trace — a big, sloppy grin splashed on his face. Only Maanika and Sunil seemed to be missing. The Egyptian brothers were there, the one who played the piano and the one who clearly fancied the Polish guy, and others she had seen in the hotel but not met. And there was the Polish guy, and a woman with Roland, the massive young guy.

As they approached, there was a silent hush, and the guests stood quietly waiting to hear what would happen. It was Trace who spoke first.

"This beautiful angel, Zendaya, she is the one who saved me at my worst moment."

Les came forward and dramatically threw himself onto his knees. "Angel Zendaya. Thank you for helping me keep my beautiful fiancée," he called.

"Ladies," shouted Tracey, "I feel like I'm turning into one of those people who walk up and down the street with placards on their back advertising something! But I am not sad. I am the happiest I have ever been, I am advertising the joy of loving a wonderful man. Some of you know — I was dumped at the altar by my previous fiancée, so you can imagine weddings have been even more traumatic for me. Les's love largely healed me, but as our wedding has got closer I have been driving him mad with menus and recipes and guests and venues and nearly ruined it all."

"And I was just working and working to pay for a wedding and losing all the joy I had found in Trace. Bashed up by bride magazines," said Les.

Mary, transfixed in her wheelchair, held tightly to Deborah's hand. Was that her too? Would the sea hurt her? Reclaim her?

Doris squeezed her husband's hand. This was all very strange, but Christians did all sorts of strange things. No. She corrected herself with embarrassment. People just do strange things. Her parents had used rude Yiddish words — *shicksa* or *yok* — to name people who were not Jewish. But then Ashkenazi and Sephardi looked down on each other, too.

She burst out laughing.

Daniel smiled at her. "What made you laugh?"

"A Puritan proverb. 'All the world is mad except thee and me and even thee is a little mad sometimes.'"

Dan burst out laughing. "It is wise. It is true. We just need two people to have two opinions. Who was it who said, "There are as many opinions as men?'"

"Don't know, but you can even have opposing opinions in one person" added Doris.

There was a sudden flash.

"What's that?" asked Maureen.

"*The Sunville Herald*," announced Charlene proudly. "We have told them that the first marriage that will be held in Hotel Mirabelle will be our trusted driver who works with Wonderful Wheelchairs and makes these holidays possible. And," she added, turning towards Naresh and Zen, "I believe I have permission to announce that the co-director of Wonderful Wheelchairs, Mr. Naresh Singh, has just today announced his engagement to Ms. Zendaya Brown."

Trace and Zendaya hugged, while Naresh threw the pink confetti in the air. It dropped like autumn leaves over all of them.

Chapter Fifty-Three

Muhammid's throat was already feeling sore. After "She'll Be Coming Round the Mountain When She Comes" and "I Do Love to Be Beside the Seaside," he had been belting out Whitney Houston's "I Wanna Dance With Somebody" for the third time, accompanied by half of the coach. Tom and Steve had both added their fine tenor voices, while Les sounded like a pantomime dame, exhorting the others to sing.

Trace, sitting in splendour next to Les, was also singing her heart out, petals of confetti still falling from her as she moved. Behind them, Maureen and Jane were clapping in time.

"Is this the wedding or a practice wedding?" asked Jane.

"I don't think they care," said Mary, "they are just happy."

"I agree," said Steve, "but let me not to the marriage of true minds admit impediments."

"Shakespeare," chortled Maureen. "I am getting good at Shakespeare."

"You are," said Mary warmly.

"What about the Shakespeare twin?" called Jane.

"Tom — did you hear the challenge from Jane?" asked Gerry smiling.

Tom smiled and exuberantly declaimed. "Shall I compare thee to a summer's day? Thou art more lovely and more temperate."

"Yippee," called Maureen. "Instead of numbers and letters, we have the Shakespeare twin fight."

"It is not a fight, it is a marathon," smiled Deborah.

"Nice singing," called Roland. He turned to Andrzej who sat next to him. "Nice wedding isn't it, Big A. Are there biscuits?"

Andrzej smiled at him. "I'm sure there will be some soon."

Roland turned to Ibrahim and Olena in the row behind. "Does she fancy him?"

Ibrahim nodded.

"Yes. They are free to get married and they fancy each other."

He and Andrzej looked at each other. Roland reflected on it. "And I am a man, and can fancy someone if they are single — a man or a woman."

"That's right," called Olena.

"His mum is not going to like that, though," she whispered to Ibrahim.

Roland thought for a moment. "But where? Where is the person who fancies me? I am free but I haven't got anyone," he screamed. "No-one on this coach for me. No-one fancies me."

For a moment the singing could not be heard. Doris shrivelled closer to her husband. Violence never felt far away. There was a moment's silence that spread through the coach.

Even Les stopped singing, and then spoke. "Roland, you don't know me. But it has taken me years and years to find Trace. I must be twice as old as you and I have only just found someone who loves me and fancies me. You don't just get someone because you are single. But it is good you know you are single."

Roland was amazed. "You are twice as old as me and have waited all those years without anyone? How do you do that? How will I do it?"

"Really good question, Roland mate," said Les seriously. "I have waited all my life to meet Trace. I am sorry I have made everyone think about weddings, but it is because it took me so long and I had to work hard to be ready."

Maureen turned round. "You are a good boy-man, Roland. Stay being good, and you will get chocolate biscuits and someone to love. I am single, but I don't want to get married. You don't have to get married. You can have friends instead."

"Like me," said Jane loudly.

Mary found she had tears in her eyes. "That is true, Maureen. Roland, listen to Maureen, she is very wise. I am older than Les, and I am happy staying single but having a lovely companion, Deborah, who lives with me."

There was quiet on the coach again. Then Les's voice came loud and crackly on the microphone. "Ladies, lady ladies, and doctor ladies, numbers, letters and Shakespeare twins, single people and married people, and people who want to be married and people who don't: we are now already in Brighton on this Wonderful Wheelchair life adventure coach."

Everyone cheered.

Charlie pointed out to everyone the Winged Angel of Peace. Just then, the coach hit a traffic jam. They could hear drumming, and they all looked at the crowds of people under the peace statue.

There were flags of black, white, and green. Men, women, and children of all ages and backgrounds were chanting "Free Palestine."

Doris gave a little moan before covering her mouth with her hand.

Dan put his arm around her.

"This is like Speakers' Corner in Hyde Park, my darling. Everyone can have a say in a democratic country. Today it is for Palestinians, another day it could be for Israel, or for or against Iran or Afghanistan. This is what England fought for."

Doris could not speak. The unknown figures raising their arms and chanting joined the hordes of Cossacks and Nazis in her nightmares. They were against her, against her kind.

Muhammid, who was sitting just behind the Ricksteins, felt his heart sink. Poor Doris had no means of telling the difference between loyal humane wishes for peace and murderous wishes to all Jews.

"Your husband is right," said Muhammid softly.

Doris put her right hand over her heart. It was racing, galloping. The faces were filled with hate and they were coming for her and Dan. They would overturn the coach, and it would lie on its back, helpless like a stranded beetle. And how quickly they would find her and Dan, the Jews. Their knives were out, their horses racing, hate pouring from their mouths.

"Mrs. Rickstein," a voice was gently saying. Time collapsed. They knew her name. They knew how to kill her. Her mother facing the horses in the battle of Cable Street. Her grandmother in the pogroms.

"Doris," said a familiar voice. He was alive. Her Dan.

"Mrs. Rickstein," said the other, gentle voice.

The galloping stopped. She opened her eyes. Muhammid and Dan were looking at her. Dan had his arm around her and Muhammid was holding her hand.

Chapter Fifty-Four

It was a coach trip like no other they had ever been on. Les and Trace, covered in confetti, and with her beautiful long white dress crumpled from the journey, were going to The Lanes to look for rings. Their voices were hoarse from the singing and shouting but their smiles rang small bells of happiness in each of other. To cap it all, when the coach pulled up for its first stop, Les walked up the stairs behind the driver seat to be on the same level as the rest of the coach. Then, he knelt down proposed to Trace all over again in front of everyone. Trace croaked "I do," and the coach erupted with cheers and claps.

"You are supposed to throw flowers," called Maureen.

"We'll do that at the wedding! You are all invited," announced Les.

"I got a flower," said Roland, proudly. He was wearing his smart light summer jacket. At lunchtime, Olena had put a fern and three dainty yellow and pink flowers through his buttonhole from the vase on their table. Taking them out of his buttonhole, he handed them to Andrzej. "Give it to the bride," he instructed.

"You are lovely, Roland," called Maureen, and Roland beamed.

Trace walked all the way down the coach to give him a hug. To the amazement of Olena, Andrzej, and Muhammid, he accepted it gladly. She walked back down the coach and, before descending to her seat next to Les, dramatically threw it over her shoulder. Jane caught it.

"Ooh! You are going to get married Jane," laughed Maureen. Then, noting Jane's look of shock, she added, "Don't worry—you don't have to."

"But, it is very good if you want to," said Gerry.

"Hear, hear!" agreed Steve.

"I want someone to fancy me," said Roland.

"You carry on being a nice boy and not shouting and someone will," reassured Maureen.

"What about you, Maureen?" asked Mary.

"I said it before. Not for me, numbers lady. I am like you. I have a best friend and don't need a wedding."

Jane relaxed. "I can keep the flowers for having a best friend then, me and Maureen."

Maureen smiled at her and held her right hand. In her left, Jane proudly clutched the flowers. "Thank you, Roland."

Roland sat looking confused. Andrzej congratulated him on his very good manners. So did Olena and Muhammid.

"It would not have been such a good wedding proposal if there had not been flowers," said Olena, "and you were kind enough to give them."

"You are not cross I gave them away when you put them in my jacket?" asked Roland, confused.

"No," said Olena. "It was one of the nicest things you could have done. You are a nice man, Roland."

"Nice man," repeated Roland, savouring the words on his tongue.

"You see," whispered Dan to Doris. "You were frightened of him because he has a disability and can get angry if he does not understand, or if he is frightened. But if things are explained, you can see how sweet he really is. That was a genuine moment of kindness."

She squeezed his hand. Standing up from her seat, she turned towards Roland. "Thank you, Roland. You made that even more lovely for all of us." She sat down again.

Les cheered her as he opened the coach door. "Lift about to start, but first I must carry my bride out." Darting out of the coach to the other side, he carried Trace onto the tarmac. She smoothed her dress and went around to the lift exit, ready to help people coming out. She knew all about how this coach worked, but had never seen it with his real-life passengers.

The plans had all been made. Charlie and Muhammid were with Mary, Deborah, Maureen, Jane, and the Ricksteins. Maureen was determined to help Jane and Mary into the sea. The Shakespeare twins, with Gerry, Marion, Louise, and Susan, were going to explore The Lanes, where they had not been for over twenty years. Roland was going straight to the pier in search of candy floss, fruit machines, and doughnuts with Andrzej and Ibrahim.

"Man trip. I am a man going with Big A and Ibrahim." With great relief, Olena said her goodbyes to him and joined the swimming party.

"But remember, you are off-duty when you are not with Roland," said Charlie firmly.

"Yes, But you need another woman to help change clothes if anyone is brave enough to go in."

It was a glorious sunny day, with Brighton at her best. The creamy regency buildings shone in the sunlight, seagulls soared and swooped against the big blue sky, and the sea was still and calm.

Hermione was smiling for the first time in months. She was not used to the feeling. Naresh, his motorbike and wheelchair: how they had expanded her vision. How moving, to have been part of their declaration of love! They knew immediately. So had she and James. If he had not fallen from his horse, she would have said what a wonderful marriage they had. Wonderful, despite her loss of Vadim, despite the babies she had longed for, despite his first marriage and his spectral daughters.

Or was she deluding herself? If he could change like that towards her after his accident, did that mean they were not right in the first place?

But such beauty on this trip! The Egyptian brothers. Zendaya's face and her beautiful skin. She thought she should join the party on the beach. Charlie had given directions.

Charlie had found the easiest accessible beach with a gentle slope down to the shingle. How the pebbles sparkled in the sunlight. Even Doris had removed her cardigan and was smiling tentatively.

Dan was brimming with pride. This was his Doris. How she used to be. The marchers around the peace statue had now dispersed, the sunny air somehow containing their pain and hurt inside itself. The winged angel Statue of Peace had seen it all before — every international hurt found its way to the holding space around her. There was room for them all, and Doris felt this suddenly, as her husband had said it, not as some distant idea but a true feeling.

She took a deep breath and smiled at the group. Muhammid's presence had eased her, like a dock leaf to the nettle she carried inside herself. Her Danny Junior would have been around his age. She would have been proud if he had turned out to be a wise young man like Muhammid. "Blessed shall be the peacemakers," her father had always said. He would have liked Muhammid.

Her gold Star of David sparkled in the sun like Muhammid's delicate cross. The warm air held all of them.

Mary was pale and exhausted. Only Deborah knew the difficult night she had endured. Only Deborah knew the dream.

Here was the sea. A beautiful calm surface. Not even a ripple to disturb it. And there she was in her dream, swimming with the numbers, 64 to the left and 64 to the right. And then she lost her numbers and didn't know how to find them. Deborah had been as good as any therapist when she finally told her.

"Oh, that is so sad and brave," said Deborah. "Your whole adult life has been linked to a love of numbers. So, of course, in trying to think of how your identity will change with Alzheimer's, you are expressing it through a loss of numbers. But what you are forgetting is your life is not just about numbers. It is feelings, too. I have feelings for you that are not about numbers, and you have feelings for me and Maureen. The fact we like numbers might help that, but it is about the feelings."

The wheelchair could go easily down the little slope onto the back of the shingle beach. The question was whether to go further down the beach.

“A shame there is no boardwalk, especially in an inclusive place like Brighton,” said Olena, as she opened up two of the four-fold-up beach chairs Les had given her. “Mr. and Mrs. Rickstein, two of these are for you. I will help Mr. Rickstein walk here.”

Dan held onto his walking stick with his left hand and took Olena’s arm with his right. Doris stood on his left, close to his walking stick. Down they went, step by step, crunching on the yielding shingle.

“Your workout for the day, Dan,” called Charlie.

He smiled, turning his face to the warming sky. There was crunching in the gravel behind him. With an arm under each arm of hers, Mary was being gently lifted. Charlie to the left and Muhammid to the right. Down they went, with Maureen and Jane beside them.

“I’ll bring the other chairs down to the sea edge and the towels,” called Olena, leaving the Ricksteins happily sunning themselves.

Step by step, Mary could have wept. This tiny little hill. Tiny. She would not even have noticed it a few years ago. Would have just run down it. Jumped down it. And now it was an Olympic event for two kind strong men to carry her down. And this was before she even tried to go in.

At the edge of the sea, the edge of the infinite, she watched the tiny bubbles of foam fall like hushed tears onto the stones. And there was Olena, smiling at her, opening the other two chairs. Breathing heavily, Maureen and Jane caught up with them.

“I’ve got towels for Charlie, Muhammid, and me,” said Olena. “Would you like the chair, Maureen, since you are helping people to swim?”

“Yes, please,” said Maureen happily. “I have got my swimming costume on under my T-shirt and skirt, so it will be easy for me. I told Jane to do the same.” She sat down heavily on the open chair and looked out at sea. “Oh, I do like to be beside the seaside,” she sang as she pulled off her top and skirt. “Do you like my beautiful swimming costume?” she asked. “I have water shoes, too.”

“You really know what to bring, Maureen,” said Olena.

"Numbers lady, why aren't you talking?" asked Maureen.

Mary took some deep breaths.

"So sorry, Mary," said Muhammid. He turned to Maureen. "She is tired from Charlie and I carrying her."

"No," said Mary. "I am not talking because I am frightened."

"I'm frightened, too," said Jane, struggling with her dress.

"Can I help you, Jane?" asked Olena.

Muhammid was gently lifting Mary's dress over her head, and a dark blue swimming costume with numbers in white all over it appeared. The numbers seemed to glow like stars in the night sky.

"Oh, numbers lady," said Maureen in awe. "What a beautiful costume!"

"And we are both in blue," said Mary.

"Well," said Charlie, "Dr. Mullin is ready and so is Maureen. What about you, Jane?"

"Well it is a bit hard. I have got my fish costume on, but it only fits half of me."

Maureen looked confused. "Do you mean half of you has got bigger and the other half is smaller?"

Mary turned her head to look at them.

"I don't know," said Jane bewildered.

Without waiting for the towel Olena was offering her, she lifted her summer dress. Her faded beige knickers were on show, then her thin white waist and a child's patterned swimsuit were around her neck, only just held together by her arms.

Olena quickly covered her, trying to hide the tears rushing into her eyes.

"That doesn't fit," said Maureen sadly. "You can't go in the water in that."

"But you are going to hold my hand in the water," said Jane, trembling.

"Yes. But in a lady's costume. That is for a baby," said Maureen.

"Not a baby! I had it when I had my last swim and it fit me beautifully. And I was not a baby," protested Jane.

Mary sat transfixed, too worried to intervene. Muhammid and Charlie were also unusually silent. A baby seagull that had been strutting up and down in front of them also stood still.

"I know what we can do," said Deborah. "I am not going in the water, but Olena, Mary, Muhammid, Charlie, and Maureen are. So I can run along the beachfront to a little beach shop which sells water shoes and swimming cozzies."

Jane's face lit up. "But I haven't got money," she said.

"That's all right. I do," said Deborah.

Mary smiled gratefully at her.

"Right! Right!" said Maureen. "So now everyone else will help Mary into the water and I have water-wings too so she can float and then I can hold her hand."

"That is a brilliant idea," said Mary. "No-one thought of that before."

"But I did," said Maureen, taking out water-wings from her large holdall. "Please blow them up," she said to Charlie.

"You are going to do it," Deborah said to Mary, firmly. "Maureen will help you."

Muhammid, Charlie, and Olena sprang into action as Deborah hurried away. Under the watchful eye of Maureen, the two men blew up a water wing each and adjusted them onto Mary's arms.

"One for each arm, numbers lady," Maureen nodded approvingly, smiling at the relieved Charlie.

Mary looked at her. "You know, Maureen, now we know each other so much better, I would like you to call me Mary."

"Mary?" asked Maureen, tasting it almost with her tongue. "Mary, not Dr. Mullins or numbers lady."

"That's right," said Mary firmly.

"I count on you as a friend now, and friends call me Mary."

Maureen burst out laughing. "You count on me, Mary."

"Count on you," reflected Mary wonderingly. "Count on you! Do you know, Maureen, in all the years I have loved numbers, I never realised that expression had numbers in it?"

"So I am not just a stupid mongol," said Maureen, who then burst into tears. "That's what Miss Jenkins called me."

"Then Miss Jenkins was a vile woman," said Mary, opening her arms, even with the water-wings on them.

Shyly, Maureen went to hug her on her chair, with the two men and Olena moving away, struck silent by what they had just witnessed.

"Those water-wings make you look like an angel," said Maureen.

Mary smiled. "You have made me feel braver, Maureen. So let's do it. Let's go into the sea."

She nodded permission to the silent Muhammid and Charlie, who carefully lifted her thin body, one arm each, with Maureen staying close next to her.

Maureen smiled happily, splashing ahead of them in her water shoes. "Yippee, it is warm, Mary! It is lovely. Like a big bath and no nasty big waves. All smooth."

A tiny smile creased the sides of Mary's lips as she felt the water on her body. One. Two. Three. The numbers were still with her.

Once Maureen got up to her waist in the water, she announced, "This is deep enough to swim. This is where you hold her so she is lying down to swim, and you can hold the rest of her, and I will hold one hand until she can fly with her wings."

Further up the steep incline, Doris and Daniel watched with fascination. "Look what she is doing!" said Doris. "That doctor, professor, whatever she is. She has got more things wrong with her than you, and she is daring to swim. Would you like to?"

Dan looked amazed at her. "My darling Doris, it is you who normally thinks everything is dangerous, and this is the first time you have wanted me to do something that I have said 'no' to! If we were in Italy or France or Spain, then I would love to, but Brighton, even in the height of summer, does not compare."

Doris laughed. "Look at that Maureen, she was so excited at bringing her water-wings for the other lady. No-one else thought of something like that which could help."

"Yes," agreed Dan. "There's whatever brain-power we have, but there's also how we use it. She really uses it. Her poor friend — that was heart-breaking with that child's swimming costume."

Doris opened her suntan lotion and spread the cream on her arms. Dan nodded reluctantly as she massaged it onto his arms and face.

"Do you think that if she last had a swimming costume at seven and hasn't swum since, her brain could cleverly remember she had a costume, remembered where it was, and remembered to pack it, but it could not realise it wouldn't fit?"

"Or someone didn't want her to grow up and never helped her or allowed her to realise?" wondered Dan.

Doris gave a little cough, and then Dan continued. "Do you think our Danny's death has frozen a bit of our family life? Not being allowed to see how time has passed?" He spluttered, reaching for a tissue. Tears were pouring down his face. "It's why I booked this, isn't it," he said.

"I am glad we can sit here by ourselves to have this conversation. Thank you, my love. There is a lot we need to do when we go back."

They squeezed each others' hands and looked back out at sea.

Charlie and Olena were swimming by with great muscular strokes, dividing the water, much further out than Muhammid, Mary, and Maureen. Maureen was walking in the water, holding Mary's left hand while Muhammid slowly supported her body.

"Can I do it alone with the water-wings?" asked Mary. "Will I be safe? What a stupid question. Fancy not knowing the answer. But before, when I was in the sea, and when I swam here almost every year with my mother, I did not have this condition, and we could swim, both of us — breaststroke."

"Well, Dr. Mullins," said Muhammid gently, "I will walk alongside you so I can put my arms around you and lift you the moment it is difficult, and Maureen is also on the other side of you. So we are like another arm each, and you have the water-wings, thanks to Maureen."

"It feels good, doesn't it," said Maureen, breaking into a few breast-strokes. "The water lifts you up."

Light sparkled on the water, like glittering beads, reminding her of her first childhood necklace. Brighton was where her mother had taught her to swim. Where they swam every year almost up to her mother's death. "I feel like a baby learning to swim for the first time," she said.

"You are a woman with a disability bravely learning her new body," said Muhammid, seriously. "And learning something new makes us think of being babies."

"I've got a disability," said Maureen, "but it is not new."

"I am ready," said Mary, splashing her legs up and down while the water-wings held her aloft.

"I thought I would have to count to 64 if I was swimming here, but I don't," she said.

"No," said Maureen, "You only need one, and two, and three — for you, me, and Muhammid.

"And four for me," said Jane, now in the bright red bikini Deborah had bought for her. "But you have to hold my hand, Deborah won't come in."

Deborah, instead, went to sit with the Ricksteins. When she approached, Mr. Rickstein offered her a ten-pound note.

"Please take that as our contribution towards the bikini for Jane."

"Thank you," said Deborah. There was something strong in his tone that brooked no disagreement. She then looked out on the water to where Mary swam with the others. And the sun carried on shining, glinting on the pebbles and waves.

Chapter Fifty-Five

The sun shone on Brighton Lanes as the group browsed its quirky and bright shops and stalls. Though some of the terrain was difficult for wheelchairs, and there was not enough room for them to walk abreast, they stayed together.

The conversation was fast and intense. First, it was Tom and Steve discussing Grendel intensively. Then, Gerry and Marion managed a whispered conversation about Gerry's hospital letter. Gerry was already feeling more positive about it. It could mean anything, and she was wasting energy leaping to the worst possible conclusion. She would phone tomorrow, at a time when she would be able to talk to Marion about it.

They then rejoined their husbands. After a quiet few moments, Susan and Marion, to their own surprise, continued their conversation in French to the amusement of the others.

"This feels like old times," said Steve merrily, distracted from thoughts of Grendel. "Looking after me has held you back in these discussions, and in your work. It is lovely to be reminded of your talent," he said.

Susan and Marion smiled at each other. It was typical of Steve to be so appreciative of his wife and un-envious of her potential to carry on working when he could not. They both agreed he was very similar to Tom, who was behind them with Gerry and Louise.

Susan could manage a really deep discussion in French, which gave her an extra emotional security. She was able, to her surprise, to ask Marion how she managed her tutorials when also worried about Steve needing attention. By contrast, they both knew Gerry had retired from her work, which had never mattered to her, and making time for Tom had never been an issue. But then Gerry was a decade older. Marion, to Susan's delight, had even suggested that, when the break was over, she might offer Susan some freelance French work for those she had no room for.

When Steve noticed a French pavement café, they all agreed to sit there together in the sun for a pastry and a drink. Gerry thought on how it all seemed so much simpler because they were in a group: when she crossed the narrow street to look at the shops on the other side, she did not have to worry about Tom: someone else was there with him. If he was dying—yes, say it, she told herself—then there would also be other people there to help. It was a huge weight lifted off her.

After their orders were taken in French by a French waiter, Gerry took the crumpled hospital letter out of her bag and pointed to it so that Marion would know what she was about to do. She received a warm thumbs-up and quickly left her seat.

And some time on hold, she finally heard a human at the other end of the phone.

"Hello, this is Mrs. Geraldine Baker, would you like my date of birth or my NHS number?" And then, yes, they found her appointment date and the letter sent to her.

"Ah, it is about your anaemia," said the receptionist helpfully. "The doctor is lovely and very hot on the right vitamins. She will have your energy back to normal in no time."

Gerry gasped with relief. "Anaemia? I thought I had cancer."

"Bless you," said the receptionist. "It says tiredness, fatigue are common in the elderly with anaemia, and iron and B12 will certainly be recommended."

Gerry took a deep breath. "So I don't have a terminal illness?" she repeated.

"No," said the receptionist. "Hold on, there. This was a useful age check-up. There is always something that needs tweaking as we age. The doctor considered your tiredness was not just the stress of being a carer, but an actual deficiency of iron."

"So, I come and this will be explained to me and I will get a prescription."

"That's right," said the receptionist.

"This is a beautiful day," said Gerry. "I feel like singing and dancing."

"Well, you just do that, bless you," said the woman.

"Thank you. Thank you for telling me. I will be there. Thank you."

Gerry ran back to the table and hugged her surprised husband. "I have just phoned the hospital about an appointment they have given me for next week. It is about anaemia. I need iron and B12 tablets, and that is why I have been so tired."

"Then, angel, it is not just because of me wearing you out," said Tom.

"No darling," she said, kissing his face over and over.

"I noticed you have been worried," he said.

"How did you know?"

"You think I don't know my angel because of my dementia?" he asked gently.

"Love is not love which alters when it alteration finds," quoted Steve, wiping a tear from his eye.

Chapter Fifty-Six

Everywhere they looked there were Pride leaflets. Pasted onto walls, onto lampposts, in neat piles in cafes. Andrzej and Ibrahim looked at each other and at Roland, who was happily eating his candy floss, little pink rivulets rolled over the sides of his wheelchair.

"What's Pride?" he asked.

"What do his mum and key worker say about such things?" asked Ibrahim seriously.

"His mum won't speak on any issue of his sexuality. She has babied him in all kinds of ways. He is all she has, and she wants to keep him like a little child."

"Ice cream," called Roland happily, licking the remains of candy floss from his fingers.

"It is lovely and warm, isn't it, Roland, and ice cream is nice on a hot day," said Ibrahim. "Shall I get the sticky bits off your fingers first?"

Roland nodded. "Were you talking about people fancying me?" asked Roland.

"Would you like us to?" asked Andrzej.

"Or would you fancy an ice cream instead?" asked Ibrahim.

Roland looked perplexed and then burst out laughing. "You are a silly care worker!" he chortled. "You can't have sex with an ice cream."

"That's true," said Ibrahim smiling.

"It would be very messy," agreed Andrzej, laughing.

They looked at each other.

"But isn't it interesting, Roland, that you use the same word "fancy" for food and sex. Maybe, just maybe, fancying food means it takes your mind off thinking about a relationship because you are too busy eating."

"You mean if I didn't have the candy floss, I might have seen someone I fancied?"

"Sorry, Andrzej," said Ibrahim, "I think I have made this harder."

Andrzej put the brakes on the wheelchair and they sat on a bench beside him. "This is really, really difficult, Roland. There are people like

Mary who don't think of food much but they are happy on their own and they don't need to fancy anyone," said Andrzej slowly.

"Like you, Big A."

Andrzej shrugged his shoulders. "That is not quite right, Roland. You see, I would like to find someone, but only if they really were the right person."

"So people can be single and happy, single and happy but looking forward to meeting someone they like, and they can be married and not happy," added Ibrahim.

After a thoughtful silence, Roland concluded, "But if I am eating an ice cream, a single man, no-one will fancy me," concluded Roland.

"I don't think we are helping," said Andrzej with an ironic laugh. "Let's all have an ice cream!"

"We all fancy ice cream," laughed Roland.

"Chocolate, strawberry, or vanilla?" asked Andrzej.

"And what is Pride?" Roland asked again, pointing to a big poster.

"Good reading," said Ibrahim, shrugging his shoulders. "I will get the ice cream."

"You can ask Olena," said Andrzej, with a rare smile on his face.

"Good idea," said Ibrahim, walking towards the ice-cream stall, "that we have given her a day off."

Chapter Fifty-Seven

Watching from the promenade, Hermione could see the Ricksteins, their bodies growing and transforming under the sun like shy creatures who had just emerged from cramped cold shells. With them was Deborah, who had brought Jane the bikini, but clearly did not want to swim herself. Further down, large dots at the edge of the water were Muhammid and Maureen, holding Mary between them with her water-wings. Mary looked like a small chrysalis held up to the sparkling air, ready to transform, and next to them, Jane in her proud new red bikini, paddled alongside. Farther still, smaller and glittering in the sun, were Charlie and Olena swimming vigorously between two groynes.

Her sketching hand wiped the water running from her eyes. James would never have come here, never have admitted his disability publicly or allowed himself to find any pleasure after it. What a tragedy for him and for her.

Hermione considered Mary again. She had swum with her mother every year in Brighton until her death, and now she dared to try again. She was not the same body she had been, but she was still embodied. Perhaps she could still feel in the water the memory of her mother and herself, connected to the larger ocean of being and the goddesses of the sea.

James had no god or goddess to pray to, only his outward-turned rage. Nothing godlike about his fall from grace. The Shakespeare twins would have more to offer. What a phrase — "Shakespeare twins!" She had Shakespeare, too. All the words she had not allowed herself in his lifetime, nor in the initial years after his death, now came back to her. It was Richard III: "Deformed, unfinished, sent before my time into this breathing world scarce half made up." How Shakespeare's Richard hated women, just like James had hated her. Perhaps he had hated his first wife, too. Perhaps the hatred had always been there, and that was why he had fallen in love with her painting. Perhaps it was her painting he had fallen in love with and not her.

There she was at her exhibition, twenty-five years ago. She was holding a glass of champagne in her hand to keep herself steady. There was no real joy in her. She was still in mourning for Vadim and their non-existent babies. The art correspondents were praising her work, and so was the gallery owner. Little red stickers kept appearing on the frames, each signalling another success. Especially "Wonderland," the most expensive, and the one bought by James. It was the first painting of hers to reach a six-figure sum.

It was her largest painting. The background was a huge stone wall representing one wall of an art exhibition. On the wall in her painting were three paintings of equal size, each within a golden frame. The first painting included her missing babies. Babies on shells floating in the sea, babies in the petals of flowers, babies playing on puffball clouds in the sky, all with the same shining dark eyes and skin. They were the babies she dreamt she and Vadim would have before he disappeared. In the second, a lake turned into a dangerous waterfall plunging onto jagged rocks, showing the way her first love had turned to horror. But James claimed he fell in love with her looking at the third painting, her Icarus high in the sky but on a black stallion and, below him on the ground, a wheelchair.

She could not help obsessively going over and over it, just as Trace could not help going over and over how she met Les. Perhaps all humans were going around in small circles, repeating the key themes in their life.

Somehow, James recognised himself in the painting and bought it. She thought she had been seen and acknowledged at the deepest level, and he had thought so, too. He had lost his children through a scheming ex-wife, and she had lost her spirit babies and her eternity lover. Were they the same? Had he let go of his real children too easily?

Two years had gone by since her Icarus had fallen from a black horse. No wonder he had turned against her. No wonder he said she had cursed him.

Vadim would be 70 now. What had happened to him? She had not even tried to search for him after that first few months of disappearance. His email account had disappeared. No sign of him in cyberspace. He had disappeared, just like Lucinda and her daughters. How could they both have lost loved ones like that? Had she given up too quickly?

Her hand began sketching furiously with a life of its own. Maureen did not give up, and nor did Mary. Naresh had not given up despite the depression that had marked his life. And beautiful Zendaya, pauper to princess — she had not she given up, either.

Hermione understood: this was why she had come on this holiday. Vadim. She had a right to know. Even if he was dead. Even if he was ill. Even if he was happily married with children and grandchildren.

Zen and Naresh had fallen for each other in a matter of seconds, the rumble of thunder and a flash of lightning, and already knew they were a match. Had she and James felt like that? It seemed like it when he recognised himself in the painting. But he never really cared about the rest of the painting, the lost babies, the beautiful lake that turned to horror. He did not really see her, except for how she understood his plight, how she had felt for his loss of his children. They had names and histories, unlike her frozen babies. But he had never asked about hers — he had been glad that she did not have children to confuse matters.

She turned a page of her sketchbook, and looked out at the sunny sky and still blue sea. There in her mind was the coach, filled with frozen people except for Maureen. And there, outside the coach, were the healing sun and waters. The people on the coach would all thaw; they would come out of their long dark freeze. Les was their Charon, the boat keeper who drove the departing souls across the water of Hades. But Les was the coach driver who drove the lost souls out of Hades into the light of the sun. This was where they would thaw.

Where was Vadim, and where did he go? How dare he? If he was not dead, then he had no excuse for not writing to her, even years later. Suddenly, she was in the school playground and the girls were all in a circle, dancing. "I sent a letter to my love and on the way I dropped it. Someone must have come along and put it in their pocket. It wasn't you! It wasn't you! It was you!"

Her silver days, 70 years old. Time was a subtle thief. You come out of the freeze and you have travelled in time. You wake up old. There was that young woman who fell in love with a man who suddenly disappeared, and then the older woman who married a man whose love for her disappeared after an accident. And why had she disappeared? Disappeared on herself? On her art?

Hermione whispered to the air around her, "I am half sick of shadows."

Chapter Fifty-Eight

Les and Trace wandered up and down Brighton Lanes while people stared and smiled. Her wedding dress was creased and crumpled, but neither of them cared.

Les was preoccupied with their lack of a ring. They had already gone into a small specialist jewellery shop where Les had expected Trace to choose one. But she had not been impressed. Even when the assistant took out a tray from the window of beautiful antique gold and silver rings costing over £1000, Trace showed no interest. He was beginning to feel worried.

"But they had everything there and that is the biggest shop," said Les. "We haven't got much longer before I have to get the coach."

"Look!" said Trace. And there it was. It was an outside stall with lots of Indian earrings, bracelets, necklaces, and rings. She picked up a crystal flower ring, with an outer circle of red and green petals of gemstones and an inner gold circle with crystals. "I love it," she said, eyes brimming with tears.

Les thought she must be joking.

Picking it up she tried it on her finger. "Look, Les. It fits!"

The man smiled at them. "£16, that comes from India. But if that is too much, we have got single circle ones for £8, too."

Les looked at her bemused. "I have saved hundreds for a ring."

She smiled at him. "I know."

"What are you saying, Trace? I want you to have the best."

"But I do have the best. I have you. And that is what the ring signifies. That we are to be wedded to each other. That is it. And it stays on my finger. I love this ring. And it can go with the plain little gold one there."

The man smiled at them. "And what about the gent? There is a matching one for that."

"Me?" asked Les.

"You!" said Trace. "You are getting married to me and I want you to have a ring so women know you are already taken."

"Very important, my missus says," added the assistant, holding out the large plain band for Les to try on.

"Me?" asked Les again.

"You, my darling. I was wasting all our time and missing what was important."

Les suddenly beamed. A cloud travelled all through his body and out of his head. He was covered in sun and gold. "Then the two matching rings for you and me, the extra one for you, and a gold bangle."

"A bangle?" asked Trace.

"Naresh and Maanika will like that. I know from Fatima, at the Hen and Horse. It is Indian custom to wear wedding bangles rather than an engagement ring."

"Oh, you are lovely," said Trace kissing him.

"£40 for all of it," said the man, smiling, and because it is for a wedding, I will give you ten percent off. That's £36."

Les unrolled two twenty-pound notes from his wallet. The man handed him two black velvet pouches, and Les handed one of them to Trace. "There you are, Almost-Missus," he said happily. "And now we have more money to go away on a honeymoon."

"Or a year's drinking allowance for you at the Hen and Horse," smiled Tracey.

He kissed her warmly. "And where would you like to go?" he asked.

Trace beamed at him. "Anywhere, but not on a coach!"

Laughing, Les replied, "Even though everything happens on my coach? Look what it has done for everyone, where it has brought them. It really is a magic carpet."

Chapter Fifty-Nine

Susan had finally found the moment to call her mother. While everyone was seated in the sun, she told them she would be back within half an hour. How thrilled her mother would be to hear from her right now. She found a quiet place in an alleyway and phoned, her heart, to her surprise, racing with excitement. It rang and rang. She began to feel worried. Her mother was always in at this hour.

Could she be ill? Had there been any text messages? No. How could her mother not be there the moment she was free to call her?

What a selfish adolescent I am being, she thought. *I am expecting my mother to be there instantly when I want her and not to be there when I am feeling independent*. How had her mother managed her absence? It was, after all, just the two of them.

She left a voicemail message.

"Hi mum, ignore all the repeat calls, It was a wonderful free moment to phone you in! Let me know when you are free next. I am really enjoying myself. Thank you for finding the job."

While she carried on thinking about her mother, she turned the corner and bumped into Tracey and Les, the driver and his fiancée. They looked so happy, despite the crumpled and dusty look of the once-beautiful wedding dress. *Mum*, she thought, *mum would be the answer to it.*

"Hi Tracey, Les," she said. "Just trying to phone my mum while the others are eating, but sod's law she's out."

"Maybe she has a nice guy she keeps hidden who she can bring out with you away!" laughed Les.

Susan looked shocked.

"Don't frighten the poor girl, Les," said Trace.

"I didn't frighten her. She is not a girl. She is a grown-up. Been to university, too," said Les.

"You did frighten me, Les," smiled Susan. "I was really surprised my mum wasn't there, like a baby, but then, you are right, anything is possible."

"She could be sitting down with a gin and tonic reading a nice magazine," reassured Trace.

"But that's all irrelevant," concluded Susan, "what matters is: did you succeed in getting what you wanted?"

"Yes. Yes," they both chortled, holding up their velvet pouches.

"If you liked it, then you should have put a ring on it," said Les bursting into a Beyoncé song.

"Oh, wonderful! Well done," said Susan.

"And the wedding will be in Betty's Restaurant?"

"Yes, with drinks after in Bert's Bar," added Les happily.

"The whole wedding is sorted," said Tracey, looking lovingly at Les.

He beamed back at her.

"I feel a bit bad about asking — but what about the dress?"

Tracey grinned. "Who cares? This dress served my dreams, but I like reality. And reality means it is the man I am marrying, not a dress."

Susan put her hand on Tracey's arm. "But who says you can't have both?"

Tracey and Les looked confusedly at her.

"My mother is one of those magical menders! She makes clothes all wonderful and new again. I would like, if you let me, to get your dress restored for your wedding by my mother."

Les looked uncertain. "Are you being a baby again?"

"Les!" remonstrated Tracey.

"No," said Les, "this is you imagining your mother will agree to your request without asking her first."

Susan burst out laughing. Fancy being told about manners by Les. He was right, and she was more like a teenager than a young woman. "You're right, Les. Thank you. Thank you. I never had you down as a Mr. Manners, but you are quite right."

Tracey nodded affectionately. "He has a heart of gold, my Les. No-one knows how much help he gives people who need it."

"Okay," said Susan, "before I say anything else wrong, please allow me to ask my mum and I will get back to my group."

Just then the phone rang. "It's my mum. Please?"

Les looked at Trace. "What do you think, Trace? Would you like this beautiful dress to be nicely washed and ironed for you to try on as new again?"

"Is that all right, Les? I thought without the dress, I wouldn't be a bridezilla."

He gave her a huge hug. "The dress is here, we have it and look at the money you have saved us in rings. It is a yes from me," he added with a flourish of his hands.

Tracey beamed excitedly. "And a yes from me, if your mum agrees."

Susan picked up the phone, "Hello mum. I really missed you."

Chapter Sixty

Charlene, yet again, was in her owner's flat lounge, changing her high heels for a pair of fluffy slippers. Even if it was only for ten minutes, it made a difference. She found she retreated to her flat whenever there was a break from the constantly unique demands of this venture of hers, however small that break was.

An electrical fault in Room 8, a toilet blocked in the Room 12 wet room, a missing kitchen assistant, a double booking for the largest room, not enough choice for vegans — all these issues that could have been sorted by someone else.

But it was working. Really working, like all the parts of an oiled and exquisitely fashioned watch. How good her wonderful chef and his deputy chef, were, there to watch over all the kitchen staff. The food was just as she had hoped for, and Bert's Bar was the perfect spot to wash it all down in. Justin's idea of an inclusive three-course meal with wine meant that people felt freer to experiment with the cocktails in Bert's.

It was better than she had hoped. Reviews were appearing on social media, and the disability organisations had picked up on the hotel and Wonderful Wheelchairs. The *Morning Live* programme had booked them in, and *The Sunville Herald* had been proud to announce a scoop, ahead of the major daily newspapers, of first-romance and a wedding at Hotel Mirabelle. *The Sunville Herald* had also quoted Della on how her grandparents couldn't get to the Mirabelle to eat when they became disabled and how nobody had a problem with such exclusions at that time.

So, the problem was not that it was starting well, but that it was already too successful. Bookings were overwhelming the receptionist, and Charlene could see she needed to add to the infrastructure to aid its growth. Having twenty bedrooms that could hold forty people was one thing, with its own demand for cleaning and laundry. But Betty's held over double that number of covers. Christmas was already filling up, and also the weekends leading to Christmas.

Could Della work with her? Would that be trapping her at an age when she needed freedom? Was it selfish to even think of asking her? Was she holding Della back?

Charlene felt a sudden twinge of loneliness. She spoke to Irene daily — how wonderful to get her bestie back at this age, how she would love to work with Irene all the time! But Irene was loyal to Wonderful Wheelchairs, or to Maanika. Could they amalgamate? Would Naresh and Maanika want to? Would Zendaya do something with My-Lights? She needed to speak to her accountant. Then she needed to speak to Della and then the others.

She wanted children and adults with a disability to have a proper holiday. They needed the hotel. Yes. But they equally needed a carer or relative with them. This meant Hotel Mirabelle and Wonderful Wheelchairs needed each other and were made for each other.

A sudden excitement swept through her. What a team that would be: her and her daughter, Maanika and her brother (and his wife), and her bestie. She wouldn't need anything else in her life.

There were people phoning to book a hotel weekend with a partner or friend with a disability, but they were also realising they needed help. They wouldn't manage outings for the most disabled if they just booked the room. It therefore made sense to join up. There were experienced carers already there. And Susan, her daughter's new friend — maybe she would join, too?

The intercom squawked. It was the kitchen, checking what time the coach would be back. She'd put Della onto that. Oh, and Ibrahim and Irene had noticed on the check-in information that Maureen would be 64 the next day. A cake was definitely in order.

Chapter Sixty-One

Hermione sat on the promenade bench near to the coach. There were fifteen minutes to go before they left Brighton, and the sun was still bright in the sky. She took her silver shawl off her arms, since there was no danger of sunburn now.

People walking past turned back again to look at her, perhaps wondering if she was someone famous they ought to recognise. Hermione was used to this, to being stared at for one reason or another. Her appearance, her title, her art, and now the sunglasses made it even worse. Far from hiding her face, they added to her mystique.

Hermione had decided to go back with the others in the coach, her mind filled with ideas for paintings. Especially, she imagined Les and his coach as the boat taking souls through the underworld, but into the light instead of to Hades. She wanted to watch their faces as they appeared. She would go on last. She did not want to take someone else's favourite seat.

The group boarding the coach looked very different from the group which had first arrived at Sunville. Their faces and arms were browner, their clothes were looser. But there was something else in their spirit — they had been transfigured.

There was Les, her apparently-tough Charon with the soft heart, ready to cross the waters of the underworld and bring his passengers home safely. His voice was a little less loud, his smile was shy and deep. Tracey stood by him, a glorious bride in a white creased crumpled dress. When Les saw her, he burst spontaneously into song. "Cinderella Rockerfella." "You're the lady. You're the lady that I love."

Hermione beamed at them. "That song is from the 60s! Fifty years ago — how can you young ones know a song like that?"

"I remember that," said Gerry delightedly, as the rest of her party took up the remaining promenade benches near the coach.

"Yes," agreed Tom. "Cinderella Rockerfella. You were probably too young for that one, Steve," he added, turning to smile at Steve.

"Well," said Hermione, "when everyone is settled, I will tell you all the lyrics. Maureen would love the words."

Andrzej and Ibrahim then arrived with a happy Roland, his shirt stained with bits of melted ice cream.

"I fancied ice cream," he chortled happily.

"And it looks like ice cream fancied you," agreed Les.

Roland looked utterly bewildered and remained silent, while Andrzej and Muhammid made signs to each other. Tom, in his fine tenor voice, started singing "I scream for ice cream" as the others arrived, all smelling of sun lotion and the sea.

Olena went straight to Roland. "I missed you, Roland! I am so pleased to see you."

"You came back to me," he said. "You did not go away."

The rest of the group turned to look at Mary expectantly. Tiny as she was, she seemed to expand in her chair, with a proud Deborah looking at her intently.

"I did it," she said.

"Mary did it," endorsed Maureen with a thumbs-up.

"Thanks to you, Maureen, and Muhammid, and everyone."

"And me," added Jane.

"Everyone means everyone," laughed Mary.

And I had a new bikini," shouted Jane.

Les and Trace started singing again. "She had an itsy-bitsy teenie-weenie yellow polka dot bikini."

"It was red," corrected Jane.

"Another old song," laughed Hermione. "That was around 1960, although it did come back in the 1990s at some point."

"Thank you for my bikini, Deborah," shouted Jane.

"Well, it was from Doris and Dan too," said Deborah.

"Well," said Les, "I have got a whole lot of beautiful mermaids to take back to Hotel Mirabelle."

"I am not a mermaid," said Roland.

"No. The ladies are mermaids. You are a merman."

Roland looked urgently at Olena. "Olena. I am not a merman."

"No. You are a man. A single man," said Olena, smiling at Andrzej.

Roland relaxed. "I am a man."

"Look at your dress," said Maureen, turning to Tracey.

"Jane needed a new bikini, and you need a new dress. You look like a woman in a film who runs away in her wedding dress."

"Well, I did do that," smiled Tracey, turning to Les. "I ran away to my husband-to-be before the wedding."

"And there is news about the dress," said Susan. "Do you want to tell them, Tracey?"

Tracey moved back to stand on the first step of the coach. "Susan's mother does invisible mending and ironing and repairs, and she is going to have my dress all beautiful again for the wedding. And you will all be invited."

Chapter Sixty-Two

Wearing trainers — rather than her high heels — and a velvet lounge suit, Zen walked to "their" usual Chesterfield. She did not have to look at the lone men sitting hopefully on the armchairs or crowded round the bar — this was her territory, her home, and her man was waiting for her upstairs.

She had delayed her meeting with Di, as Naresh had been on the radio: the BBC and local. She had sat opposite him, listening to him on the phone, giving him encouraging looks.

He sounded so positive. After the broadcast, he had sobbed for his dead friends, men who lost their lives in Afghanistan, and then he sobbed for his family who lost their lives in India. Zen had held him, and he had held her as she wept for her great grandparents, slaves of Mr. Brown. And then they toasted the Wonderful Wheelchair Company and Hotel Mirabelle, and then his prostheses and her boobs, and they hugged each other, asking each other again, "What do you want to do with your life? Where do you want to live?"

It all seemed very simple to them.

Zen said she would like to live in Bert's Bar, as that was where she had met him. Failing that, she wanted to work as a hairdresser in Hotel Mirabelle, if Charlene would give her a job there. She wanted to live with him and did not mind where.

"But not too far from a hospital," she added wisely. "And that could be for me let alone what you already have."

Naresh loved the Wonderful Wheelchair Company, but he did not have the energy to add on new ideas for trips every year. He liked the idea of the two companies working together, but he did not want to live there. A move to Sunville would be fine, however. Also, he knew Maanika and Sunil wanted a child, and so Maanika could not take on all the management. They would all need to meet together to work the details out.

"So what are we waiting for, loverboy?" asked Zen. "As soon as I am done with Di, let's all get together."

So here she was. Bert's Bar, where it all began. As soon as she sat down, one of the waiters came and asked if she would like her usual. This was belonging! This was having a home. So she smiled and thanked him, knowing the bowl of nuts would come, too. She remembered the times when she had depended on those bowls of nuts to stay alive.

Di arrived in her high heels and breasts standing to attention, click-clacking towards her, eyes looking in all directions. "Where have you been, bitch? I've been calling and calling. And what you done up like a hoodie for?"

Zen didn't know what to say. Was it really only a couple of earth days that had passed?

"Sorry, sister," she said.

"Sorry? You don't usually say sorry. Even when you should. Are you all right? Has anyone spiked your drink?"

The waiter returned with Zen's drink and the bowl of nuts. He bowed politely to Di, and asked if she would like the same as Madam, on the house.

"On the house?" asked Di, a wicked grin on her face. "You get a deal going here, Zen, with this lovely man?"

The waiter looked confused.

"Yes. The same for my friend please, thank you, Mark," said Zen.

The waiter bowed and hurried away.

"What's going on here?" asked Di. "What are you up to?"

Zendaya leant forward. "Naresh."

"Legless?" interrupted Di.

"Yes. Well, we are engaged."

"Where's the ring?" asked Di, staring at Zen's fingers.

"Oh, we were too busy to get it today," said Zen. "We were going to get it in Brighton, but we had so many other arrangements to sort out."

"No ring. No guy. All a scam to get you into bed," said Di.

"Will you fucking listen?" said Zen, suddenly losing all the great calm of the last few days. "I am in love. We are getting married. He has a suite in this hotel and he runs the Wonderful Wheelchair Company."

"Blah, blah, blah," said Di. "No legs, no ring, and a fake ID, and you are getting too soft in the head to fall for it."

The waiter came with Di's drink and looked worriedly at her.

"Don't like what you're looking at?" she mocked. "It is my friend who is the fool here."

Zen stood up. "It is too much to say now, especially as you can't hear me. But if you speak like this to me in this room, I will have you barred." And out she walked.

Chapter Sixty-Three

"Where is my Grendel?" shouted Steve.

Marion looked around with surprise. It was the first time he had spoken in such an irritated voice for two days.

"Grendel?" she asked. "We brought your last paper on Grendel with us, darling. It is in the file."

"Well, where is it? Because I keep asking for it, and you deliberately keep it away from me."

Marion opened the drawer of the bedside cabinet and took out a bright blue foolscap file. In it were both the printout of his last published paper on Grendel, and also his new notes. Nothing had changed for months. He could not manage it, and he could not accept he could not manage it. She gently handed it to him.

He opened it up avidly, and then his face fell. "That's not my Grendel. That is old. It is rubbish. Those notes are not my new notes."

Marion had a sharp intake of breath. This had not happened before. "Shall I put the television on?" she asked.

"Good idea," he said in his normal voice.

Turning on the TV, she went through the menu to see if anything excited him. There was an old jungle movie with people walking warily around a swamp.

"There," he said, "There. That's where Grendel is. Thank you. You finally found it." And he stared intently at the swamp, waiting to see Grendel.

Marion dug her nails into the soft palm of her hands. He hadn't done this before. Was this the next stage down?

A nubile "native" girl walked around the side of the swamp in a bikini fashioned from rags. This really was an old film. Colonial. Misogynist. But Steve was not interested in the girl at all. His eyes were fixed on the swamp.

"It is Grendel."

There was a pause. The girl walked away. The dramatic music changed. There were lush trees and bird sound.

"Where did Grendel go? Where is Grendel?" he howled. "His mother has to avenge him. This is what they did to him." And he sobbed loudly.

Marion did not know what to do. She'd read about it, heard about it. But that was different. She had not seen it, not in her Steve. Poor Grendel, poor monster. Grendel was an outcast, descended from Cain, doomed to wander the face of his earth. Poor village outcasts, the unwanted, the disabled, thrown out into woods and forests, and then feared at night-time. Grendel, hating the music and light of the mead-hall. And his mother, out to avenge the death of her son. Grendel at least had his mother to fight for him. France, the land of enlightenment, yet Descartes had wanted to think it had no monsters. Then where did Quasimodo come from? She would phone Gerry, and then she would see if Charlie or Ibrahim were free.

"What are you doing?" shouted Steve, watching her type a message on her phone.

"Just checking what time Gerry and Tom will have dinner tonight so we can go together," she said in her reasonable bright voice.

Steve stared at the screen, the light in his eyes having gone out. In a few seconds, his head drooped down and he was asleep. Marion instantly stopped texting and phoned instead.

"Gerry? It is me. He has just gone to sleep, so I am phoning instead of texting. He was shouting at me, and he never shouts at me. He thought I had stolen his precious Grendel notes, but he can't let go of the fact he will never write more about it."

"Hi, Marion!" Gerry said. "First, thank you. I cannot tell you how much I appreciate the help you gave me. It has transformed everything. Worrying about mortality at my age alone is one thing, but when you are also a main carer it is doubly worrying. Anything I can do to help you? You poor love. It is the illness, not him, that is doing that, and it could have been a bit of a hallucination, too. I am lucky, it is still rare for Tom to get like that, but when he does, I feel I am holding an umbilical cord to a gigantic, depressed baby, and it is a lot to take on."

Marion began sobbing quietly. "Yes. It is just like maternal preoccupation, but with an adult who used to share all your problems."

"Yes," said Gerry, "and we so feel for the burden they are carrying, we tend to not want to notice how it affects our health."

"I wondered whether to think more about Grendel to be able to discuss it with him," said Marion.

"I tried that with Shakespeare, but I can't keep up, and it is not what I ever did," replied Gerry sadly.

"I have been thinking about monsters in French literature," said Marion, "and, of course, I have been thinking about the meaning of a handicapped outcast, deprived of joy and light and becoming murderous." Her breathing had calmed. "I feel better, Gerry, just talking to someone who understands. What is Tom doing at the moment?"

"He is sleeping, bless him, before he was even washed or changed. Now that I am not frightened of dying myself, I can see how he sleeps more and more, apart from pockets of Shakespeare."

"He really loves Shakespeare, doesn't he," agreed Marion. "It is his food and drink, his basic words."

"Shakespeare twins," reflected Gerry. "I am so glad we came on this holiday."

"Yes. Holiday is the wrong word, though. It feels somehow like a pilgrimage. Let's hope Steve doesn't shout at you and Tom," said Marion worriedly.

"Don't worry about that. I would not take it personally," said Gerry. "It would not matter."

"Thank you."

"Do you know," said Gerry softly, "when Covid began, it was a strange pleasure for us. We were just disabled like everyone else. No-one could visit. Her grandson Zoomed and our son and daughter-in-law Zoomed. We called them the FaceTime Phantoms!"

Marion laughed.

"We could look out of the window like everyone else," continued Gerry, "and look at skies and clouds and pavements unaffected by humans, slowly taking over more space. We had deliveries. Everything was plastic: aprons, gloves, masks. We were living in a surreal world. And then I started feeling tired, and I did not know if I was tired because I should be tired. An old woman looking after an old man. Then, I wondered if I was depressed. But I have never had a bias towards depression. And then, then, all my mortality fears came to rest on that symptom, and I went to my GP. I left Tom on the phone with our son as I didn't have anyone to be with him while I went to the doctors. And then when I got the letter from the hospital, I was sure it would tell me I had cancer."

"Do you think," Marion asked after a pause, and then she started again. "Well, I am not a psychologist, but do you think that in worrying about cancer, you were also wishing for something organic to happen to allow you to get more help with Tom? He is a kind and lovely man, and you clearly love each other. But you are with him all the time and are his main carer."

"Oh my goodness," said Gerry, emphatically, "You have done it again, Marion! That is absolutely right. Goodness. Because the first thing I thought when I phoned the hospital and I was given my reprieve was that I have to get live-in-care."

"It is so good to talk to someone who understands," agreed Marion.

"Yes," said Gerry. "Because what I get from our son and family is to move in with them. I love them, but that is not the life we have had, and I prefer my independence. And many of my friends sing the praises of respite care and care homes, but that is not what I want for him. We did visit one old friend who was now in a residential home. A beautiful posh one. Manicured lawns, flowers, bird tables. Individual rooms that looked lovely. But basically, old people are left alone in their rooms, ringing the bell for someone who does not come, because the poor care staff are so overworked and overwhelmed. If my friends are like that with me now when I am over a decade younger than you, it will only get worse."

"Angel," said a loud velvety voice through the phone.

"Ah, it is my Tom — he has woken up," said Gerry with a softness in her voice.

"Then ring me when you are ready to go down to dinner," said Marion. "Thank you again."

The room was quiet apart from an almost imperceptible hum from the Clever Mattress. It did something every so often to help avoid bed sores, and was definitely better than the adjustable bed they had at home. She would ask the hotel where they had ordered the bed from. She realised there was all kinds of help available if she looked properly. The folder on the bedside table full of outings also included leaflets from the Alzheimer's Society and Dementia Hubs all over the UK. They were a disabled couple. She had a husband with a disability. He was no longer a lecturer in English Literature. He was no longer an expert on Anglo-Saxon literature. He was a lovely man whose brain was being stripped from him while he lived.

"Grendel!" he suddenly called in anguish.

She went to the side of the bed and put her arms around him, then spoke softly. "Poor Grendel. Poor lonely outcast Grendel. No wonder he felt so awful. But he had a mother who loved him and was ready to fight to the death for him."

He opened his eyes. There was a light back in them. "That was a good sleep," he smiled at her. "Sleep, the innocent sleep, sleep that knits up the ravelled sleeve of care."

"Good evening, Mr. Shakespeare. Shall we go and find your twin?"

"Excellent," he said. "Ring one of those nice men to help. I don't want you straining yourself."

And she kissed his cheek, furtively wiping her eyes.

Chapter Sixty-Four

Mary and Deborah had invited Maureen to come to their room before they all went down for the evening meal. Mary was agitated, wheeling her chair up and down the large bedroom.

"What is it?" asked Deborah. "It has been a really big day for you, hasn't it?"

"Yes," said Mary.

She wheeled herself to the mirrored wardrobe and looked at her face intently. How thin it was. She had aged, but in her eyes was a spark she had not seen for a long time. "I have an idea. I would like to do a maths book for people with an intellectual disability, like Maureen, who are so clever, and so kind. It could be called Count on Me."

"Oh, my goodness," shrieked Deborah. "That would be wonderful! It is exactly what you and Maureen have been doing all this time."

"Yes," said Mary, putting on a pearl necklace.

Deborah watched with tears in her eyes. Although she had packed Mary's slim jewel case, Mary had not yet worn any necklace or bracelet on the trip. She said nothing.

There was a knock on the door. Deborah opened it, and Maureen wheeled in apologetically. All her radiance from the coach had disappeared. She looked devastated.

"Was too tired to walk."

"How sensible of you, Maureen! We are allowed to rest," smiled Mary.

Maureen took a deep breath. Deborah offered her a drink, but Maureen clearly had something on her mind and did not want anything yet.

"Maureen, I have something important to ask you," said Mary. "It is good news."

Maureen looked confused. "I am bad," she suddenly said and burst into tears.

"What is it, Maureen?" asked Mary, wheeling next to her and taking her hand.

"It is my birthday tomorrow, Mary. I am 64. God thinks I am bad. I should not have been born. I wished Miss Jenkins was dead. Mr. Grass didn't remember me, and you won't remember me." And then a huge wave of shudders passed through her body.

Deborah was struck dumb, but it was Dr. Mary Mullins who saved the day. "Now, Maureen," she said, in her most formal teacher voice. "I have something very important to tell you. First, I have to ask you if this is a song you know."

While Deborah and Maureen looked at her with bewilderment, she typed onto her phone. In a moment a familiar song filled the room.

"Will you still feed me will you still need me when I am 64."

The two women continued to look at her with confusion, but then a light dawned in Maureen's eyes. "Numbers lady! I am 64 and the song sings about being 64." A slow smile appeared on her face.

"You are 64, Maureen, and that is a special number that asks if someone will still be needed when they are 64; it's about if they will still be loved when they are old. And I love you and I am 64, so we are like the Shakespeare twins."

"And I am 64 – or will be tomorrow," said Maureen wonderingly.

"And I will love you tomorrow as well," said Deborah, a hand on her mouth to silence her sobs. "And I love Mary."

"Do you want to hear the good news I wanted to tell you about?" asked Mary, still holding Maureen's hand. "It is a birthday present. A very special kind of present."

Maureen took a deep breath and let go of Mary's hand, who then continued. "Well, Maureen, you know I love numbers, and I write books about numbers, and you know I love you and really also love the way you love numbers, too."

A further sigh passed through Maureen's body.

"Well, I would like you and me to write a book together called *Count on Me*, and it will be about us swimming in the water and you saying I did not have to count to 64; I could just count to three."

"But it was more in the end, it was me, Muhammid, Jane, and then it was Olena, and Charlie too."

"You see how good at numbers you are!" said Mary. "That is why I wanted you to write this with me. You don't have to do the writing; you do the speaking, and Deborah and I write it down, and then we get an artist to draw the pictures for us."

Maureen seemed to contemplate this, and then Mary continued, "Yes. I do have a disability which is not like yours. You stay the same and mine gets worse. Is that what happened with your Dr. Grass? My memory is still good, even though my walking days are over. And in the end, my memory will go, but it could take a very long time or it could be short, or something else could happen to me, like a heart problem, before my memory goes. None of us know what will happen to us."

Maureen reached for Mary's hand, and Mary took it warmly before adding, "I don't know who Miss Jenkins was, but she sounds like someone bad, and you are someone good, who does not like to have bad thoughts about people. So let us hope Miss Jenkins grew up to be a nicer person and say sorry. But you are allowed to be angry with people who are not nice to you."

"My mum, she got rid of me. Right from the start. Right when I was born. She left me on a step."

"What step was it?" asked Deborah suddenly, a light in her eyes.

"It was a convent with five steps and she left me on the top step."

"Then that is how *Count on Me* will start," said Mary happily, beaming at Deborah.

"So it is all right I was born?" asked Maureen.

"You bet it is! And you know what? I bet that lovely Muhammid can play 'When I'm 64,' and I will ask him to play it tomorrow."

They all looked at each other, suddenly aware they were all holding hands. "Look at that, Mary," beamed Maureen, "three people holding hands makes six hands."

Chapter Sixty-Five

Hermione drew feverishly in her room, filling her sketch pad with ideas. There Les was Charon, and there was Zen, her hair loose, long, and frizzy.

Who gave a damn about James' stupid fecund first wife and the spoiled daughters? They knew her address and her name. She was not Hermione waiting for them, frozen in innocence in a permanent *Winter's Tale*. She did not need their approval.

Their mother had left James before she had even met him. How dare they rubbish her history like that? Let them go to their graves not knowing about their father. It was not her responsibility anymore. And nor was Vadim. What had he done? Why hadn't he written?

Vadim Isak Abramovich. She would get an agency to investigate. Damn it! She was 70. She only had a decade left, and there was nothing she could be sure of. She was not going to be burdened by other people's secrets.

Vadim Isak Abramovich. He would be 70, too, if he was alive. And if he was alive, she would feel like murdering him.

Lucinda, Virginia, and Emma. She felt like murdering them, too. How dare they treat a living man as if he was dead? He was not a father who had left them. He had an unfaithful, gold-digging wife who ran off to the other side of the world with her children.

Poor James. His careful files and boxes of cards and details of everything sent to them along with the date. Virginia and Emma. They weren't innocent children now. They were in their 30s, old enough to take responsibility for a broader picture than the lies their mother had fed them. If they had been proper family, he might have felt different after his accident. He might have accepted his disability. If they had been proper family, he might not have become that kind of a rider or risk-taker. He did not have a family to rein him in. Fortune, his beloved favourite horse. Would he have loved Fortune so much if he had had living children who loved him?

Stop there, Hermione told herself.

The past was another country. No point in "what if" and "if only." But she did not have to carry their dead weight on top of everything else.

She would offer Charlene the coach painting for the reception. What a wonderful place. A magical transformational place. And she knew exactly what she was going to do first. She stopped drawing and closed her sketchbook.

There was a meaning in this holiday—this holy day.

Chapter Sixty-Six

Roland was sitting on the armchair in his room, watching cartoons on the television. He was unusually quiet, and his brow was furrowed. Andrzej and Olena watched him with concern.

"You okay, Roly?" asked Olena.

He did not reply.

"What is on your mind?" asked Andrzej.

"Nothing," said Roland. He turned around to look at them. "My mind is in my head. It doesn't have things on it."

Olena sighed. "I keep forgetting how literal he is," she said to Andrzej.

"What is it?" asked Andrzej. "You are doing some important thinking."

Roland sighed a big sigh. The two workers looked at each other with concern. "You can tell us, Roland. We will think about it with you whatever it is."

Roland turned round in a sudden violent action. "It's about the ice cream."

They looked at him, surprised. "The ice cream?"

"Yes."

"I said I fancied ice cream."

Andrzej sighed and looked worriedly at Olena. "Yes. That's right. You did," he said.

"And Les said the ice cream fancied me."

There was a long pause, and then Roland added, "He said that because ice cream melted on me."

"Yes. I remember," said Olena gently.

"When I said I fancied ice cream, I didn't mean I had sex with the ice cream."

"That's right, Roland. You didn't. You meant you liked it. Words are funny, aren't they?" said Olena. "Because, in English, 'fancy' can mean you find someone attractive and sexy but it can also mean you just like something."

Roland breathed a sigh of relief. "So no-one thought I had sex with ice cream?"

"No," they both agreed.

"And when Les said the ice cream fancied me, he didn't mean the ice cream wanted to have sex with me and the white stuff on me was from sex?"

"Ah," said Andrzej happily. "What a brave, clever man you are. When a man feels sexy, white stuff can come out of his penis. But it's not ice cream."

Roland laughed. "I don't have ice cream coming out of my willy."

"No, you don't. So Les wasn't saying that. He was making a joke, like 'I like the sun and the sun likes me.' When the sun shines on me I feel it likes me, but it doesn't know me. It doesn't think about us humans."

He looked at Olena, who came to his aid. "English words are very difficult, Roland. Les was making a joke. You said you fancied ice cream and he thought it sounded funny to say it the other way round."

They could see the effort on Roland's face. "So, it was a joke."

"Yes."

"But no-one was laughing at me, because no-one fancies me, not even ice cream."

Andrzej did a high five with him. "You are a brave single man who is free to fancy someone, a person, and you are free to fancy any food or drink you like as well."

"Or television programme?" he asked.

"Yes."

"So I could say 'I fancy a cartoon now,' and someone could say 'and it could fancy you,' and that would be a joke?"

"That's right," said Andrzej triumphantly. "You've done it, Roland."

"If I see Les tonight and tell him I fancy ice cream, and he says 'I bet the ice cream fancies you,' I could laugh because it means it is a joke and no-one is being mean to me." Roland smiled and laughed happily.

"But Roly," said Olena, "he might not say it at all, because when people make a joke, they don't usually plan it. I hope it won't disappoint you if he doesn't say it."

"I could tell Maureen and Jane," said Roland. "If Les is not there I can tell the whole thing. I could say 'I fancy ice cream' and Les said 'And I bet ice cream fancies you' and then I could laugh and they would know it did not mean sex-fancy but just meant I liked it."

"What a lot of work you just did," said Olena happily. "You amaze me." She turned to Andrzej. "And don't think I don't know you fancied ice cream, too."

Andrzej blushed. "Early days," he said.

Roland picked up the TV controls and made the sound louder. "Quiet please. I fancy a cartoon now. But you don't have to tell me it fancies me because we have already discussed the joke."

Chapter Sixty-Seven

Irene was delighted. The bookings were unbelievable. The bank manager would be delighted. She would like nothing better than getting her teeth into the hotel business, linked with Wonderful Wheelchairs. And now it looked as if this was going to happen without any conflict of interest.

Naresh and Zen were absolutely clear in their aims, and she wished them luck, she really did. They deserved happiness. He had done less and less in the last few months, and it was she and Maanika who had shouldered the burden. How good for Sunil that the gamble had paid off and she could replace the money she had given from her personal account.

All the staff had worked wonderfully so far, hotel and restaurant and bar staff as well as the carers. Zen and Naresh. Zen and Maanika. Susan and Della. Les and Tracey. Muhammid and Ibrahim. Maureen and Mary. Ibrahim and Andrzej. What amazing and moving combinations!

She didn't need or want a man in her life again. What she wanted was a career. Hotel management. And here it was, without any job interview needed. It was the best kind of promotion.

Everybody wanted everyone. It was as simple as that. The aim was so simple. The cause. People in wheelchairs, people with dementia, carers and partners did not get the kind of break they needed to aid their immune systems, their sense of curiosity and pleasure. And here was a hotel and a travel company that did that and knew what was needed.

Lawyers would be needed and contracts would need to be drawn up, but that, for Irene, was the easy part. What mattered, to all of them, was the instinct. The mission statement and the aim had come authentically and naturally from Naresh, and everyone else shared his vision.

Wonderful Wheelchairs would be a separate division, answerable to the over-arching executive group — Charlene, Irene, Naresh, and Maanika. There would then be issues of accountability over My-Lights and checking out Zen's capabilities there. And housekeeping? Della would need to consider the areas she cared about. PR? Liaison? Fundraising for people to have holidays?

But look, whatever they did, at this stage of her life, she was in her prime and she loved it. Hotel Mirabelle and the Wonderful Wheelchair Company. It was wonderful.

Chapter Sixty-Eight

"That's a Russian Jewish name," said Doris to Dan, standing behind her by the Betty's Restaurant doors.

"Pardon?" asked Hermione, frowning. That little round woman who had looked so collapsed had a new confidence about her.

"You were saying it loudly, so I could not help hearing," said Doris.

"Saying what?" asked Hermione.

"Vadim Isak Abramovich."

Hermione held onto her golden walking stick. "How do you know that name?"

Daniel intervened for his wife. "Apologies, Lady Hermione. You kept repeating the name aloud, and because it is quite a common Russian Jewish name my wife responded. Our families came from Russia, you see."

Hermione relaxed. "I am so sorry. I had no idea I was speaking my thoughts aloud. How rude of me. Please join me for dinner, unless, of course, you have other plans."

Doris beamed widely. "We would love to, Lady Hermione."

"Please call me Hermione," said Hermione as she moved to her usual table.

Once they were seated, she turned to Doris. "It is so strange I did not know I was speaking that name aloud. But — would you know if it is possible to trace a Russian Jew, when all you have is their name and not even the part of Russia?"

The Ricksteins looked at each other. To her husband's delight, Doris spoke. "Yes. It is indeed possible, even though it is hard. Is he a refugee? Is he political?"

Hermione took a deep breath. "He is a good friend I knew half a century ago. So he is the same age as me. When he graduated, he was supposed to come to London, but he suddenly disappeared and no-one knew where he had gone. The university records state he returned to Russia. It was a public fact, so they were willing to let me know that. But nothing else is known. In my clearing-out, I found I have some pictures that are his, and it is that time of age for me where I want to make sure I am not left with other people's things."

The waitress appeared at that moment. "Wine or juice?" she asked them.

"Juice, please," they replied.

"Could I have pineapple juice?" asked Doris happily.

"I'll have pineapple juice, too," said Hermione. And then, she turned to Doris. "It is a strange way to say a proper hello, but I must say that you are looking wonderful, Doris. Something about this break has been good for you."

"It has," said Doris. "I had got frightened of going out. I had kept everything frozen, rather than facing up to things."

Dan squeezed her hand.

"I feel rather similar," said Hermione. "Since my husband died two years ago, and the period when he was invalided from a riding accident for a couple of years before that, I have hardly left my house."

"I am so sorry," said Daniel. "It is my condition that keeps me disabled physically, but mentally I am feeling luckier than my wife."

A feeling of calm settled on the table. "I apologise for hijacking you to this table, but you seemed to find the name I said familiar."

"Life moves in mysterious ways," said Daniel solemnly.

"Our families come from Russia and Ukraine, like Olena," explained Doris, "They were immigrants from the Pogroms before the Holocaust. We know the Jewish names. Isak and Abramovich are Jewish."

Hermione looked shocked. "Do you know, I never knew that. He never mentioned it."

There was a silence, and then Dan said, "Unusual. If he had changed his name, that would make more sense, but in keeping such a name he was not hiding it."

"He was an artist," said Hermione, a little defensively. "He had all his plans for London when he graduated and then he disappeared without a trace."

"Sounds like my mother's side of the family," said Doris.

Daniel frowned at her. "Hermione might not want to know."

"No. Please continue," said Hermione.

"My uncle came to England to study, and he fell in love with an English girl. And he was suddenly called back to Russia and never returned. It turned out that when a new wave of antisemitism started, the attack was on being 'cosmopolitan' or 'Western,' and if you had family members in America or the UK, you were seen as being disloyal. It was bad enough having Western connections anyway, but being Jewish and having Western connections was dangerous. So he could not write or phone because that would have betrayed Western links."

Hermione's whole body was shuddering. "So, someone could disappear just like that. Just like that. Disappear, and you would never know."

"Yes," said Dan. "But that does not mean it happened to your friend. People can disappear for lots of reasons."

"But if they are Russian, Polish, Ukrainian, or Jewish, it adds to the number of reasons why people disappear or are disappeared."

"That is awful," said Hermione. "I had never considered that possibility."

"But you can try some of the sites on the internet," added Doris. "I can give you the names of some of them."

"Thank you," said Hermione. "That is very kind."

They looked towards the door after hearing raised voices. Olena and Andrzej were with Roland, that enormous young man, and he was beaming happily.

As they nodded back in greeting, Olena came up to the table. "Mrs. Rickstein, apologies again. When I spoke about Ukraine. I wasn't thinking. And your history—I did not mean to upset you."

Doris smiled at her. "Olena, you do not know how you have helped me to speak again. I felt better for speaking."

They smiled at each other, and Roland intervened. "I have got a joke. Do you want to hear it?"

"Yes," said Dan.

"I said I fancied ice cream and Les said the ice cream fancied me." He burst out laughing.

Olena and Andrzej gritted their teeth, but Daniel smiled. "That's a good joke, Roland!"

Roland smiled. "Thank you. It is a joke. It does not mean the ice cream wanted sex with me."

Doris shuddered, but Hermione burst out laughing. "What a good thing to discover, Roland! That is a good joke."

Roland smiled, nodded, and pointed to the buffet table. As they moved on, smiling with relief, Roland lifted a hand up, signifying he wanted to stop.

"So, Big A, what is Pride?"

Andrzej looked helplessly at Olena, who looked unwaveringly ahead.

"Pride is when you are proud of yourself for something," said Andrzej hesitantly. "And you should feel pride, Roly, for understanding all the difficult English conventions for the word 'fancy.'"

Roland smiled.

"But in England and other countries, it is also a time when people who are different in some way say 'we are proud of who we are.'"

Roland nodded. "So I am double Pride. Because I know what 'fancy' means and I am different."

Andrzej moved to the front of the wheelchair. "I feel so proud of you Roland, and if numbers lady was here, she would be proud of you understanding 'double'—two things."

Chapter Sixty-Nine

"It is a surprise," said Mary.

They were going down in the lift, and Deborah and Mary were beaming at Maureen. She was nervous, though, and ran her hands through her hair. Her face was paler than usual.

"It's not going to be something frightening, is it?" asked Jane.

"I hope not," said Mary.

"Where are we going?" asked Maureen, all her usual energy depleted.

"Bert's Bar," said Mary.

"I don't go in bars," said Maureen. "There are drunk men and they are nasty."

"This is a Hotel Mirabelle bar. It is different."

"This is a bad day," said Maureen.

"Why?" asked Jane.

"It is my birthday."

"Happy birthday, Maureen," said Jane excitedly. "I will buy you a present when we go to the shops."

"You don't have to buy me anything. I don't like birthdays," said Maureen.

The lift doors opened and Mary wheeled the way ahead to Bert's Bar. Maureen covered her eyes nervously.

"Look!" said Deborah.

The bar was largely empty except for the smiling staff and Muhammid sitting at the piano. When he saw Maureen, a huge smile crossed his face and he started playing the piano. "When I'm 64," sang Muhammid

Big sobs racked Maureen's body. "And you still love me and need me, numbers lady. And I am 64. I thought you would go away and leave me today."

As Muhammid carried on playing, a restaurant waiter brought in a birthday cake with candles.

Maureen looked around amazed. "My mother dumped me. Got rid of me. Didn't want me born. My birthday is a bad day."

“Was a bad day,” corrected Mary. “You are with friends here.”

“And there is something else for you, Maureen,” said the waiter. Hurrying back behind the counter, he returned with a bouquet of flowers and two large cards.

“For me?” asked Maureen.

“Look at the envelope,” said the waiter.

“M–A–U–R–E–E–N,” spelt out Maureen with wonder. She opened the envelope carefully. On the cover was a beautiful garden full of flowers. And inside the card it read: “To a beautiful woman, who is now 64. From Alice and everyone from Cherry Tree.”

Maureen burst into tears. “Alice does not forget me when I am away.”

Deborah took the card to put on the table, pointed out the gift card on the bouquet, and then read it aloud. “To Maureen, our first 64th birthday guest at Hotel Mirabelle, from Charlene, Naresh, Maanika, and all our staff.”

Maureen took a deep breath. “Even though I wished Miss Jenkins was dead.”

“I would wish Miss Jenkins was dead. She was awful,” said Mary emphatically.

“Really?” asked Maureen.

“Really,” said Mary and Deborah together.

Muhammid stood up from behind the piano and said “Happy birthday Maureen. I will play that song for you in the evening when everyone is here. We all wish you a happy birthday. And I am your piano-playing birthday present from Mary and Deborah.”

Maureen then unclipped the little yellow teddy bear that lived in her bag and handed it ceremonially to Jane.

“This is for you, Jane Edwards.”

Chapter Seventy

The wedding invitations sat on the table. It was for Sunday, the last day of the trip, and everyone was invited.

"Are you going?" asked Gerry.

"To be honest, I am rather dreading it," said Tom. "If I can't find — find — find — oh, what is it?"

"Words?" asked Steve.

"Yes. Words. Words. Those beautiful dying things," said Tom sadly.

Gerry put a hand on his arm. "Is that what it feels like, love, when you can't find them?"

"That's not what I wanted to talk about. It's about the — what is it?"

"Where the wedding is?" asked Marion.

"Wedding?" asked Steve.

"Yes," said Tom, with energy. "Wedding."

"I don't really know them — the people getting married."

"None of us do," said Marion.

"It is not that. People here do listen and they are not friends. But they listen. And — and people you call friends don't talk to you."

There was a silence.

"It was beautiful when Muhammid played 'When you are 64' for Maureen's birthday," said Gerry softly. "And it made me cry. And I felt so full of love and pride for her. Even though I will probably not see her again, and she is not really a friend."

Marion responded thoughtfully. "People listen who are not friends, and you can feel the deepest feelings for someone who is only in your life for a short while. You can remember a moment all your life. But with you two, I feel we have made new friends of a very different kind."

Steve shrugged his shoulders. "When I think about Grendel — "

Gerry and Marion looked at each other concerned.

"Friends don't want to hear."

Gerry opened her mouth but then changed her mind. Steve clenched his fists. "'In the end, we will remember not the words of our enemies but the silence of our friends,' Martin Luther King, Junior."

A thoughtful silence followed.

"People are so frightened of getting close to disability and death. They feel it is catching, like Covid," offered Marion.

"Maureen and Jane have had it from birth," said Tom, "Bless them. They are so brave. But we have only had it since we got this. We are not used to it."

"No," said Steve. "It is why being Shakespeare twins has helped me so much. I feel Shakespeare is imprinted deep in my heart."

"Yes," said Tom. "Give sorrow words. I am losing the words that were my passport into the ordinary world of work and friends. Outside of family, people will not try to find out what I am thinking. The weight of unsaid words will grow." He reached out for Gerry's hand. "You are amazing, Gerry. You stay there, translating back and forth. But I am not speaking another language. But to old friends, some old friends, that is what it is like. Even the words that do come out — they — they — oh words!"

"You can find it, Tom," said Gerry.

"Some old friends can't even hear the right words, the words that come out right."

"That's true," said Gerry. "They turn to me asking for a translation when you have been very clear. They are too frightened to talk to you directly. They don't know how they would manage if they had what you have."

"That's true for me, too, Tom," said Marion. "Old friends and colleagues come over to be nice to Steve and say hello and then try speaking to me for the rest of the evening."

"Hello! I am here!" said Steve, "I feel I have to wave my arms or give a quote of the day. Earn my right to be seen as a human. If I did not loudly quote Shakespeare, people would think I had a learning disability."

"And does that matter?" asked Tom.

"To me. I have a degree, several degrees. I studied. And people think I am totally incapable and uneducated. But if I quote Shakespeare, they think I am educated and mad. I prefer that."

Marion poured them all more water. "So," she said, "with all these important issues in our mind, do we or do we not wish to go to the wedding? And we may all have very different ideas and that is fine."

Gerry held up her glass. "I am so happy being married to Tom, but I do not feel like the tiredness of going through a wedding, something so intensely personal, for people I do not know and do not expect to have further contact with. However, as the hotel and Wonderful Wheelchairs are paying for the wedding, I feel going for lunch is something very different and I would like to do that with you all."

"Phew! Thank you," said Marion. "That puts it into words really helpfully for me. I see you two as friends who will listen out for my words and Steve's words, and so having a celebratory lunch with you as part of a wedding will be lovely. But not the ceremony."

"Settled," said Tom. "I think I will have a Shakespeare rest. I watched the man — his — you know — the man, the director — created this." His voice got louder.

"Naresh?" asked Steven,

"Yes. Taking off his prostheses. Is Shakespeare my prosthesis and yours, Steven? We can go to more places with it, but at times it is nice to-take-take it off."

"I don't know if I can," said Steve. "When you said 'settled' and we all agreed to go to the lunch, I nearly said 'exit stage left followed by a bear.'"

They all burst out laughing.

Chapter Seventy-One

It was a bright and sunny day. Balloons were hung in the entrance hall to Hotel Mirabelle. Betty's Restaurant was filled with floral decorations and red, heart-shaped helium balloons. There was a bottle of red wine and white wine on each table, as well as water and orange juice. There was a red carpet unrolled from the door down to the sea-view windows, and tables had been arranged on each side of it with a top table at the end. That had a golden candelabra as well as little bouquets of flowers. Outside of Betty's was a huge sign:

THE WEDDING OF LESLIE DAWKINS AND TRACEY MILLER.

Bert's Bar had been similarly festooned, with little bowls of peanuts and crisps on each table. In the kitchens, in Mirrorland, and in the rooms and offices, there was an excitement that filled every space. There was even a reporter from the *Sunville Herald* there early to look at the new facilities.

"You will be having a wedding each week here when my piece appears," he said proudly. "And the scoop I got from Les and Tracey. A happy ending and story of redemption after he rescued her from being stood up at the altar."

Les had invited his friends from the Hen and Horse, which meant the pub almost had to close down with all the key regulars deserting them. "Not real friends," he had confided to Tracey, "But they are all I have got."

Tracey had invited a few friends from work. "Not real friends," she whispered back. "Just making do after everyone stayed clear of me at my non-wedding."

Tracey had asked Zen to be her matron of honour, since she had helped her at her worst moment. Les had asked Naresh if he would do the honours as best man, seeing as how he had given him his job and his sense of worth.

Les had arranged for another driver to take the Wonderful Wheelchair people who wanted to be part of it to the local church for the ceremony and then to bring them back for the reception. On this day, he was not going to drive.

Mirrorland was filled as never before, with women trying on their clothes and doing their make-up. Even Doris had dared to go down, with Olena showing her the way. She had taken out of her make-up bag a special tube of red lipstick that her mother had given her and she had never worn. It was in case of a special occasion. And this was.

"Goodness," said Olena, "I know that from my country's history in the Second World War. That is Montezuma red. It was for women in service. Women fighting Nazism."

Doris looked at the tube of lipstick. Elizabeth Arden. "I did not know."

"Put it on. Put it on. You will be wearing history on your lips."

"Thank you. Thank you," said Doris, feeling tearful.

"Hitler hated red lipstick. Imagine. He tried to ban it. My grandmother wore it."

"So if I wear it, I am frightening Hitler."

"Yes. Put it on."

And Doris did.

"Lovely wedding," said Roland.

"Yes," said Ibrahim. "It really was. They love each other."

Olena and Doris joined them. Seeing his wife, Dan said, "You look beautiful."

"It was Olena," smiled Doris. "She told me the history of my lipstick. It was victory lipstick."

Roland stared in fascination. "Can I wear lipstick?" he asked.

Just as Olena worried about what to say, Dan stepped in. "Anyone can wear lipstick if they want to," he said gently.

"Because I have a victory," Roland said.

Olena put her head in her hands.

"Les, who got married in the church. Nice man. I told him I fancied ice cream and he said ice cream fancied me, and I was worried he thought I would think the ice cream was like a person who fancied me but it wasn't — it was a joke."

"And you got the joke!" said Dan warmly. "That is a victory, with or without lipstick. You can show a victory in all sorts of ways."

Doris took a deep breath. "Olena comes from the same country my parents came from."

Roland looked at her intently. "You don't look like you come from the same country. I don't see anyone from the same country as me. I am Black. Naresh is brown. Zendaya is Black, but she doesn't look like me."

"We are all lots of different colours, aren't we, Roly?" said Olena.

"My mother is brown," said Roly. "I know colours."

Charlie joined them. "That wedding service was so beautiful. My mum always cries at weddings, and I thought she was soppy but I felt like crying there."

"Why does she cry, Charlie? Is she upset?" quizzed Roland.

"It is a nice upset, sometimes, when people cry at weddings," said Charlie carefully.

Roland looked across at Ibrahim and Andrzej. "So when are you two getting married?" he asked.

There was silence.

"But you fancy each other. You are single men so you can marry."

Everyone looked at him, amazed.

"You are right, Roland, they are single, and they might," said Dan.

Tom, Gerry, Steve, and Marion sat with Susan, Louise, and Hermione. She had phoned to ask if they would find it an intrusion. She was also feeling very nervous about a painting she had completed for Hotel Mirabelle, which would be unveiled after the lunch.

She told them she had been painting and painting while listening to a recording of Shakespeare's *Winter's Tale*, and she thought that Tom and Stephen might be pleased to know she, now for the first time, enjoyed the vindication of the end of the play.

"Ay and makest manifest where she has lived or how stolen from the dead."

That was it. That was her. Stolen from the dead. She was not the Lady of Shalott. She was not a zombie. Juanita, her cleaner, was right. She could paint. She was alive.

Mary, Deborah, Maureen, and Jane moved to a table together.

"How amazing to have watched a wedding on a holiday like this," said Deborah, wiping her eyes with a tissue.

"Yes," said Maureen. "Lovely wedding, but Mary and I are not getting married. We love each other, but we are friends and we are writing a book named *Count on Me*."

"That is so exciting," agreed Mary. "I will have a cab pick you up to take you to my place so we can work there when we are all back."

"And I have your number!" laughed Maureen.

"That's funny," said Jane. "Numbers lady has your number. And you have my number, too, because I am your best friend too."

Betty's Restaurant was filling up. There were men from the Hen and Horse, work friends of Tracey, staff of Hotel Mirabelle and Southern Lights. In the background, the bridal march suddenly began.

"They already played that," said Jane, "in the church. But perhaps everyone didn't hear it."

"Shhh," said Maureen.

And down the red carpet came Tracey, in her beautiful fairy-tale white dress, and Les, in a dress suit, shirt and tie, followed by Zendaya and Naresh, Charlene, Irene, and Della. Along with them was a wary-looking woman, Joan Moreau, who'd come to Sunville just to fix Tracy's dress.

As they reached the top table, one of Tracey's friends rushed up and threw a bag of confetti over her. There was a roar of laughter.

"Now watch it!" called Les in a pantomime voice. "You leave my missus alone. She'll make our house a right mess if you carry on like that."

There was a flash of light as the *Sunville Herald* reporter snapped away. Then, when everyone was seated, Zen called for silence and invited the bride to speak.

"Ere, what about Les?" called a man from the Hen and Horse.

"Ladies first," shouted Les.

Tracey stood up. "Hello everyone. My wedding. A real wedding. Me and Les. And everybody here. It is everything I ever wanted and it is everything I needed because it is real. Real—but it has angels, too.

"It has this angel of a woman, Zendaya, who found me crying here in my bridezilla state and made everything come right, even though she had never met me before. And she found another angel, Joan, who restored my dress which was all creased and crumpled, so I could have my wedding and my dress. And then I am given a wedding by a hotel filled with angels who care about disability.

"But perhaps the biggest angel is Les, the man who took me on when I was at my lowest point and has helped me ever since. He helped me restore myself, even if it meant he needed some drinks to do so."

The entire restaurant erupted in laughter and cheers.

"Thank you, Charlene, Hotel Mirabelle, and the Wonderful Wheelchair Company, because you are wonderful. And thank you for all you do for guests and staff. You are my new family."

There was a huge round of applause. Men from the Hen and Horse Table started calling out "Les, Les, speech, speech!" and Les stood up.

"I have always lived my life in journeys. In cars and coaches. Always travelling. But it was never really a proper journey until I met Wonderful Wheelchairs. The guests here are so brave and so courageous with whatever they have to put up with. So I started feeling more proud of my driving and the coach. I felt it was a magic vehicle that could not only take you somewhere new, but change your life in the process. And without it, I would never have met my Tracey. I didn't know how to talk because despite my handsome appearance, my wonderful taste in clothes."

"Hear, hear!" called the men loudly.

"— I had only ever had one other girlfriend in my life."

"Shame," called the men.

"Lucky man — you spared yourself," called another.

"And she wasn't really a proper girlfriend. So I didn't know what to do. But my Tracey did. She just turned up again when I thought I had blown it, and luckily she is good with words. And I am just so happy. So please enjoy your meal and we can have some music and dancing after."

And then Charlene stood up. "Welcome to Sunville, Hotel Mirabelle, and the Wonderful Wheelchair Company. Sunville has been seen as the most boring depressed old-fashioned seaside town in the UK."

"No!" came the indignant cries from around the room.

"But what we are showing is that the smallest, most boring place can be the most magical and the most advanced! Sunville is where the sun lives, the sun of human relationships and hope.

"And in honour of our first marriage here, and hopefully the first of many, we are delighted to announce the engagement of Naresh to Zendaya. We can now announce that Hotel Mirabelle and Wonderful Wheelchairs will be merging together, and to celebrate it, we are also thrilled to unveil a painting by Lady Hermione Lambton, who has agreed to be our Artist in Residence."

She rang a bell in the midst of the cheers, and two waiters carefully carried in a large painting and an easel. "Lady Hermione, please stand."

Hermione stood up timidly, warmed by the approval of Tom, Gerry, Steve, Marion, and Susan. And then Charlene said, officiously, "Hermione Lambton's new painting, *Waters of Remembrance*."

The cloth was removed and there was the painting. There was a coach next to the sea, driven by Les, standing in for Charon. Next to him was Tracey, in her wedding dress, a goddess aiding their movement to freedom and life. Then, there were Naresh and Zendaya — the god and goddess of the Underworld — coming out of oppression and injury into life. Naresh sat on the cushioned seat looking out at the water, and Zendaya's legs were rested across his, hiding the emptiness of where his thighs ended. His hand around her shoulders partially hid her breasts. They were both covering each other, making each other whole.

Maureen was there, a small nymph of love with flaming hair, next to the Shakespeare twins tossing words to each other, like a lifebelt. Doris Rickstein was changing from a chrysalis into a butterfly. And there were Muhammid and Ibrahim, like Egyptian gods, looking out to sea. The others were smaller figures And standing outside the coach on the shoreline were Charlene, Maanika, and Irene, three Graces.

A little plaque underneath the painting read:

WATERS OF REMEMBRANCE, WITH THANKS TO HOTEL MIRABELLE AND THE WONDERFUL WHEELCHAIR COMPANY, AUGUST 2023, LADY HERMIONE LAMBTON.

About Valerie Sinason

Valerie Sinason is a widely published poet and writer who was on the council of the British Poetry Society and ran Poetry West Hampstead with acclaimed writer Bernard Kops. She was also for four decades (now retired) a consultant child psychotherapist and adult psychoanalyst focussing on trauma and disability. Her previous novel was *The Orpheus Project* and her classic renowned textbook is *Mental Handicap and the Human Condition: A Psychoanalytic Approach to Intellectual Disability*, which included a chapter on working with Alzheimer's. Alzheimers and intellectual disability are also lived family experience for her.

About Sul Books

Born from a collaboration of two long-time independent esoteric publishers, and named to honor the Suleviae — the sisterhood of goddesses revered at springs throughout Europe — Sul Books is dedicated to publishing works that manifest aspects of the sacred sight that heals what humans have harmed.

Each of our imprints is guided by a commitment to pluralism, dissent, and the autonomy of humans, with a core focus on the importance of indigenous, animist, and non-exploitative ways of being in the world. We're especially supportive of autonomous, restorative, communal, low-tech, and land-based philosophies and actions.

You can find all our titles and support our authors at SULBOOKS.COM

Helpful Resources

Helpful UK Organisations

Airbnb (via Accomable acquisition): Since acquiring Accomable, Airbnb's platform now includes accessibility filters to search for accessible features in accommodation, although not fully specialised as a tour operator.

Cherish Dementia Holidays – Midlands Bespoke holidays / day-trips for people with dementia & their carers: CHERISHDEMENTIAHOLIDAYS.COM

Dementia Adventure: Offers supported holidays and breaks for people living with dementia and their carers. DEMENTIAADVENTURE.ORG

Disability Destinations: Wheelchair-friendly UK holiday properties. DISABILITYDESTINATIONS.COM

Disabled Holidays: -Wheelchair-friendly UK holiday properties DISABLEDHOLIDAYS.COM- 01612602218

HCPT – The Pilgrimage Trust - A charity organising pilgrimage holidays to Lourdes (France), for disabled and disadvantaged children and adults. HCPT.ORG.UK, +44 (0)1788 564 646

Helping Hands: HELPINGHANDSHOMECARE.CO.UK/HOME-CARE-SERVICES/CARER-SUPPORTED-HOLIDAY -0330 173 0627

Jumbulance: Holiday travel via adapted ambulance-coaches JUMBULANCE.ORG.UK, 07483 414330

Limitless Travel: Holidays with full care and accessible support. GO.LIMITLESSTRAVEL.ORG/UK/DISABLED-FRIENDLY-HOLIDAY

Mencap: MENCAP.ORG.UK

Mind For You: Specifically adapted holidays across Scotland for families who are living with dementia. TRUSTEDCARE.CO.UK

People First: PEOPLEFIRSTINFO.ORG.UK/GETTING-OUT-AND-ABOUT/THINGS-TO-DO/ACCESSIBLE-HOLIDAYS

The Downs Syndrome Association: DOWNS-SYNDROME.ORG.UK/

Tourism for All: Directory for accessible destinations/attractions. TOURISMFORALL.CO.UK/CHARITY

World Accessible Holidays: Organise fully accessible trips and equipment. HOLIBREAKPLUS.ORG.UK/DESTINATIONS/WORLD-EXPLORER-HOLIDAYS

Helpful US Organisations

Easy Access Travel: Accessible cruise vacations and land tours for persons with physical disabilities. easyaccesstravel.com

Hammar Travel: All-inclusive vacations for adults with intellectual and developmental disabilities hammertravel.org

New Directions Travel: (New Directions for People with Disabilities, Inc.) Leisure and educational travel for adults with mild to moderate intellectual / developmental disabilities. NEWDIRECTIONSTRAVEL.ORG

Society for Accessible Travel & Hospitality (SATH): a New York based non-profit organization founded in 1976 and dedicated to the promotion of accessibility in the travel & tourism industries. SATH.ORG

Special Journeys: Vacations for people with physical and developmental disabilities who need assistance. Fully guided / chaperoned vacations; transport, hotels. SPECIALJOURNEYS.ORG

Trips Special Adventure: Vacations for travellers 18 and older with intellectual &amp developmental disabilities. TRIPSINC.COM

Helpful Global Organisations

Wheel the World: provides listings and experience bookings that include accessibility details. Useful for those wanting to travel domestically or internationally. WHEELTHEWORLD.COM

Books

Sinason, V *Mental Handicap and the Human Condition: An Analytic Approach to Intellectual Disability*

Sinason, V & Hollins, S (2022) *A Refugee's Story*

Hollins, S, Sinason, V, and Access All Areas Artists, (2018) *Belonging*

Veiga, A & Sinason, V (2026) eds. *Disability Psychotherapy: What it is and Why it Matters.*